*Sir Norbert
and The Purple Haze*

Sir Norbert
and The Purple Haze

Gordon Strong

mutusliber

LONDON

First published in 2012 by Mutus Liber

BM Mutus Liber
London WC1N 3XX

A CIP catalogue record for this book is available from the British Library.

ISBN-13: 978-1-908097-10-1

www.mutusliber.com

Curiosity will conquer fear even more than bravery will...

James Stephens

'...he who loves must share the lot of the one he loves.'

Mikhail Bulgakov

To dream the impossible, that is my Quest.

Cervantes

Foreword

Some readers may detect a certain similarity between all this and *Sir Gawain and the Green Knight*, the fourteenth-century tale so beloved of the Medievalist. I readily admit to having purloined a theme or two and quoted certain verses as epigrams, but there any resemblance ends. As T. S. Eliot remarks in his notes to *The Waste Land*, '...I have obviously departed to suit my own convenience'.

John Massey of Cheshire – the most likely candidate for the chronicler of *Sir Gawain* – was known to be serious but 'not without humour'. The following pages have laughs by the trebuchet load. In any era, fun is there to be had if only you know where to look for it.

I did not deliberately set out to write a sequel to my previous mystical outing – *Dawn of The Goddess* – although the Dark Ages setting is more or less the same. The world of these tales may appear harsh and unforgiving, but when the *iPod* and the *iPad* are removed from our own times, life seems to me to appear remarkably similar. References to the modern world in the narrative will hopefully provide an amusing counterpoint.

After completing the book I discovered the statue of a St. Norbert in the city of Prague. A brief epitaph describes him as, 'a miracle worker'. I like to believe that the devout fellow was at my side when I composed this tale.

Thanks are due once more to Sean Martin at Mutus Liber for diligently editing the manuscript as well as offering his most pertinent suggestions.

Gordon Strong
Portishead
July 2012

Dramatis Personae

King Arthur
Guinevere
Merlin
Sir Lancelot
Morgan le Fay
Sir Norbert
Sir Gadroon de Montaigne
Sir Wayne
Abbot Speckle
Scriven
Sir Edmund Wooslak-Bascoombe
Lady Malinda
King Brime of Anghard
Lady Lardiana
Croop
King Tirhadeth of Tomberg
Edrith the Wizard
Nouvin
Willowpetal
Athilde
Hendrique the Minstrel
Lapin the Jester

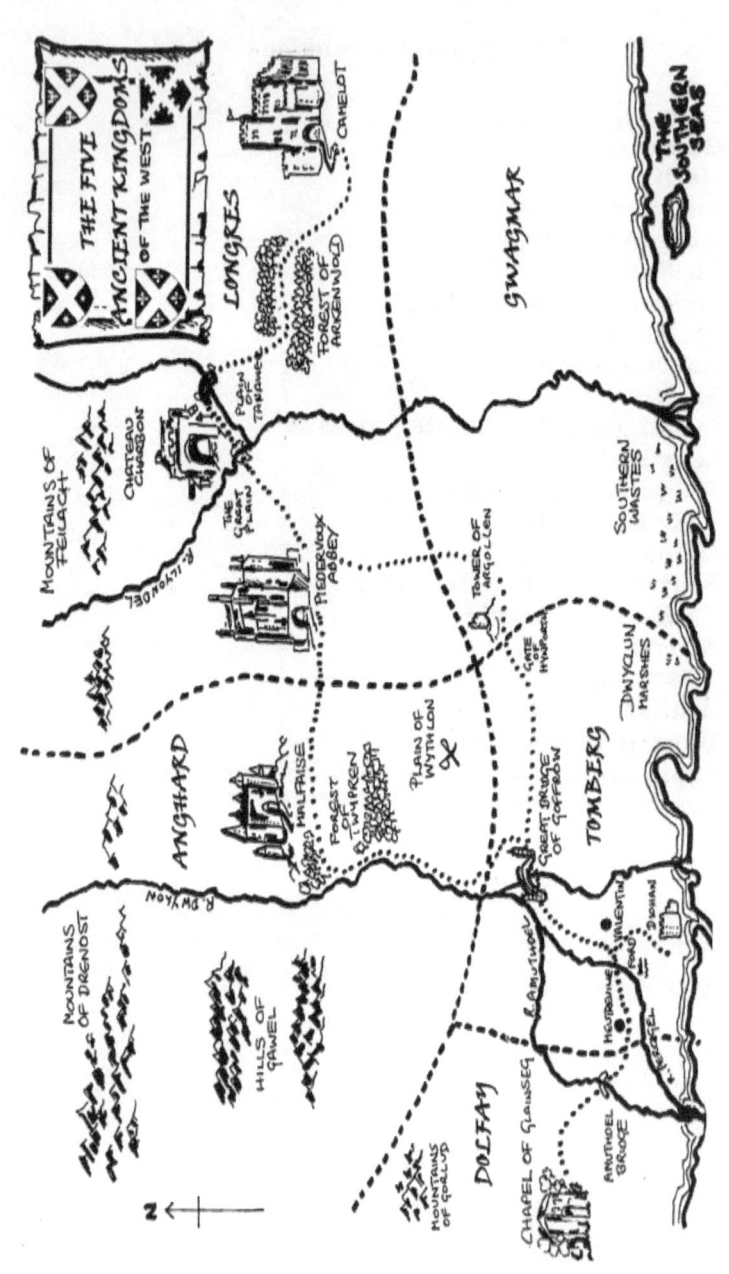

For Camelot's Christmas feast was fifteen
Days, as full of food and laughter
As feasting could be made, loud and happy
And glorious to listen to, noisy days,
Dancing nights...

Even though we can't actually see Time we always think we know what it is. The difference between yesterday and today depends on something we call memory. What's happening now will eventually join the rest of what we think of as then. Or will it? That's the problem with Time, you can't say anything definite because it doesn't exist.

Our tale is set in what we might call the distant past – maybe a million yesterdays ago – but how far away is that? Even if measured precisely, it doesn't really mean anything. Maybe it's easier just to assume that everything that has ever happened still exists, it's just been tucked away somewhere. Parallel universes? That might be the answer. Not a bad try by someone, anyway.

Being particular about Space is just as much of a problem. Is what we think of as 'here' really 'there' in another place – 'over there' maybe? Do we ever get to see all of anything? What about corners of space, or the space round corners? Wouldn't a big space be a small one to a giant? How about endless space? Surely, it must stop somewhere?

Sometimes a glitch appears in the fabric of the cosmos, and life is created where none ought to be. Very occasionally such an aberration is also given the power of reason and the ability to communicate. The

Purple Haze was just such a thing. Unfortunately, it wasn't very nice.

*

Being made out of lumps of frozen rain, snow is wet. It is only ever attractive on a Christmas card or when observed from somewhere else. Preferably, a place that's warm, dry and comfortable. Even a small garden shed would do the trick. Having lots of the stuff dumped on you from an unforgiving sky is no fun at all – just ask Sir Norbert, the hero of our tale.

This noble knight had been riding for the whole of the short winter day. If alternative employment for the last six hours had been available he would have taken it – even for less than the minimum wage. By noon the gauntlets he had been wearing – leather lined with wool – had turned into a pair of frozen tea cozies. The very worst sort of damp and cold had invaded his jerkin, and got right inside his boots and hose. He would not have been surprised if an area of low pressure hadn't settled inside his codpiece. Not that the equipment residing there owned much heat anyway. Norbert was a man who had never known a woman – poor chap.

In a timeless tradition (as these things so often are) every knight in the realm gathered at Camelot for the Yuletide celebrations. Wildburn, the town Norbert had left that morning, was but 'a day's journey' from King Arthur's castle. Said like that, it might have seemed like a merry jaunt; signing up for a Ten Tors Trek was probably nearer the mark. Even though the thick cloak of Winter disguised much of the land, it was still just possible to follow the principal ways which traversed the kingdom. Norbert calculated he would have to ride for at least another league or more before he would find shelter. The snow had obligingly agreed to leave off – just for the moment.

The noble knight continued on his way, at intervals humphing and grumphing – but always with what modestly be termed true grit. The Dark Ages had a habit of being trying – frequently and unexpectedly. It was the way of the times. Getting from one place to another was never an easy business. The average peasant never went out of the village where he was born if he could help it. He might venture over the hill to marry his cousin, but not if her sister lived nearer. Exercise for its own sake was not considered sensible. Avoiding starvation or being killed used up most people's energy.

Just as dusk had begun – inconveniently – to fall, a horseman joined the way a little ahead of Norbert. The rider was so intent, urging on his mount, that he appeared not to notice anything else. The snow had started to fall once more, and any sound from the horses' hooves was lost in this sullen world of whiteness.

At a wide bend in the way the two knights became aware of each other. Norbert could see that the newcomer was riding a courser, a steed fit for war. His own palfrey would be of little use in battle and, in the strict order of chivalry, the stranger's mount indicated he was of higher rank than Norbert.

"Master Knight, do you journey to Camelot?"

Norbert's cry caused the other to quickly turn his horse.

"I do that."

The two regarded each other.

"Then..."

"It would seem best for us to ride together... if it is to be our fate to die... frozen in the snow... at least we may perish together."

Norbert rode alongside and offered his wet gauntlet. Just as gamely, it was accepted.

"Sir Norbert, son of Cuthbert the Aledraper."

"Sir Gadroon de Montaigne."

The handle certainly had a classy ring. Norbert made a mental note to look up this particular nob in Debrett's.

"Have you travelled far?"

"I have journeyed from Noome where I enjoyed the hospitality of the Earl there. I am certain Lady Noome hath some notion that I wish to be betrothed to one of her daughters... in her eyes it seems not to matter which one... any of them, it seems, will do..."

Norbert, not really *au fait* with the posh life, could offer no comment.

"...and thou, Norbert... hath travelled further than myself to judge by the dampness of thy cloak...."

"Indeed... from Wildburn... where I bought frankincense and olive oil as gifts for our liege and lady. Also a vial of worm physick for the stables."

Gadroon's chuckle echoed merrily in the grey surroundings.

"From the top to the bottom, it would seem."

Norbert smiled, but in a minor key.

"You are a lover of the jest, Sir Knight?"

"To laugh is to live... some would say to live profoundly. Come... we may talk as we ride and make the leagues we still must gain become shorter. Tell me thy tale and what befell thee in this world that thou became a knight... we being men of a chosen band, after all."

Norbert responded brightly to such flattery, as Gadroon had intended he would. Thus, easily did he begin to confide in his new companion.

"I sported at quarterstaff and hunted the hare... as every youth... then I became squire to Sir Sainsbury Morrison and my learning began in earnest. It was he, when I swore my knight's oath, who presented me with the finest *bacinet* and an engraved *cuirasse*... costing much in silver I was later told..."

"Is that so?"

Norbert faltered in his words, and could hardly continue.

"Sir Gadroon... forgive me... I am from lowly birth... 'tis true."

Gadroon regarded him frankly. Well-bred chaps are trained in that sort of thing

"Come, Norbert... there is no shame in what thou hast told me. A churl may be as noble as a king... sometime more so."

Norbert sighed.

"I am gladdened that you regard my humble blood in that light, Sir Knight. Some at Camelot... of higher rank than myself... have shunned me since first I took a place at the Round Table."

Sir Gadroon gave all this short shrift.

"What odds? A plague upon those who cannot see further than an emblazoned surcoat... or some pretty device upon a shield! It is they who own the greater loss."

Thus encouraged, Norbert was inclined to pipe up a bit – on his own trumpet, as it were.

"I know I have been trained as well as any other knight of Arthur's Company. My lord taught me to hunt the wild boar. He used to say the killing of that beast was no different than piercing a man with a lance. And he would have me run a league before he would allow me to break my fast... and that in every season."

Gadroon could not help but smile, imagining the squat figure of Norbert puffing and blowing through the woods on a brisk Eostur morn. As the dusk gathered about them in earnest, they rode on. Gadroon, in his turn, was willing to share some part of his own life. As a youth he had been hotheaded, his pride forcing him to accept any challenge fearlessly. Even if confronted with an opponent twice his size, Gadroon never considered that he could be defeated in combat. To him, all was a sport, and in victory he was always magnanimous. Only once did Gadroon regret his openhandedness when, after returning the sword of a defeated opponent, the other made to stab him with it. His anger at such insolence nearly caused him to cut the man in two, but wiser counsel prevailed. Fascinated by all this, Norbert politely asked questions – a bit like a new bug at boarding school.

"And you were quartered as a page..."

"Indeed... in the manor of Sir Siburg a friend of my father. Full seven years I served... aye... and often slaved... until I became his squire."

Beneath his hooded cloak, Norbert inclined his head.

"Sir Siburg?"

"He fell at the Battle of Stamphill... and I wept many tears as we buried my master. It was my first taste of death... and also of one I truly loved. He was often harsh in his ways but in his heart always generous... and I was taught much by being at his side. I won my spurs and was given the accolade but a few months after that battle... yet I was sore grieved that Sir Siburg was not there to see me wear the red tunic. The honour I felt that day... when I accepted my sword belt... meant so much less to me because of that. My triumph was empty without my lord's eyes upon me."

The stillness of the scene – the trees silhouetted against the pale land – bestowed a great melancholy upon his words.

"Thou art a knight who is loyal and true, Gadroon. Yet I tell you freely there are greater powers than our own which decide the way we are to take. Man is helpless before He who is in heaven... the One who giveth and also giveth not. We must accept these things and yet keep our faith in divine providence. Is that not so?"

Gadroon wasn't used to blasts of full-on piety, especially before supper, but he kept his cool.

"I only know that those who insist upon hearing the truth seldom welcome it. Wisdom is a rare dish... not to the taste of all. It is also poor counsel to always be listening to others... even those reputed to know. The heart is thy best witness and most loyal friend. Of that I am certain."

Norbert *did* humph at this, and audibly, but he decided to divert the conversation into a side road, one that avoided the metropolis of 'religious matters'.

"And your forefathers, Gadroon?"

"I am from warrior stock. My ancestors were of the Old Kings that are told of in *The Ancient Tales of Our World*. The greatest fighter among them was Swordslayer... great of beard and girth... he would make three of any man."

Norbert appraised Gadroon, who sat most tall in the saddle.

"And *thou* art no scullion boy to look at you."

" 'Tis said Swordslayer stood always on the left side of his Chief when they advanced against the enemy. Thus his sword stroke was always made away from his leader...so there was no risk that he would strike him in the heat of battle. They say also that none could stand against him... men ran when he came towards them. Any who stood against him would be slain."

Sensible. Discretion... valour... better part of... and all that.

"And his fate?"

"Like many who go to war... an end without glory. Fever in the camp... tainted water... who can really know? That is what the tales handed down from many years ago report..."

"Methinks it is not the way a great warrior would wish to die."

Sir Gadroon nodded and allowed himself a brief 'Nay'. They plodded on into the darkening day and, most fortunately, the moon suddenly rose to light their way. Within an hour they had reached the brow of the great hill that overlooked Camelot. The buildings that clustered about the castle wall seemed to be desperately seeking shelter in its shadow. The knights halted, their breath visible in the moonbeams shimmering in the air. Gadroon spoke.

"Whatever differences we may have, good Norbert... we shall be brothers-in-arms, that I know."

Norbert could feel Gadroon's eyes upon him.

"I am certain that will be, also."

They rode past the gatehouse into the outer court of Camelot. There the steward greeted them, the ostlers taking their horses to lead them to the stables. Their mounts were rubbed down, to take the chill from them, and were given fodder. The two knights strode across the courtyard towards the Great Hall. Norbert was particularly anxious to find fodder for himself.

*

Those who served, and a select number who ruled, made up the occupants of Camelot Castle. Everyone knew their place – either up or down. It was unlikely those on the lower rungs of the ladder ever questioned their fate. They enjoyed a secure existence, one free from doubt and one unlikely to change in their own lifetime. The old ways were more than established and, until the rumblings of revolution would come many centuries later, the feudal system would remain unchallenged.

Norbert and Gadroon had retired to their quarters and were making ready to present themselves in the Great Hall. The prospect of warmth, companionship and a laden table would be more than welcome. Gadroon drew from his travelling bag a pleated jacket of dark crimson to wear over his surcoat and tunic. The number of layers he wore might have seemed excessive, but in those days, the interior of any castle could never be described as snug, and Camelot was no exception. Rich hangings covered the walls of many a chamber, but did little to alleviate the unyielding chill of the stone walls. Gadroon's outfit was strictly practical – no preening peacock he.

He closed the door of his chamber and, sensing that Norbert was still engaged with his toilet, made his way along a dimly lit passage. Detecting the presence of another, Gadroon peered into the shadows. Standing silently in the small vestibule was Merlin the Wizard – his features still, as if observing a distant scene, one invisible to all but himself. The snowy locks fell upon his dark cloak, and the staff held by a hand used to practising magic. A silver ring, circling a blue stone, was upon his finger, glinting in the light from a rush torch above. Merlin had been aware of Gadroon for some moments, such was his power.

"Ah... the noble knight doth grace the court of Arthur! Look upon me, Sir Gadroon... and well! Remember what thou seest! For... know ye... I leave this court upon the morrow."

The knight was understandably surprised.

"Before I have had time to greet thee, O man of mystical ways? How so?"

"My time as advisor to the king draws to a close... and besides... I must away to the Lake of Nimmue where I have certain matters to attend to."

Gadroon frowned a trifle – a rare art, known only to a few celebrity chefs.

"I shall miss thee, old sorcerer. Thou sayeth that on the morrow thou travel? It is hardly the season for going about..."

Merlin smiled secretly.

"Know ye not, Gadroon... that a man of magic hath his own ways of journeying from place to place?"

"But cannot our king – Arthur – furnish thee with a guide? A page to carry your belongings at least?"

"I tell thee, Master Knight... the wizard's path is always alone, as it must be. Those of our calling have never sought friendship or aid. There is one with whom I must tarry as long as I may before I pass forever into the eternal West. A kingdom where we all must journey some day... even thee, O brave knight."

"Thou speakest only the truth."

"A wizard sees no reason to do aught else."

Gadroon regarded Merlin, unable to hide his affection for this man of magic.

"Many of the Company hold you most dear..."

"That may be so..."

"You have more to tell than the few words you have spoken... I know this to be so also..."

Merlin sighed, briefly.

"True! You have been away from the court for some little time, Gadroon. You will not find the Great Hall so full of merriment as it was in former years. Old quarrels have come to the fore and are now on display for all to see. It is not a pretty sight to behold and an old man flees from the clamour of dissension... it is painful to his ears."

Gadroon nodded briefly.

"I had heard it was thus so..."

Merlin put his head on his shoulder, resembling an inquisitive raven.

"You will depart ere long also..."

Gadroon raised an eyebrow half-mockingly.

"How is this? Does the mighty Merlin see my fate in a vision?"

Merlin smiled, in the way only a magician can – it goes with the territory

"A wizard's days and nights are spent constantly in the company of visions, Gadroon. One more... though it may concern a great knight such as thee... makes little difference. I would have let it fade into nothingness had I not laid eyes upon you... a most pleasant encounter... one that I knew would occur. Indeed... I have to tell you that you will depart from Camelot upon the last day of the Yule festivities."

Gadroon was slightly complacent.

"I see no great revelation in that, old Merlin. I had already planned to depart upon that day..."

The eyes of Merlin twinkled like many stars.

"But not upon The Quest!"

Gadroon was startled out of his wits.

"The Quest?"

"Aye! You had not thought you would go upon such a venture as that! A journey into the unknown lies before you... one that will ensure you will be absent from these walls for a year and a day."

Merlin twinkled like a New Year Sale of cut-price constellations.

"Only remember this...you will be sorely tried...aye sorely... but Angaz, the god of death, will not claim you... at least not yet awhile... of that you may be certain. One of my most gifted pupils, Edrith, will come to your aid when you are in sore danger. You will also have a trusted and loyal companion upon this journey... one you have met already. Those who are fated to be together cannot remain apart for too long.... and in that there is also another truth. But stay... if I am not mistaken, here cometh thy fellow seeker upon The Quest."

On cue, Sir Norbert appeared, his black surcoat complementing his bright yellow hose. Or perhaps vice versa. The world could now be left in no doubt as to how square of build he was. Each of Norbert's legs was like the stump of a felled oak and upon them perched a barrel that was the rest of him. Hailing him, Gadroon thought it wise to spill the beans straightway rather than open a can of the same later.

"We are to venture forth, Norbert... upon a great journey. The great wizard Merlin has told me of this."

Norbert regarded Merlin coldly. He was not in sympathy with wizardry and its ways. The magician detected this, but was not to be drawn, or even lightly sketched. He was too old a hand for playing any game

11

of challenge and counter-challenge. He gazed at Norbert's shiny cheeks with some inner amusement.

"Good eve, Sir Norbert. Thy countenance speaks of rude health."

Norbert was frigidly polite.

"Good eve to thee also, Merlin."

The knight could not, however, conceal his desire to learn more of Gadroon's tidings.

"What journeying is this you speak of, Gadroon? I confess to having no great appetite for such a prospect... having just seen a tired horse stabled but an hour ago."

Merlin was all smiles and reassurance.

"Fear not, Master Knight! 'Ere you depart there will be time enough for taking your ease before the Hall fires... and letting your *appetite* off the leash... as I know you are inclined to do."

Norbert was inclined to be superior, not a good move where men of magic are concerned.

"I demand you tell me all!"

Merlin slowly and deliberately held up his staff. It glowed a dull orange in the darkness – a sign for silence. Not surprisingly, the trick always worked.

"Knights... nor any other men of this world... do not demand of wizards, Master Norbert... it is not meet to do so. But hearken ye both to me. When I addressed the Company for the last time, it was my sacred duty to inform the king that his loyal knights should now embark upon the Quest for the Holy Grail."

Gadroon interrupted.

"I was not of the Company when this was spoken of, Merlin. I beg of you, tell me all... I know not even what The Grail may be."

Merlin did more than fix the knight with his gaze; he gave his soul a strip-search as well.

"I perceive that... truly you do not know of this marvel, Master Knight," Norbert said. "I will tell you

12

now that, among many of its great wonders, the Grail is anything a mortal may wish it to be."

Norbert could not stop himself – words hissed out of him like steam from Thomas the Tank Engine's boiler.

"It is the highest of all the high..."

Norbert took off on a flight path to ecstasy, his eyes dazzling with divine light. Devout thoughts filled his head until it nearly exploded in a shower of rainbows.

"It is the most marvellous thing... the very essence of purity and spiritual love. Therein is the celestial... the..."

The other two let Norbert ramble on for a bit, until Gadroon was aware that the hunger in his own vitals was of a more earthly kind. He would have willingly swapped any amount of devotion for a venison pasty or two. Norbert's sermon eventually fizzled away, leaving Merlin to add a footnote.

"Thy faith in things eternal does thee credit, Master Norbert, and all this and more will be revealed to you in due time. Remember only that the journey holds as much fulfillment as the end."

Gadroon nodded gravely.

"I believe that to be so, Merlin... and I am certain many lessons will be learned upon the way."

The two knights followed the wizard into the courtyard and there, Merlin raised his staff once more. He saluted the heavens and, in acknowledgement, the waxing moon painted its shaft silver with celestial light.

"Farewell, Sir Gadroon, Sir Norbert... the Quest awaits thee! I will see thee both in some other time!"

Merlin seemed then to be swallowed up by the night, a proceeding that only added to Norbert's unease. He was muttering to himself as they made their way to the Great Hall.

"I do not trust these wizards..."

Gadroon was solid in defence – a straight bat.

"Merlin is the greatest of them all..."

"I care not. Sorcery is the plaything of Satan."

Gadroon took a more sober view. Most would.

"I cannot know whether that be true or not... having never met the worthy gentleman of whom you speak. Perhaps you may have that privilege one of these days, Norbert... then you may inform me of his devilish ways. I speak only of what I know... and I am certain the deeds of Merlin will one day be celebrated in legend."

Norbert stiffened up even more, particularly in the gills area.

"Darkness breeds greater darkness."

"It would not do to be constantly blinded by the light. One must have shadow also."

Norbert, not used to having his beliefs so roundly questioned, was most put out, to the extent of looking like a stuffed pike.

"I am sure we will have many hours of debate when we venture out upon The Quest, Gadroon. *If The Quest will happen...*"

Gadroon bowed graciously.

"I feel certain that it will, Norbert. And I look forward to the pleasure of talking with thee... already it is one of the delights of my hours."

Norbert, greatly flattered, softened up a bit – like a favourite pair of slippers.

"I thank thee. Thy company gives me great pleasure also, Gadroon."

A touch of mutual back-slapping followed.

"Come, Norbert... a cup of wine will cheer us... and the smell of roast boar beckons also."

As they entered the Hall, the herald announced their names with due ceremony, and at top volume. He didn't need an amp. His voice was already set at 11.

II

And trembled, sitting motionless in that noble
Hall, silent as stones, as corpses;
All speech was swept away as if sleep
Had dropped
From the sky...

Merlin was absolutely on the button when he confided
to Norbert and Gadroon that all was not well at
Camelot. Ninety per-cent of the problem could be laid
slap bang at the feet of the king. Arthur's big hang-up
was that he was more at home with his knights than he
was with Guinevere. The Queen responded to this by
hardly being at home at all, but that is another story,
and one we shall shortly relate. At court Arthur never
failed to be deferential to his consort, but there was
always a distance as wide as the Grand Canyon
between them. Even when Arthur was being pleasant
to Guinevere, right in the back row of the stalls, they
could see the flame of love had been snuffed out.

Some said the king's vitality was ebbing away which
was not good, whichever way you looked at it. If Arthur
lost his power then that would bode ill for the kingdom.
If the king has no sun in his heart, then the land
becomes cold and sterile, so the legends went.

Arthur had fathered Mordred, a child born of
Morgan le Fay in a night of Beltane passion hotter than
a jumbo jar of jalapenos. Nobody knew about his one-
night stand and Arthur wanted the secret to stay as
dark as Morgan's laciest lingerie. Yet, even after so
many years the guilt-trip still lay as heavy on the king's
heart as a Led Zeppelin solo.

Result: a family more dysfunctional than any in
Eastenders. Mordred had turned out to be a crazy
mixed-up kid, much more high-maintenance than any
regular teenage punk. He didn't see his mother because

she was too busy with sorcery, and he hated his father worse than a helping of Brussels sprouts. It was all bad, bad news. Eventually, this hatred would spell the king's doom. That's spelt D-O-O-M, just to show how serious it is.

Arthur had filed the memory of his encounter with Morgan le Fay under 'Worst Possible Sins'. Since that night he had gone around weighed down with mega-denial on a daily basis. His game plan was that being painfully pious would provide a balm for his tortured soul, but that scheme was a total washout. A stag night in Amsterdam's Red Light District would have been a much better solution, but alas in the Dark Ages, EasyJet wasn't around.

Arthur had watered his guilt with bitter tears, a horticultural innovation Percy Thrower would not have recommended. Perhaps Sir Norbert would have understood the king's subsequent renouncing of all sensual pleasures. Though regarding our hero, it was a case of not missing what he had never known in the first place.

It was hardly surprising that Guinevere had sought solace, and a bit of rumpty-pumpty elsewhere. She found what she wanted in the arms – and other bits – of Sir Lancelot. Just like Elvis, whose missus ran off with her karate instructor, the King of England and the King of Rock 'n' Roll had both been cuckolded good and proper. Apart from Merlin, no one in King Arthur's court would admit that the good ship Camelot had hit the rocks. A knight might own a keen blade, but he wasn't always the sharpest knife in the box.

Chauvinist types in the Company were also thicker on the ground than Daily Mail readers in Dorking. This lot considered Guinevere as merely someone who prevented them hanging out with His Majesty. Lancelot was of a different stamp – a rare Penny Black, probably. Of an evening, when Guinevere withdrew from the Hall with her maids, he felt that a light had left their midst.

He would grow sullenly silent, as well as silently sullen, and grasp his goblet of wine as if he wished to shatter it in a thousand pieces. If a touch of hyperbole was needed – always handy for writers – the spilt vintage was as the blood from his broken heart.

Into this deep pit of angst came Norbert and Gadroon. As they entered the Great Hall and checked out the magnificent blaze upon the open hearth – servants spooning up stoups of spiced wine and other spiffy scenes – they might have believed all was hunky-dory. They bowed low to Arthur and Guinevere up on a dais above the throng, rather like the Big Wheel at Blackpool. This pleasantry fulfilled, they duly took their places at the Round Table.

Cheery churls promptly laid loaded platters of venison before them. Just as quickly, horns of wine and flagons of ale were placed within their easy reach. Cursory nods of greeting to their fellow knights were all they could manage for some time, getting as much grub as possible being the only item on the immediate agenda.

Even though the original intention of the circular shape was to impose a natural democracy, a definite hierarchy still hung over the Round Table. A-List celebs like Sirs Percival, Sir Galahad, Sir Bors and Sir Kay congregated near the King, like the Rat Pack buddying-up to Frank Sinatra. The remainder of the Company – Division Two – consisted of the landed gentry, along with a smattering of upstarts and nouveau types. A ripe example of the latter was Sir Biston – a five-star prune – who happened to be sitting opposite Gadroon and Norbert.

He began by regarding Norbert in silent disdain, not that he noticed, being too busy tackling a surfeit of lampreys. The bearded and bumptious Biston leaned towards Gadroon, attempting what he imagined to be a bold sally.

"I see you wear a silver ring, Gadroon. Has that vulgar practice not been disallowed by the Courts of Chivalry and the Crown? Come, sir... it is *the law...* you know."

Gadroon promptly booted this bollocks into touch.

"Not any law that I follow, Biston. This ring was given to me by my knight-master and I wear it with pride."

Having said his piece, Gadroon then maintained a deliberate silence. He would have been in accord with Merlin in believing that words had their own power, and could be more precious than pearls. Gadroon did not slosh them about like swill for swine, and Biston owned about as much wit as a packet of pork scratchings.

"Unholy pride, eh? Do you not recall the rules of chivalry expressly condemn arrogance in a knight, Gadroon."

"I do most certainly. I also recall that a knight behaving like an ale-house tosspot is not considered seemly either."

Sir Biston's countenance lit like a flaring lantern and he would have reached for his sword if he had been carrying one. Had not Arthur decreed that no arms were to be carried in the Great Hall for exactly this reason? Too often in times past a temper, too swiftly ignited by liquor, had brought a bloody duel in its wake. The moment could have turned very black indeed had not Lapin the Jester appeared. The world was all of a sudden turned upon its head.

This famed and frenetic Fool wore a fantastic hat that gave him such a great height he resembled some exotic plant. Feathers and bells were attached to this headpiece and, with his loose doublet – one half yellow, the other blue – Lapin had a carnival air. He always pranced, never walked, and his grin was the widest ever seen in the world. The careless abandon of his attire served to disguise the precision of his wit. The ever-changing look in his eyes constantly echoed his jests – clear, yet fathomless.

"Ho, knightly nights... the night is nigh, nine by the candle clock. When a man's candle doth burn too brightly 'tis a sign he may soon go out in a trice... or even a trance. But where can he go when he hath no light to guide him? A candle burning in a bedchamber is not loved by the night or the knight... for it bringeth light. Yet the knight must need of the light if he needeth to make water in the night. Thus fire and water are good companions though they be of opposing stuffs... thus all beneath the heavens is of different matter but in troth the same."

Goodly guffaws greeted this shower of sallies, and joy once more settled upon The Round Table. Lapin leapt into the air, landing neatly between a dish of capons and a pigeon pie. He regarded the king impishly, and his majesty ordered the jester to remove himself from the festive board. With a sudden jump Lapin returned to the floor where he twirled himself about on one foot, all the time unleashing an unruly riot of verbal cross-reference and contradictions. A plethora of puns and paradoxes a-plenty were popped in there somewhere too. Lapin had trained his words to jump all over good sense in big red boots and make it freak out.

"He who doth not fall into a hole in the ground cannot climb out again... and he who reaches for the sky will touch it one day. He who doth fly... knowing it is not possible for a man to fly... will surely fall. But he who falls knowing that he may fly if he wishes... may be as any bird on high. The night owl owns both light and dark and 'tis said every dog has his day... but there hath yet to be seen a dog with wings."

Thank heaven for laughter! A five-star, high-octane invention bestowed upon the crown of creation by a deity who had woken up one morning with a sense of humour. God had been dreaming that the universe might not actually be anything to do with Him! He cracked up at that and couldn't take anything seriously any more. Everything that came into the Universal Mind seemed absolutely ridiculous... a penguin's chuff with a wig-hat on... a doughnut dancing on the end of a bicycle pump. Why was every bunch of atoms always trying to look like it made sense? No way!

Right at that moment the crew at Camelot were going to need a few gallons of giggles to get them through what happened next. The doors of the Great Hall burst open with a sound like seventy-six trombones being played loudly and, it has to be said, badly. Or at least not in the same key. *Something* was out there. In the gap that should have been just a slice of darkness, they beheld a very extraordinary sight... *The Purple Haze*.

Years later, scribes and chroniclers tried hard to recall that moment. They had about as much chance as sneaking up on Winston Churchill puffing on a rollie. If 'seeing is believing' then everyone in the Hall – from knight to knave – was posing in three pairs of Ray-Bans. The Purple Haze wasn't *just purple* it was *awesome* – about thirty-five feet high, almost as wide, and with a sort of human shape. It really didn't seem to give a hoot for anybody or anything, and just slid silently into the middle of the Great Hall like it owned the place. Not that anybody was going to call security, the biggest bouncer in club land would have asked for the night off. Things were so freakin' scary that even the fire, a moment before roaring mightily, took to smouldering weedily.

How do you describe a mirage? How about – 'it floats around kidding you it's something else'. Okay. 'Mist doesn't move it sidles.' 'Fog appears and disperses'. *A haze* is a bit different though, especially a purple one. This one spoke. Not that anyone could understand a freakin' word it said – except Lapin the Jester. He *could savvy the lingo* and that made sense, because the Purple Haze talked *non-sense* and who better to

20

interpret that kind of sense than a fool? Sensible, eh? Lapin, being an old trooper and no pooper, quickly turned the whole thing into just another bit of funny business.

He started off with a few light quips to ease any neurotic neurons there might be, coaxing them back into their brain beds, snuggled up nice and tight. Anger and fear he dealt with by telling them not to be so silly (or properly silly). Anything else disturbing the peace got sorted out by a hologram of the laughing policeman.

"Yes... it is a Purple Haze, my liege... lords... and noble knights. It could have been The Pink Fairies... Orange Blossom Special... Mellow Yellow... Green Onions... Red Sails in the Sunset or Black Betty Bam-a-Lam. But no... just think of it as just a purple passage in the book."

From the minstrels' gallery, a couple of sackbuts – an early half-arsed version of a trombone – honked in encouragement. The Purple Haze was not impressed; it had come here to deliver an ultimatum. Lapin concentrated on translating the weird sounds (half-way between a smoker's cough and streaky bacon frying) the Purple Haze was making.

"A true and virtuous knight must seek out the Holy Grail. This sacred vessel is to be found in the Chapel of the Blue Moon at Glainseg in the Kingdom of Dolfay. The Purple Haze will return... in a year hence. If the quest is unsuccessful then all Camelot will be turned into a Purple Haze... all around... up or down... day or night... until the end of time."

Lapin delivered this totally straight – a bit like the Queen's speech. He never got the chance to slip in any chequered chestnuts. One of Arthur's knights leapt out of his seat, settin' the Round Table a' rockin'. The high-flyer was Sir Wayne – Arthur's nephew.

"I... Sir Wayne... am prepared to undertake this most arduous task, O my king. The Quest will be fulfilled and that most precious thing, The Holy Grail, I shall bring in triumph to Camelot, and the Company shall rejoice."

Arthur began making the sort of noises that accompany someone who is dithering dreadfully.

"Er... um... er... well..."

A flinty tone interrupted this feeble performance – Lancelot, sounding as if he was spitting gravel.

"I vouch it is the duty of the king to let this knight embark upon this venture... and with thy blessing, my liege. If he doth succeed he may bring much glory to Camelot, and the kingdom is sore in need of such I trow."

The king ceased to flounder like a netted dab, or even dabble like a flounder.

"You are wise as always, Lancelot. Wayne must certainly venture upon The Quest."

Wayne was unctuous to his uncle.

"I shall never forget the great honour you have bestowed upon me, my liege. I shall indeed bring the greatest glory to Camelot."

This was Wayne laying it on with a coal shovel. Arthur, playing the gracious king, was stuck with his lines in the script, too.

"Thou brave knight! The kingdom smiles upon thy courage. May great good fortune go with thee."

The sackbuts started up again, even more squeakily than before, providing some kind of soundtrack to the next bit. Brimming goblets were raised high. They toasted the new number one in the charts – Wayne Banana and The Grail Benders – over and over again. The cheers were deafening, as they always are when some daft sod has volunteered to do a job nobody else wants to. Wayne grinned, more like a Cheshire cheese than the celebrated feline, and returned to his place at the Round Table. They all looked in the direction of the Purple Haze to see if it had okayed the deal. This now started to resemble one of those annoying T.V. films of

22

clouds speeding up. Lapin did his best to interpret these new smoke signals.

"The Purple Haze is satisfied... but gives warning such a promise must not be broken. If this should come to pass the kingdom will be forever laid waste."

They listened intently, but not soberly – not after all that mega-toasting.

"He also says, 'A Very Happy Christmas and a Prosperous New Year to you all.' "

Lapin had made the last bit up, of course, just to keep morale high. When the Purple Haze at last departed from the Great Hall, many were greatly afeared, and spoke anxiously among themselves of the dread portent of such a visitation. Lapin didn't join in, he just watched the misty vision gradually fade away and singing 'smoke gets in your thighs' quietly to himself. Drinking horns were topped up again, troubles were packed up in their old kitbags and they were smiling, that's the style. Particularly featured in the grin department was Wayne, carrying on like a dog with two tails and a street full of lampposts.

It was not long before a desire for slumber crept up on our heroes like a mugger with a sock full of wet sand. They bade goodnight to King Arthur and the Company and left the Hall, bound for their beds. As they made their way across the courtyard Norbert piped up with a query – a talent he had acquired over the years.

"Gadroon... what think thee of Sir Wayne?"

Gadroon didn't actually think a great deal of him. If he was the one marking Wayne's end of term Chivalry Paper, he would have been lucky to get a D-.

"He desireth honour that is certain..."

Norbert waited for further insights, but got only a wodge of silence. It did speak volumes – a whole library's worth – but Norbert wanted more. Just the facts, ma'am.

"You believe Wayne is sincere?"

"Most certainly I do not. Did thou not think it strange that Wayne almost *knew* The Purple Haze was to appear? He leapt up like a rising salmon to make his pledge to the king."

"Wayne is a most unlikely hero to my mind. I trust him not. To place a purse of silver in his keeping would be the act of a mad loon. It is beyond belief that such a knave should set out upon any Quest for the Holy Grail."

Gadroon was quietly sage – a rarely found herb.

"You may recall that Merlin swore we two were chosen to embark upon The Quest."

Norbert snorted like a pound of sausages – or, how they would have carried on in their previous incarnation.

"Did I not tell thee I had no love for these sons of sorcery, Gadroon? Every one of them is in thrall to the Father of Lies."

Gadroon shrugged.

"No matter. We shall see what the morrow brings."

Later, while lying abed in his chamber, Norbert wondered if Gadroon was not right, and that the die was cast. Moments later he was in the arms of Morpheus, dreaming he was beneath the stars, alone in some strange land. There, the light of The Grail was blinding in its intensity, but he could not banish the spirit of Merlin from within it.

*

The night had been no less eventful in the Royal Apartments. Horny Guinevere had been midnight creeping – seeking out her favourite knight's mighty lance. At breakfast in the solar the next morning, the queen had a coy smile about her. She declined a helping of porridge, having had more than her fair share of oats. Arthur hardly noticed his queen languishing in the Garden of Earthly Delights. He was more concerned with divine portents – namely a comet.

"It is an omen, I swear it."

Guinevere wasn't listening.

"What is?"

"The comet."

Guinevere looked absently towards the ceiling.

"Where?"

"No... no... not *in here*... in the sky... last night. I saw it with my own eyes. A fiery trail of cosmic... er... fire. Profound... meaningful and... um... terribly full of meaning."

"And you think it to be an omen?"

"Yes... of that there is no doubt. Such a mysterious happening in the heavens is a great sign... one for us all to heed."

"What doth Merlin say concerning this?"

Arthur was impatient at this.

"Ha! The wily wizard hath taken himself off last eve. I cannot consult with him nor enquire of his wisdom... even if I had wished it. I shall have to use my own."

"Is that a good idea?"

Arthur looked peeved.

"What canst thou mean, Guinevere?"

Guinevere ignored him.

"So... tell me... what be this comet an omen of then, Arthur?"

"Of that I must consider. A few hours meditation in the chapel... and all will be revealed."

Guinevere shivered at the thought.

"It's as cold as a widow's whatnot in that chapel..."

But a light had come into Arthur's eyes; he was off on a spiritual safari, hitting the highway to the highest good.

"Suffering must always play some part in the great Quest. I shall reflect deeply upon these matters."

Guinevere yawned, still vaguely aware of Arthur chuntering on. The monarch seized his kingly robe about him, and went flying from the chamber.

*

While kneeling devoutly in the chapel, Arthur reflected that Guinevere was absolutely right – the place was accursedly cold. Dibble, the priest who administered at this holy shrine, had earlier been shivering and shaking so much that Arthur sent the pathetic prelate off to the Great Hall to sit by the fire. The king reflected that Dibble's predecessor, Father Staple, had been even less of a success. A hopeless sot, he had a penchant for collapsing intoxicated behind the altar. His snores could often be quite clearly heard during the mass he was supposed to be conducting. Arthur reflected glumly that the sound was on a par with the present incumbent's wretched groaning as he turned a delicate shade of blue.

After some intense inner deliberations, Arthur left the chapel. Encountering the steward in the courtyard, he ordered various members of the Company to be sent to the royal chambers forthwith. The man hurried away on his errand. Arthur then ascended the stone stairs to his quarters vaguely hoping he would not find Guinevere there. He need not have been concerned the queen was in her private bower, enjoying a hot bath and planning the next night's frolics.

When Norbert and Gadroon entered the king's presence, Arthur greeted them warmly – a little too much so. Warning bells were jangling away in Gadroon's head, trouble was brewing like a pot of cyanide soup. It was merely a question of how big were the bowlfuls being handed round. The arrival of a third party – Sir Wayne – changed Arthur's demeanour from effusive to twitchy. Gadroon took this as a hint as to how the cookie was about to crumble.

26

"Noble knights, I greet thee all... those of our illustrious Company. Sit ye down... I have great tidings to impart that will shape the destiny of Camelot... and perhaps all of the known world."

Gadroon took a place opposite the king while the other two settled for seats in the stalls.

"Didst thou see the comet in the skies last eve? Nay? No matter... I admit freely to being sorely tried by its presence. It seemeth the true way of destiny was disturbed. Verily, the stars were moved from their accustomed place in the heavens."

Ham stuff.

"...and I have seen a vision of The Quest... and which of my noble knights shall embark upon it."

Arthur was careful to avoid Wayne's eye when he said this. Gadroon thought the odds on an early substitution were high.

"Although thou art truly of my blood, Sir Wayne... one of such courage that none could ever doubt... it is not wise that your king should spurn the experience and maturity of others in the Company."

Gadroon could see all this was not going down well with Wayne.

"It is my decree that Sir Gadroon... with Sir Norbert as his companion... are the two knights most fitted to fulfill this great task."

Merlin's prediction had come true! Wayne was scowling like Billy Bunter being refused tick at the tuck shop. Gadroon already had his acceptance speech well-prepared.

"This is a great honour, my liege... as I am sure Sir Norbert will agree."

Norbert was like one of those nodding dogs once to be seen in the back window of a Rover 90.

"...and I realize how difficult your decision... one that must have hung heavy upon the royal shoulders... since the very moment when you observed the portentous heavens..."

Gadroon was in imminent danger of signing up for the old gammon club himself, while Wayne was looking like he'd swallowed a ferret, muzzle first. Lapin chose that very moment to make his entrance, stage left. Arthur, although secretly relieved by the diversion, knew he ought to preserve some modicum of royal dignity.

"Ho, jester! What brings thee to the King's Chamber? Canst not see I am in converse with the most noble knights of the Company?"

Lapin took this on the chin, before applying a merry massage to the monarch's funny bone.

"Their nobility is without question, my liege! It shineth as the sun at noon. Yet the sun of the king is greater still even when the moon confineth herself to the night skies."

All laughed merrily – no prizes for guessing who didn't join in. Wayne's pout would have made a good flying buttress. The king addressed Lapin as if he were a Medieval seaside postcard.

"Hath thee some wit that is not of the quipping kind, jester?"

Lapin bowed low.

"I'll surprise thee, good king, and tell thee it is indeed so. The Purple Haze did impart a secret to me, but 'tis only for the ears of the true Grail Seekers."

The hint was about as subtle as a series of Benny Hill. They all looked at Wayne, who went the colour of a Bloody Mary prior to adding the Worcester Sauce. Anger oozed out of him like a volcano having a teenage moment. Arthur then came on like an old scoutmaster – and just about as sincere, too.

"Fare thee well then, Sir Wayne... thou most loyal of knights."

Wayne made his farewell speech, looking about as cheery as the Black Hole of Calcutta.

"Sir Norbert... Sir Gadroon... I bid thee good fortune upon thy quest. That the Holy Grail be returned to Camelot is my dearest wish..."

When the door of the chamber had closed behind Wayne, the jester leapt in with his lecture.

"There will be Five Wisdoms encountered upon the way. Each these must be learned and that fully... before one may continue upon The Path of The Quest."

Lapin spoke of the sacred significance of the number five – how there were five virtues, five senses and five points upon the pentacle – as well as a lot of other transcendental toot. During all this, the knights listened intently, sticking mental post-it notes on their chain mail. Arthur then rose, now doing a passable imitation of the headmaster encouraging the leavers to 'play the game' and put their 'best foot forward'.

"Destiny and Heavens have together seen fit to guide you, my noble Norbert and Gadroon. May all fortune go with you and I bestow upon you... your king's blessing."

There not being any other business to discuss, the meeting was declared closed. The two knights bowed low to Arthur and Lapin did the same, though he was a bit more jangly, what with the bells and all that.

Arthur was left to ponder. It was most strange that nobody else would admit to having seen the comet. By Saint Basil's Choad! He had definitely seen it! The cursed thing had a hugely long tail and filled half the sky!

III

Gawain was seated near
The queen; he leaned
Forward: 'Hear me,
My lord. Let this challenge be mine.'

The Yuletide feasting and carousing carried on for absolute yonks. After the umpteenth goblet, Norbert and Gadroon privately agreed the roast boar was getting to be a bore. The vibes were pretty heavy too, particularly those coming from Sir Wayne. The thwarted knight had a tendency to glare at them, like a Volvo with its headlights on full beam. Our heroes were almost relieved when the time came to embark upon The Quest.

As Gadroon set out from Camelot that morn, into the bleak country beyond, the ancient motto of chivalry – *I seek in order to serve* – echoed in his mind. Norbert too was aware of the great significance of their adventure; he knew they would not return the same men – if they ever returned at all.

Snow still lay round about – deep and crisp and whatnot. The horses' hooves often slipped upon treacherous ground, so they made slow progress at first. Though, as Norbert reminded himself, if they were to journey for a year's round, what matter the pace? Behind them the sun rose, as if blessing their endeavours. By noon they had left the plains that surrounded Camelot to descend into a valley. A stream, edged with ice, ran beside the way and they halted there to let the horses drink. Norbert pulled a wheaten loaf from his pack and, with a piece of cold beef added to that, satisfied his hunger – for the present. Gadroon was content with a long draught from the rushing waters – thinking how fine was its taste.

Refreshed, they continued on their way until they found themselves approaching a small hamlet. They rode past a few humble cottages with their wattle and daub roofs. If there were any folks within, they seemed little inclined to quit their firesides to gaze upon strangers. Only when they came upon a dwelling larger than the rest, sporting a green bush over the lintel of the door, any life became evident.

Norbert's horse shied as a figure dashed out of the door of the alehouse, for this it was. Though not clad in motley, he recognized Lapin.

"Master Lapin!"

At Norbert's cry the jester turned a complete pirouette.

"Compliments with no complaints I give thee freely, O noble knights. I see thou art in the world, and by the size of your saddle-bags the world is soon to be in thee also."

Gadroon smiled at these japes.

"Forsooth! Thou art cheery and without care this day... while all around draw closer to the hearth and pray they have gathered enough logs for the winter months..."

Lapin's limbs jerked from side to side like corn waving in the breeze.

"The heart is always warm that smiles at the foolishness in the world. He who spends all day and night in judging his fellow man... hath a coldness... a dozen of doublet and hose will never make to flee from him."

Gadroon looked arch. On a good day he could impersonate a complete viaduct.

"You are far from Camelot... and not, I believe, only for the wish to find an alehouse..."

Lapin knew he had been rumbled, crook, line and stinker.

" 'Tis true... the ale of my mistress is most fine... but my purpose is to journey to Malfaise Castle in the

31

kingdom of Anghard. There I have a friend... a minstrel named Hendrique... who hath sent word that a place as jester to the court awaits me there. Camelot has become dull and most dreary... this new living promiseth to be more than comfortable I am told... so thither is my destination."

As if he considered this was too serious a speech, Lapin paid homage to the gods of mirth by performing a neat somersault in the air.

"To Malfaise is also where we go, merry Lapin. Would thou wish to accompany us?"

The jester bowed low.

"I thank thee, Sires Gadroon and Norbert! I will agree to do in part what you say – as the rogue who lied said to the honest man."

Norbert was determined not to be excluded from all this banter and badinage.

"Come, Master Lapin... your riddles would be too difficult even for the devil himself to solve."

"Nay, Sir Norbert... I would say that the quip walks hand in hand with the puzzle – as close as lovers do. As to the Devil... with all his evil he has become so dark none may see him... which is good fortune."

Gadroon returned to this witty fray.

"Give us Light! Reveal what it is that is within your heart, Lapin... I beg of you!"

"Exactly as the lovers promised to each other!"

Gadroon made to throw his gauntlet at the jester who then mimed catching it.

"Speak, thou prince of folly!"

"For thy sake I will, O noble knight. Though there is more sense in folly than the other way about where, I vouch, there is rarely enough for my liking. I journey this day as far as the edge of Arkenwold Forest there to visit my brother Reygard who is a ranger in those parts. That far I will go with thee. That is if such men of standing would wish to be seen in the company of a man of wit such as I... though I swear it be an honest

32

trade. More so than the lawgiver I'll be bound, who maketh the rules so that he may rule all but himself."

Lapin climbed up behind Gadroon and the knight was about to spur his horse when a woman appeared at the door of the alehouse. She had long red hair, and her gown was cut worryingly low. But briefly did she acknowledge the two knights, for all her attention was fixed upon Lapin.

"Do not be too long in returning, Master Lapin. It is hard for any man who tarries here to make an alewife smile, but you have done that in a dozen ways."

Her wink was rude, nearly lewd.

"Fear not, marvellous mistress... I will come to sup with thee again afore long. My hunger is like the beggar's tale... or indeed the serpent's tail... one without end."

He pressed some silver coins into the woman's hand and squeezed it long and hard. With a wave of farewell the travellers joined the way once more. Gadroon was thoughtful for some moments, finally calling over his shoulder to Lapin.

"The lady's ale must be most fine for you to reward her so well."

"The price I pay is how much I have spent... not *with* my mistress... but verily *within* her."

Gadroon laughed. Norbert, even if he had heard the jest, would have been most perplexed.

*

The brief day was drawing to a close by the time they gained the Forest of Arkenwold. Of all the woodlands in the kingdom of Longres, this was the most mighty. Even in the starkness of Winter, its majesty was still undeniable. Much of the ground it encompassed had never felt the foot of man or heard his clamour. The fierce boar, the mighty stag, and the stealthy fox ruled here, while badger and hare also made it their home.

The wolf had long been driven from these parts, but his human counterpart – the thief and bandit – was to be found hiding in its depths. Whole gangs of rogues had taken to haunting the forest. Of these, some were true outlaws – exiled for their crimes – while others simply preferred a lawless society to their own. If travellers were unlucky enough to come upon these roving bands they would be robbed and viciously murdered.

Well aware of its reputation, the prospect of entering the forest was not a welcome one, but for the knights, their way indubitably lay within. Lapin left them at a run to gain the ranger's cottage, and his brother, hearing the jester's light footfall, appeared at the door. The two were then seen to embrace most warmly.

Norbert and Gadroon entered the woods cautiously. The path was wide enough for them to see some distance ahead but soon it began to grow dark and the need to pitch camp became more pressing. The way was now only a rough trail for cattle, and trees on every side forced them to ride in single file. They continued in the growing gloom until a great oak bough across their path, prevented them from going any further. Forced into the forest, and venturing too far, they were unable to find their way back to the trail. Gadroon halted.

"We shall have to make do with staying where we are for the night. At least we have blankets enough to wrap about ourselves... but we dare not light a fire."

Norbert agreed, though somewhat reluctantly. A vision of the cheery blaze in the Great Hall now seemed only a distant memory.

"Nay... 'twould not be wise to burn down the forest."

Gadroon was stern.

"Neither should we wish to show any who might be watching that we are here. This place is a haven for all manner of varlets."

Norbert stared into the darkness, desperately trying not to see sinister figures creeping through the undergrowth.

"The wicked do not feel the chill it seems."

"I know not... but there is nothing else for it... and we must make haste. The moon has not yet risen... so there is hope that we shall not be seen."

They set about tethering the horses and opening their packs, mislaying things, and stumbling over tree roots. When it came at all, sleep came fitfully, yet their very wakefulness was to save them when the attack came.

The outlaws had known of their presence as soon as they had entered Arkenwold, the rarity of travellers at this time of the year making the knights even more conspicuous. Gadroon was shaken out of his slumbers by the sound of a sharp crack in the undergrowth. He reached for his sword. He freed his other arm from beneath his cloak to shake Norbert firmly.

"Mmmf... wha..."

"Shhh."

Gadroon's sword was of the finest Damascus steel and a masterpiece of the smith's art. With a grip of sharkskin and gemstones set in the pommel, it also had all the balance of a cricket bat. Gadroon was known as a hard-hitter. At first they could not tell how many outlaws came at them; Gadroon only knew how many he struck down. The foremost of his attackers fell with a scream, a second went down likewise. Norbert thrust with his sword at a third who had launched himself at them from the branches of a tree. It soon became apparent the odds were heavily against the knights and they were fighting for their lives. Alarmed neighing, and the crashing of hooves, told of the horses being set free. Knowing this only added to their plight.

Things might well have gone very badly indeed had not help arrived in the person of Reygard the Ranger. Several of the outlaws were wounded and two lay dead, but the arrival of Reygard, his woodman's axe swinging in a deadly arc before him, turned the tide. Loud yelping suggested that one or two of the outlaws had not been able to avoid the blade. Realising that the contest was now not so one-sided, what was left of the band made off, the wounded stumbling along behind them as best they could.

Norbert was puffing and panting, his countenance scarlet with effort, while Gadroon leant on his sword to catch his breath. He looked up at Reygard.

"Thank thee, Master Woodsman... I think we were in sore danger. But for thee I would not now be standing here."

A pale light was breaking through the trees as Reygard wiped the blood from the blade of his axe.

"As soon as Lapin told me you had entered the forest I was sore troubled. The way is not easy to follow even in daylight. I rose in the early hours and sought you out..."

His teeth lit in a deadly smile.

"...the outlaws made so much noise my search was made the easier."

Norbert, still not capable of speech, clasped Reygard's shoulder. Gadroon then suddenly remembered the horses.

"Our steeds..."

"They will not have gone far, the outlaws have no use for horses... their taking them was only to ensure you could not escape. They are a cowardly rabble."

"Still... we must find them... we have a long journey ahead."

"Aye... Lapin told me you have embarked upon a Quest..."

"Indeed..."

Reygard smiled once more.

"...as Arthur's knights are wont to do."

Gadroon allowed himself a brief smile also. Norbert, now having regained the power of speech, was eager to quiz Reygard of the likelihood of the outlaws returning. Before he could answer they heard a familiar voice sounding from the depths of the forest.

"Is a horse without a rider more content than a knight without his steed? Only he can tell... the four-footed party stays silent on the matter... though I have spoke with him in as many languages as I know... which is but the sum of none."

Lapin came into view leading their horses. Their saddles and packs were seemingly intact and, on closer inspection, it seemed the knights had lost none of their belongings. Gadroon was the first to give thanks.

"Not a jester but a man of miracles thou art, Lapin."

"If all the world were miracles constantly... which it is... none would consider but a slight thing to be remarkable. Thus the jester would be no more. But if this is not so... then the jester returns... to bring the strange to strangers."

Norbert slapped him on the back, Lapin then pretending to tumble backwards into the undergrowth.

"Hi, Sir Knight... thy blow was as the wind – blowing mightily. Thy limb has the strength of a storm that may take the limb away. From the mighty oak the bough falls... so thou art the king of the forest and master of the storm – and all at one moment."

As was his way, Lapin made their spirits merry once more. The words of his brother Reygard were more practical than paradoxical.

"I shall lead thee both back to the path. From there thou must needs follow the way once more to the west. It is but a day's ride to the edge of the forest... at an easy pace you will be there by the forenoon."

Norbert mused.

"And the outlaws?"

Reygard crossed his arms defiantly.

"I shall send word... in my way... throughout the forest that you are not to be molested. Not any in the whole of Arkenwold will harm you further... of that you may be sure."

Norbert seemed reassured. Now came the dawn – through the trees they gazed upon a sky slashed with pink. The clear light glinted upon sword and axe blade alike. The forester led them back to the path and the knights rode on, the growing beauty of the morn accompanying them.

IV

They'd all seen wonders, but nothing like this.
And some said he was witchcraft, a phantom.

Even had it been a bargain break, Norbert's favourite holiday destination would never be the Forest of Arkenwold. After an hour, the two knights were lost once more. The sombre wall of trees surrounding them looked on mockingly.

"What now, Gadroon?"

"Every possibility lies before us."

Norbert looked down at the dead leaves on the ground before him. As many possibilities as there are of these, he thought.

"Mean you that we should consider every one in turn?"

"That would take a lifetime or more."

This kind of conversation can go on forever, like the Circle Line.

"Then what?"

Gadroon looked hard at his companion.

"It seems we have no choice..."

Norbert was getting a little tetchy.

"What mean you now, Gadroon?"

"Honest sense is the greatest ally any man may have... but there is another...."

"What is that?"

"Faith. Follow the heart."

Norbert made an obvious point.

"But if we take the wrong path..."

"What of it? We have nothing to lose... we gain nothing by remaining here one movement longer."

"The way seemed so simple..."

"Aye... and to Reygard... who knows every tree in the forest... it was so."

And so they continued, but it was not long before misfortune came upon them again. As before, the way became so narrow the knights were eventually obliged to dismount and lead their horses. The further they went, the more oppressed they were by all that surrounded them. The very trees began to assume a forbidding appearance, like giants lying in wait for the unwary. Gradually the scene changed, and Gadroon hoped they might be nearing the edge of the forest, but it was not to be. He halted and leaned wearily upon his horse.

"'Tis utter madness. We have ridden and ridden yet we seem to have come but the distance a peasant walks from his hut to the turnip field. All reason is lost. I fear, Norbert... that we have strayed into an enchanted part of the forest."

This news sent Norbert out of his comfort zone and into the Twilight Zone. The fears of the previous night were a mere frisson compared to the malignant presence he could feel growing around him. They seemed to be on the edge of a glade where the snow still lingered – a pale powder that made the scene even more spectral. A sound that at first they thought might be the wind came but, as it grew louder, resembled more the call of birds unknown. By the time they entered the glade, this had become an unearthly tone.

With horror, Norbert saw the very ground before them was beginning to move. The earth had abandoned its very nature and become as another element – Water! Such a rocking back and forth resembled the surface of the sea! Great cracks began to appear, and all became a seething, tormented mass. More terrors followed as, from these gaping rents, came forth a writhing, blubbery, yellowness. Norbert cried out in fear.

"By all creation! Hell is before us!"

The ground continued to split asunder and, almost from beneath their feet, came endless coils writhing more feverishly than any serpent. More and more of this looping, contorted spawn began unwinding itself, seeming intent only to escape from the earth. The tendrils grew in thickness as they whirled and twirled in the air, and Norbert could plainly see jagged teeth erupting all over the bulbous stems. Gadroon called out to him in desperation.

"Look away! What you see is not there! These things live only through thy fear."

But Norbert was beyond reasoning, and his whole body shook uncontrollably. Oh, to be free of these terrible sights! Gadroon rushed over to him and flung the knight's own cloak over his head, certain that a world of darkness was better than anything Norbert's senses perceived. All the time these nauseous growths twisted like insane dancers. Gadroon wondered how long it would be before their whole consciousness became engulfed.

Even as Gadroon contemplated such a fate, a figure sporting a scarlet cloak stepped into the glade. He raised one arm and the air was immediately filled with a white light. Magic was afoot! Regarding the nauseous mass before him with a look of immense concentration, mixed with not a little contempt, this wizard held both arms aloft. To Gadroon it seemed the abandoned writhing suddenly halted, as if whatever life within the tendrils was aware the coming of the wizard heralded its imminent destruction. The wizard's voice rang out like a hammer striking upon an anvil

"Begone, thou worthless stuff! Return! Return to the deeps from where thou hast come! There is no place for you here. Begone! Trouble this world no more. By all the powers that are bestowed upon the magus... begone!"

The livid hue immediately began to fade, the forms to quiver, shrink, and eventually melt. All became a frothing, bubbling liquid flowing back into the cracks in the earth. These too soon narrowed and disappeared, so that within minutes all appeared as before. Satisfied

41

with this, the wizard lowered his arms. He then turned towards to his silent witness.

"I am Edrith the Wizard... and thou art Sir Gadroon, I believe. I bid thee greetings! A more peaceful time for the giving and taking of such courtesies might well be wished by us both."

Gadroon responded as best he could.

"I take the world as I find it, Master Wizard... though I thank all the powers that you have called upon for our deliverance. That you chose to come here when you did is a miracle."

Edrith smiled.

"All heaven and Earth is one great miracle, Sir Knight... and magic merely makes use of this power... to create or to destroy."

Gadroon shrugged.

"I am more than willing to engage in combat with my enemies... but the world of spirits... that I cannot hope to conquer."

Edrith smiled.

"To each of us is given particular powers."

Of all that had transpired, Norbert could have had little notion. Swathed in his cloak, in a cocoon of darkness, he now chose this moment to emerge and look about him. His relief and wonder were equal when he saw that all trace of the foul growth had disappeared from the glade. Noticing Edrith, he regarded him curiously. In his turn, the wizard looked upon Norbert, speaking in such a way that the words passed directly into his heart.

"And this must be Sir Norbert. I have heard much of thee... a noble knight of the realm..."

Norbert may have had his mind fried, twisted and blown away, but he still remembered his manners.

"I bid thee well."

Edrith pulled a small vial from his tunic.

"Your companion must drink this... it will bring strength to him once more."

Gadroon pressed the container to Norbert's lips, so that he took some of the liquid contained therein. The effect was instantaneous. No longer were Norbert's cheeks as chalk, his eye dull.

"All has passed, Norbert. We have Edrith here to thank for our deliverance."

The wizard smiled and made a mock bow towards the two knights.

"I was told you were here..."

"By Reygard?"

"The Forester? Nay... not any human creature... an owl I passed last night seated upon a branch told me of this matter."

Edrith, seeing the baffled expression upon the face of Norbert, made to offered some explanation.

"Of all the creatures of the night, the owl is the most wise. In the day... ravens and foxes are the most forthcoming in passing their news to mortal men... though I confess they are not above trickery, either."

Norbert was inclined to be on his dignity.

"You jest with us... surely..."

Edrith slowly shook his head.

"The natural world is the best teacher of all, good knight. My own master used to say that a rock would tell him more in an hour than a town full of folk in a whole lifetime."

Now sensing the identity of Edrith's master, Gadroon enquired after the well-being of Merlin. Norbert, perhaps a little too lively from the effects of Edrith's tonic, interrupted their talk. His mouth cashed a cheque his brain could not cover.

"All this talk of wizards and sorcery sickens me. Merlin is naught but an old trickster and a mountebank."

Edrith took this calmly, while eying Norbert with a gentle amusement.

"Know ye not that Merlin is the master of the night and the day... both the sun and the moon?"

43

Norbert was inclined to frown with disapproval. Edrith deliberately aimed his next words in the direction of the uptight knight, with a view to opening the doors of perception. (Kids! Don't try this at home!)

"Master Knight, Merlin holds the secrets of how the birds fly... the planets run their courses in the heavens... and why the stars do not fall from the skies. Though I am sure that at his command fall they would... if he so desired."

Norbert spluttered like a Morris Minor on a frosty morning. His religion gave no quarter to stuff like this. Unfazed, Edrith merely quickened his stride.

"If it be destined to happen... the magician cannot change but one jot anything that occurs in this world. And yet... he is able to exercise his powers whenever he wishes. If his desire coincides with the will of the universe then miracles may happen... as thy companion hath just witnessed."

Norbert started working furiously at the pump of piety.

"The Will of God..."

Edrith laughed so loudly and unexpectedly that Norbert visibly jumped.

"In ancient times men always aspired to be gods. I see no reason why mortals should not determine the form of heaven and earth."

At this Norbert got seriously puffed-up, mounting his soapbox with a hobbyhorse attached.

"Thy words are those of the Great Deceiver, the Father of Lies."

Edrith countered Norbert's pulpit polka with a fandango on the font.

"How one sees the world is how it will be, Sir Knight. The Forest of Arkenwold is most certainly enchanted... as you yourself have seen... the *manner* of its enchantment is in the mind of he who walks within it. "

Norbert was having none of it – not even one penny piece.

"It is an evil place! Fit only for the vagabonds that creep about in its shadows. Forsooth! We have been nearly murdered... and now made to endure the frights of hell... and for what purpose may I ask?"

Edrith looked upon him, kindly enough.

"Why... to test the spirit, Master Norbert... and there seems to be nothing amiss with thine. Thou art to be praised for thy resolve. But before you hear the sound of triumphant sackbuts welcoming you back to Camelot, you will need upon thy coming journey every speck of courage thou hast. Sorely tried you will be... more so than you have been this day... of that I do assure you."

Norbert did not wish to contemplate the prospect and said so, forthwith.

"It seems the Devil himself has set his foul purpose to ensure that honest and godly folks do constantly stumble and fall... perchance through no fault of their own. Ah... if that foul fiend had never come into this world..."

"But did not your god create this devil too?"

This was too much for Norbert. Theological debate was one thing, but rampant blasphemy just wasn't on. He puffed up again, this time like a flatulent frog.

"Thou wicked wizard, how dare thee insult mine own creator! It would be as well that you were struck down even to permit such thoughts to come into your mind... let alone to give them tongue."

There was no sign of any lightning bolts raining down from heaven, nor did Edrith look like he was about to run for cover.

"Master Knight... consider for one moment I beg of thee. Without night one cannot know or contemplate day. Similarly... there is light and dark within us all. All this talk of demons is of little worth. Have you not observed that all the ugliness and infamy in this world has been created by men themselves?"

Edrith, when he spoke, was as the cucumber, and his cool made Norbert's temper zap up a few more degrees – now rapidly approaching boiling point.

"Aye! And sorcery is a hideous thing to behold... for its foul and base treachery has but one purpose... to tempt the soul."

"Wizardry is a most ancient art, Sir Norbert! Older than either me or thee... and none may understand its power. It will bear insults beyond number for it knows full well that man is mortal whereas magic is eternal. Magic is indifferent to those upon the earth... all of whom one day will certainly perish. It is a gift from the gods. Remember this, O Quester upon The Path... there is more to this life than that which thou might see with thine own eyes."

Even if the lecture had a power-point presentation, Norbert would not have been convinced. Gadroon, who had been standing silently by all the while strode forward to grasp the hand of Edrith and thank him once more. The wizard looked kindly upon both knights.

"The road will be hard... but I know full well you will succeed in your Quest. Rest assured I shall be there to aid you further if you have need."

Gadroon did an encore.

"Thou art the best ally a man may have, Edrith."

"The otherworld with all its wonders and terrors is never far away. But from this moment on you have my protection. Until you leave the Forest of Arkenwold nothing will harm you..."

Norbert mumbled his thanks, he had seen a light in Edrith's eyes that was brighter than any he knew, and this troubled him greatly. He realised that his hobbyhorse might well have a wooden heart, possibly the same one Elvis sang about.

"I thank thee."

"When you take the way again you will find that it has an altogether more welcoming air. Now... farewell... until we meet again!"

The next moment Edrith seemed to be swallowed up by the forest. The knights took this as a sign they must continue upon their journey, and this they did. Norbert and Gadroon rode on through the trees. After some hours, to their relief, the path began to broaden by the minute. Even so, it was many hours before they sensed their weary exodus was coming to an end. The moon had risen, and its light was so intense as to turn night into day. In front of them was a gap in the trees – they had reached the edge of the forest. They did not rejoice overmuch, as deep in their hearts, both knights knew that Edrith had spoken only the truth. This was but the beginning of The Quest, and yet more danger and darkness were bound to follow.

V

And now, Gawain; think.
Danger is yours to overcome
And this game brings you
Danger. Can the game be won?

Their spirits strengthened anew, the companions decided to journey on through the night. The moon was now their ally. When they left the forest, the Plain of Tanawel – which meant 'peace' in the old tongue – was before them. The moon continued to bathe them in her silver light as they continued on their way to Château Charbon.

The coming of the dawn brought the knights to the edge of the plain. The wind rustling in the topmost branches of the elms echoed like a gentle sea. The thaw had set in and when the sun rose higher, the grass was lit with a thousand diamonds. An endless flat land stretched before them, and so undulating was it that, espying a clump of trees, at first they took this to be a mirage. It proved not to be so – but most real.

While resting the horses there, they discovered a well, surrounded by oak, ash and thorn. A flight of stone steps led to an ancient spring, a wooden pail lying on the ground next to it. They drew water for the horses and after quenched their own thirst. Such a sweet draught it was that came from those cool depths!

While mounting their horses once more, they espied a rider approaching in the distance. They waited intent on finding out who this lone figure could be. No hint of his identity was revealed as he approached them, except Gadroon recognised the livery of Charbon. The castle was still some distance away and it was unlikely this was a welcoming party. Two lowly knights from Arthur's court would hardly merit any kind of reception, however modest.

"Hie, Master Page, what is thy errand with us?"

At Gadroon's call the youth reined in his horse and came up alongside of them.

"Good morrow, great and noble knights. I am Nouvin... in service at Chateau Charbon."

Gadroon was quizzical.

"Thou art some distance from thy quarters, Master Page..."

Nouvin pointed towards some low hills that could be seen in the far distance.

"Aye... Charbon is now my home but yonder I was raised in a hamlet... it was named Lonwyd in the old chronicles."

Norbert smiled upon him.

"Thou hadst good fortune to have been born in such a place of peace methinks."

Nouvin's face fell, almost as far as his pointy boots.

"It was so, Sir Knight... until *the beast* came there."

Norbert turned a whiter shade of pale. You could hear the organ intro coming in.

"The *Beast*?"

"*The Ufeltan*, good sirs... the dragon. You have not heard tell of this cruel and terrible creature?"

Gadroon deliberated.

"Perhaps... but it may be that I thought such things to be tales from afar... stories that grew in the telling...."

"Nay, sir... I assure you... 'tis true...."

"Then tell us more, good page!"

"All are afeared the Ufeltan will destroy every man, woman and babe in the hamlet. I have been sent by the elders to seek out men of yore to hasten and defend us."

Gadroon was lost in thought, a place where many seek directions.

"It is the first rule of chivalry that a knight must defend the weak. So it is meet and right that one of Arthur's Company should hasten to the aid of you and your fellows and do battle with the Great Worm."

49

"Does this mean that thy very selves will come to the aid of our helpless Lonwyd?"

"Aye... it will be so. I, Sir Gadroon shall do this deed, while my companion Sir Norbert will continue with thee... to your master's estate. I think thou hast a map to show where this beast doth lie..."

With a flourish Nouvin drew from his jerkin a worn parchment. '*Here be dragons*' was plainly inscribed in the top right hand corner. Antique and picturesque it may have been, but as Medieval Sat Nav, it was totally useless.

"All is not lost, Great Master... I may show thee the path thou must take."

Naturally Norbert mildly protested that he would himself be willing to do battle with The Great Worm, but this was merely for form's sake. Neither did Nouvin look as if he considered Norbert a serious contender in the dragon-slaying stakes. The effect of Edrith's tonic having now completely worn off, he had lapsed into his usual laid-back self. Taking on the back end of a pantomime horse might have been too much for him right then.

"Lonwyd will forever be in thy debt, Sir Gadroon."

He who was addressed merely shrugged manfully, as befits all strong and silent types, and the trio set off upon their way. They journeyed some leagues before Nouvin halted to show Gadroon the way he should follow. The brave knight bid farewell, assuring them he would join them at Chateau Charbon when the deed was done.

*

Nouvin turned out to be a cheery companion, and during their ride together Norbert learned from him much of life both above and below stairs at Chateau Charbon. As Norbert had suspected, the Wooslak-Bascoombes – the family that had held Charbon since the days of King Eggbound II – were country Sloanes down to their Gothic gumboots.

The way climbed slowly and they could see in the far distance the Feilach mountains, now capped with snow. In the valley below, set on a fork in the River Ilydonel, lay Chateau Charbon. A stone bridge with immense turrets could be clearly seen ahead of them, hinting at the grand design of the rest of the castle. Crossing the eastern arm of the river, Norbert could see the towers of Charbon, offering a softer line than was usual for the times, and giving all a welcoming air. A pale sun, like a ghostly coin, hovered above them as they followed the way as it went, winding slowly down the side of the valley. At last the gates of Charbon were before them.

As Norbert rode into the courtyard, he was greeted by Tantrum the Steward. His purple cap he chose to wear at an angle that defied gravity. As Norbert got the standard welcome from Tantrum, he was at the same time assessed for the amount of deference due to him.

"Chateau Charbon greets thee, Sir Knight."

"I am Sir Norbert of Camelot and I come at the behest of Sir Edmund Wooslak-Bascoombe."

Norbert hoped he would not have to mouth that moniker too often.

"Ah... from King Arthur's court..."

"That is so."

Tantrum switched from stiff to chatty.

"...another passed by here from Camelot recently... on his way to Malfaise."

"Indeed?"

"*A Jester.*"

"Ah... yes... Lapin. We know him well."

The Steward glanced in the direction of the drawbridge.

"You have a companion, Sir Knight?"

"Sir Gadroon and I were together until some hours ago. Unexpected business took him to a hamlet near here..."

"Oh?"

Norbert lowered his voice dramatically.

"Gadroon is intent on dispatching a Great Worm."

Tantrum's face radiated astonishment and awe.

"Great Worm, you say! Ah, the Beast of Bumblebritch! The Ufeltan in the common tongue..."

"The very same I believe..."

"...and your companion hath taken it upon himself to slay this fearsome creature? My! Such great news! All here must be told forthwith. We are a community where little changeth from day to day... this will be tidings of the greatest import."

Tantrum seemed genuinely impressed at Norbert's revelations. As he led his visitor across the courtyard towards the castle keep, he continued to mutter approvingly. There currently being no other gossip, Norbert and Gadroon would certainly be frontpage news. Their standing would be high among the castle servants – double helpings of pudding coming their way without a doubt. His standing raised somewhat, Norbert was slightly less bashful than he might have been when he went to meet his host.

Sir Edmund and Lady Malinda were of prime English stock, the type that would breed Old Etonians many centuries later. Their sort got to be at the top of the feudal ladder because they had stomped on those grasping desperately at the next rung down. The future descendants of these robber barons would turn Château Charbon into a theme park – with a miniature railway, adventure playground and several burger bars. Thus they would keep up the family tradition – not giving a damn what anybody thought.

Cordial but distant – as often the way of the privileged classes – Sir Edmund received the newcomer in his chamber. Norbert introduced himself and bowed as low as his XXL pantaloons would allow.

"So... your chum... orf dealing with vermin somewhere I understand?"

"'Tis true, Sir Edmund."

"You are *knight errants* I believe. Yes... well... how absolutely spiffing for you! Don't see so many of you chaps about these days, what with the dragon count being so low these last few seasons. Not to mention maidens in distress being a bit thin on the ground too... must be a sign of the times too... eh... what?"

Sir Edmund let out a bit of chuckle, a sound like a wallaby sneezing. Norbert thought he ought to offer a grin or two in support of such masterful wit. Sir Edmund, judging this to be a pretty feeble attempt at bonhomie, decided to carry on a bit more.

"I'm a huntin' man meself. Always have been... father was the same... Grandpa Bascoombe too. Orf at dawn with the jolly old hounds after Sammy Stag, that's my idea of a bit of a lark. Might not be everybody's cup of mead but it's certainly mine. Hmmmph. Well... there we are. Bob's yer blinkin' uncle... eh. D'you hunt?"

"I regret do not, Sir Edmund."

Norbert could see his standing visibly drop innumerable points.

"No? Pity. We shan't see much of each other then... apart when we put on the old nosebag in The Hall. I'm out and about at the crack o' sparrow... then don't pop back until day is done and all that."

"Yes... I see..."

At that precise moment the leading lady made her entrance from the wings.

"Mmm... aha... my dear wife... So you two can have a bit of a chinwag now. I've got a few things must see to about the place so I'll just pop orf. Cheerio then... um... Norbert... see you in due course I expect, what?"

"Farewell, Sir Edmund."

His host disappeared, perhaps a little more promptly than was strictly polite. Lady Malinda glided in with her maids, like an elegant schooner escorted by a lot of jolly little tugboats.

"Sir Norbert! How gladdened and honoured Charbon is by your presence..."

The upper classes tend to turn on the five-star flattery as easily as drawing a bath. Poor old Norbert felt a bit out of his depth, particularly when Lady Malinda got going at a cracking pace with the chat.

"...and your companion... Sir Dragoon... he is orf chasing a gadroon..."

The maids all dutifully giggled at this spoonerism and Norbert manfully did his grinning glassily bit. Lady Malinda sensed her guest was starting to seriously flag and she certainly wasn't having any dozing off in the soup later.

"Sir Norbert... you must be so tired after your journey... all your wonderful adventures... which I shall *insist* you tell me all about later. I have *personally* chosen the finest chamber for you. I will tell Tantrum to escort you there."

"I am most grateful, my lady."

Her ladyship was all breezy and bright, as if she was about to open the village fete.

"We must have you on top form for tonight when you can tell us all about your goings on... and your friend... whose name I shan't even try to say... or I shall simply make some frightful bish again... and then everyone will make so much fun of me..."

Norbert could hear more dutiful giggles from the maidenly gaggle as he followed Tantrum to his appointed chamber. Sumptuous it was indeed – as far as anything could be so described in the Dark Ages – and he gratefully collapsed on the coverlet of his bed. Closer examination would have revealed the woven design as being a graphic depiction of rutting stags. Oblivious, Norbert lay sleeping like an innocent babe amidst the carnal mayhem.

*

The feasting, when it arrived, was something of an ordeal for Norbert. Not that he did not enjoy the fayre put before him, which was copious and most toothsome. It was the chat that defeated him – the baronial banter going backwards and forwards like a busy shuttlecock. No sooner did Norbert think of some *bon mot* than the talk shuffled off into some other territory. By the time the culinary *piece de resistance* – a swan stuffed with a goose, a duck inside that, a quail inside that and so on – was wheeled in, Norbert was bored stiff.

Lady Malinda had insisted that Norbert sit on her right. She did her best to include him in the conversation, but tended to abandon her guest when she wanted to pitch in herself. She was quite capable of braying and hee-hawing at top volume like all the rest of them. After an hour or so of this Norbert had a corker of a headache and prayed for the evening to end so he might retire to his chamber once more.

Her ladyship was certainly the life and soul of the party, and got more vivacious and unbuttoned as the evening developed. She was obviously determined to keep Norbert interested in her and at every opportunity stroked his arm or, more disturbingly, squeezed a thigh beneath the table.

After a few cups of wine her caresses, particularly those involving his nether parts, became even more daring. Norbert was becoming thoroughly alarmed when, to his relief, the Under-Steward called for silence, the hubbub receding from a Force Ten Gale to a moderate tempest.

"Sir Edmund... Lady Malinda... My Lords... Ladies... pray leave aside the sweetmeats and gather together that the dancing may commence."

This was a signal for the company to surge away from the tables and gather about the floor. The nobility were now getting in the mood to show a leg or two. For those who had imbibed freely, getting said limbs to function was a bit of an undertaking. It helped a little that the dancing of the time was not abandoned but simple and sedate. During a *rondel*, the dancers formed a ring and held hands. Somewhat predictably, they perambulated in a circle – first one way and then the other. The dancers were also expected to sing at the same time. A brace of lutes and the inevitable sackbut started up, and they were under starter's orders.

Lady Malinda grasped one of Norbert's hands, while the other was held by Lady Lumpkin. The circle twirled round tentatively, and it was obvious that many of the gentlemen participating could hardly stand, let alone dance. Norbert, infinitely more sober than the rest, found himself leading the proceedings, a role which he had certainly not anticipated. So grim was his resolve however, that in the eyes of the ladies, he was elevated to heroic status.

The next piece was a variation – The Chain – the form of which speaks for itself, and no more exciting than its predecessor. Norbert found himself at the head of the cavorting procession, Lady Lumpkin immediately behind him, Earl Gobforth next in line. The rhythm of the dance, encouraged by the minstrels, became lively, quickly building a certain amount of momentum. All went well until the Earl stumbled, and in clutching at Lady Lumpkin to save himself, brought them both down. Those behind all went over like a stack of dominoes. Lady Malinda found herself on the floor in an unwelcome embrace with Lord Lungecock.

Norbert, taking advantage of the melee, and seeing a side-door conveniently open, sashayed neatly out of the Hall. He found himself in a passage he recognised as leading to the guests' bedchambers. Gaining his room, he quickly dived beneath the coverlet and sought slumber. His first taste of the high life was not much to his liking, and he fondly hoped he would also escape the too-intimate attentions of his hostess on the morrow. In this, he was most definitely mistaken.

VI

Her face was sweet,
Her skin was white and pink;
She spoke like birds
Singing, and her small lips laughed.

A sound woke Norbert and he opened one eye cautiously. A slim hand slipped around the chamber door, followed by an equally slim figure. Norbert thought it prudent to close his eyes and feign sleep. As we have been told, Norbert's experience of the female sex hovered around zero and falling. If his libido had been a terrestrial tremor it would not have registered on the lower end of the Richter Scale. He continued with the feigned *zzzzzz* routine while Lady Malinda, most fetching in gooseberry-colored velvet robe and a wimple to match, was by now perched on the end of his bed.

"Sir Norbert..."

The words floated in the air like a pink mist. Norbert flipped on the sound and vision.

"Lady Malinda... what ails thee? Not a fire in the castle I trust?"

"Only a burning in my heart, fair knight."

Her eyes flashed like a Sixties strobe light. Norbert, more dozzled than bedazzled, began to mutter.

"...for you to enter my chamber... something must be amiss..."

"Sir Edmund is away hunting... so nothing can therefore be amiss..."

"Aha..."

"Sir Norbert, does my desire to be in thy company disturb thee... or perhaps it is thy desire that is aroused?"

For Norbert this was a puzzle impossible to solve, like a Rubik cube with half the bits missing. Norbert could only refer to the Chivalric Code, p.153 s. 27.

"A lady's wish should be honoured always."

Lady Malinda positively simpered, with more than a touch of simmering thrown in.

"And how shall I command thee, gentle knight? What pleasure could a willing woman gain from thee? One so great in its delight..."

Norbert could not help noticing that as she was talking her ladyship was moving closer to him.

"I know not, my lady..."

Her response was to advance a good foot and a half more along the coverlet. Lady Malinda was now adjacent to parts of Norbert he definitely considered to be private.

"Should you wish tutelage in such things, sir knight... you will find me more than a willing teacher..."

It was no good – such nuances went over Norbert's head like a Boeing 747.

"I would not think to place such a burden upon you, my lady."

Lady Malinda decided to give up – at least for the moment. She rose, displaying a touch of pique, and made for the exit.

"I shall leave thee to rest, Sir Norbert. I look forward to your company this eve at the feasting table."

"Indeed, Lady Malinda... I too anticipate that pleasure."

Norbert waited until he was sure the door of his chamber had closed once more. What in the name of St. Clapton of Winwood had all that performance been about? He resumed his slumbers, his dreams set in a landscape where exotic fauna like Lady Malinda were nowhere to be seen.

At the same moment, Gadroon was approaching the cave of the Ufeltan. This fabulous beast would prove to be as much of a challenge to this noble knight as a rampant aristo was to his chum.

*

A dragon, more than artfully designed by a divine hand, is a serpent with wings. Renowned for their wisdom and ruthlessness, the Ufeltan was a top-of-the-range model. The sheen of its golden scales was dazzling to look upon and could have been part of heaven itself. Gadroon was now feeling less enthusiastic about the whole business of *dragon slaying* but he tethered his horse to the statutory blasted oak, and set off towards the dragon's lair. The way led between jagged rocks and trees that had been visibly singed at some time or other. With a song in his heart he continued on, though the melody might have been in a minor key.

When Gadroon approached the dragon's cave the ambiance was exactly as he rather hoped it wouldn't be – lots of bones scattered about and more than a hint of menace. Our hero reflected that dozens of knights had known this moment; the problem was that not a lot of them had lived to see the next one. Gadroon boldly threw caution to the winds – not only a ludicrous metaphor, but rather a silly thing to do in the circumstances.

"*Ufeltan, thou foulest of creatures, spawn of the dark pit!* No longer wilst thou bring fear to mortal men! Come thee hither and make ready to face thy doom!"

Nothing happened, which for Gadroon was a bit of a letdown. A wisp or two of blue smoke came wafting out of the depths of the cave, but not much else. Time passed, as it tends to do, though at a much slower pace than usual. Gadroon repeated his challenge, this time louder and longer, though his voice was starting to crack by the time he had finished. From the depths of the cave came answer – a rasping tone, and a touch on the peevish side too.

60

"Who the dickens is making that awful row out there? I didn't get a lot of kip last night... hot flushes... that sort of thing... hoping for a bit of lie-in. Fat chance now! Absolutely no consideration for anybody else some people..."

Listening to all this, Gadroon might have changed tack, but he stuck to the script.

"*Fiend! Show thyself!* Thou shalt pay dearly for thy cruel and wanton ways! Thy life is the only repentance I shall accept... no less."

This all prompted an even more tetchy response.

"Oh, do be quiet! I've never heard such a lot of tosh in all my life! Who d'you think you are... some curate preaching his first sermon? Do put a sock in it... there's a good chap. I'm in no mood for that kind of twaddle... savvy?"

Gadroon marched boldly towards the cave and peered in. It all rather resembled the Ghost Train on Brighton Pier.

"Sir Gadroon of King Arthur's Court demands that Ufeltan the dragon come hither... that combat may commence."

In his mind Gadroon saw the situation quite clearly. You can't have a dragon without a knight – that was like a chav without a bit of bling. When Ufeltan actually appeared, Gadroon might have had second thoughts, but it was too late. Dragons were part of *myths and legends*, but if you believe they're real, the essence of their realness is that they're *big*. The wingspan alone would have qualified for Runway 3 at Gatwick. Not that the tail wasn't impressive either – the way the pointed end swished about from side to side. And this was all before the flaming bit got going too – there was obviously a lot to learn about the family of *draconis*. The beast in question – not looking terribly pleased – then emerged, to regard Gadroon.

"So, what *is* all this fuss about? Disturbing honest folks when they're tucked up nicely in bed... rabbiting

on outside my front door in some archaic lingo....
making absolutely no sense at all. What's your game,
Tin Trousers? C'mon... out with it!"

Gadroon was not quite sure what to do next.
Challenging a ton of armour-plated dragon to a scrap
might have been his first mistake. The magnificent
example of the swordsmith's art he held would be about
as much use as a propelling pencil. Our hero thought
he might try appealing to the dragon's sense of history.

"It's a tradition. The Great Worm brings fear and
terror to the innocent villagers... they summon a
fearless knight. He dispatches the beast in a bloody
combat... cuts off its head... presents it to the old
patriarch of the grateful community... many a maiden
looks on admiringly. The noble knight rides off into the
sunset."

Ufeltan listened to all this with growing impatience.

"And you think I'm not aware of all that guff? My
grandfather used to tell me these stories.... called me
his 'little firebrand' while I sat on his knee hanging on
his every word. Those were the days... peasants had a
bit of respect for dragons then. Now we're nothing but
some cute little illustration in the border of a map
drawn up by some goofy monk. 'Here be dragons',
indeed! What a blasted cheek!"

In a way Gadroon was sympathetic but felt he ought
to support the conservative view.

"I know, but the old tales must also be honoured. I,
Sir Gadroon have come to fulfill my vows of chivalry. It
is a mark of honour. We two must engage in combat...
and that until death."

Ufeltan snorted – no small thing where a dragon is
concerned.

"What an old stick-in-the-mud you are! It's about
time they wrote some new tales that reflected an
enlightened view. You wait... in years to come they'll
want to preserve creatures like me in purpose-built

parks. It'll be too late then... of course... extinct that's what we'll all be."

Gadroon was not prepared to comment; he just got on his horse, raised his lance, and posed. If there had been a wind machine handy his flowing locks would have assumed the look of a lion's mane. Ufeltan sighed with tired resignation.

"I can see there's no getting through to an old *reactionary* like you. I suppose we'd better get on with it... acting out some tired old ritual that has no meaning anymore. What a waste of time! If only you hadn't come along... demanding to breathe some life into your antiquated beliefs... I could have been dreaming about some beautiful young gryphon..."

Gadroon was in another world, one where fair maidens were there to be succoured and every wrong righted. He lowered his lance and prepared to charge. Ufeltan looked suitably laconic about the whole affair. For form's sake he whirled his tail and flapped his wings, a procedure which succeeded in creating a small but impressive whirlwind.

Gadroon spurred on his steed, the familiar coconut-shell sound of coconut-shells being clonked together filling the air. He bore down on the dragon holding his breath, waiting for the moment when his lance would strike, hopefully in some vulnerable spot. It never happened.

Ufeltan didn't move an inch, just coolly blew smoke rings – perhaps the same as the ones of your mind. They certainly blew Gadroon's mind – and he could see clouds from both sides now. He dropped his lance, and promptly fell off his horse.

The dragon smirked in a superior sort of way as Gadroon hit the deck with a noise like dustbins doing the hokey cokey in a skip. He lay there for some time.

"A knavish trick, O Beast of Evil!"

"Evil... eh? And what were *you* going to get up to with that sharp spear of yours then... give me acupuncture?"

"Twister of words! Thou fightest not fairly!"

"Oh, button your visor, Aluminum Drawers! Get yourself a can-opener."

Gadroon went to draw his sword with a view to avenging such a gross insult, but the weapon was no longer in its scabbard. It must have been flung into the far distance when he took his tumble. Ufeltan then put his huge head about three inches from Gadroon's nose.

"Now you jolly well listen to me, Sir – *puffed-up* – Gadroon. Times have changed... St. Georgie-Porgy ain't the top banana any more. He'll be no more than a football flag one day... you mark my words. The Archangel Michael had a lot more savvy than he ever did... knew that it was better to gain wisdom from a dragon rather than harm it."

Ufeltan warbled a little ditty that he had – rather obviously – composed himself.

No wool's ever been pulled o'er my eyes
Any villein will tell thee... I'm very, very wise.

Gadroon was studying the eye of the dragon from close range. He had no option. It was enough to convince him. Within that gold and emerald orb lay all the secrets of the world, from the depths of the past to the furthest places in the future. How could he have wished to harm such a magnificent creature? Ufeltan, sensing this, would have patted him on the shoulder if it wasn't for the spikes sticking out of his claws.

"There... there... you're not a bad sort of chap... just a bit too inclined to follow the Medieval party line. Now... cheer up! I've got something interesting you might like to see. Very fine and beautiful and worth an absolute fortune... you've probably guessed what it is already..."

64

"No… it cannot be…"

"The Holy of Holies… The very Grail itself."

Gadroon went all shivery at the mention of the sacred vessel. Could The Quest have already been fulfilled? Gadroon was suddenly suspicious.

"How can it be one such as thee owns such a sacred thing?"

Ufeltan was somewhat affronted.

"All dragons guard a hoard of gold and jewels… you should know that Master Gadroon. You haven't been doing your homework have you?"

For a moment Gadroon wondered about voluntarily entering a dragon's cave, but he did.

"I've been thinking of having one of those antique chappies over one day… just to tell me how much it might fetch at auction. Now… come along and see this wonderful thing for yourself."

Gadroon was suddenly aware of a mysterious light, not originating from any opening in the roof of the cave but coming from somewhere within. At that instant he espied the heap of treasure, so huge you could have hiked on it or abseiled off the top. The knight gawked at the urns brimming with diamonds, the piles of gold rings and bracelets, and the caskets stuffed with glittering precious stones. Right on the summit of this bank of baubles stood the star prize – The Holy Grail. Or was it?

Gadroon was determined to investigate. And began to wade through this ocean of opulence until he reached the holy vessel. It was certainly impressive – a silver chalice encrusted with emeralds and rubies and ornately etched with intricate scrollwork. And yet…

Wasn't there something a bit vulgar about it? A hint of the Las Vegas rhinestone jumpsuit? Gadroon closely examined its flamboyant form until he found the script on the base of the cup. 'Brierley Hill the Blacksmith maketh this'. Gadroon propped the goblet back against a stack of sapphires and clambered down again.

"'Tis but a farrago of fakery."

"Really? Not worth a churl's chuff?"

"I think not..."

Ufeltan was inclined to be philosophical.

"There you go... win some, lose some. I never quite trusted the cove I got it from... didn't like the cut of his jib. I suppose I could always give it to someone as a Christmas present..."

Gadroon agreed, absently, as he was now desirous to be off. Darkness was about to fall and he wanted to retrieve his sword. Gadroon was much relieved when the mighty blade was found poking out of a badger's burrow. The knight had been thinking about how to repay the dragon for his gracious understanding, as well as not frying him to a packet of Doritos.

"I will proclaim it abroad that Ufeltan is no more... swallowed up by some extraordinary shiftings of the Earth. That way there is no need for folks to venture near thy lair."

Ufeltan fairly beamed.

"Excellent! That would be a relief... I won't get kids chucking stones at me anymore... I'm not getting any younger after all..."

Gadroon was intrigued.

"How are old you?"

"Five hundred and sixty-three next Yule."

"Fie!"

"That's about middle-aged for us dragons. I'm definitely at the cup of cocoa and slippers stage, I can tell you."

Gadroon set off on his way while Ufeltan, all bright red and glowing gold, waved a claw. As he set his steed towards Chateau Charbon, Gadroon wondered what it would be like to have wings, and fly about the place scaring the socks off all and sundry – rather a lark, he thought.

*

If Gadroon was ever going to feel like a star this was definitely the moment. News about his exploits had spread as fast as a plague with sneakers. 'Sir Gadroon the Mighty Dragon Slayer' definitely qualified as *Hello!* magazine material. When this all kicked off Gadroon followed the golden rule that the legend must outscore historical fact every time. He certainly wasn't going to let on what had really happened.

When he arrived at Chateau Charbon and saw bunting everywhere and flags flying from the topmost towers, Gadroon assumed the king or some other blue-blooded begum was on a royal tour. He was quickly put right about that when he passed through the castle gates. Lines of trumpeters tooted merrily, sackbuts squawked and many a maiden threw flowers at his feet. The common folk put up a fine showing too, loudly acclaiming their hero.

"Hail Sir Gadroon! Saviour of the People! Hail thou brave and fearless knight!"

Gadroon felt this was all a bit rich and, although he smiled and waved like the Queen Mum during the Blitz, he still felt a bit of a fraud. Dismounting, he let his horse be led away by a whole platoon of ostlers eager for the privilege. Our reluctant hero was only too glad to escape his adoring fans and get inside the keep, planning to have a hot tub and a bit of a nap before dinner. On the way to his chamber he was ambushed by a gaggle of girlies – Lady Melinda's maids – screaming like they were pop-fans at Wembley. Lady Malinda found him lying dazed outside his chamber – post-groping by groupies.

"Sir Gadroon! You appear as a vision before us! Apollo descending from the heights of Olympus to dazzle us with your exploits and... dare I say it... your beauty!"

This was accompanied by much flashing of eye and bouncing of bodice. Gadroon responded as best he could in the circs.

"It is an honour to make your acquaintance Lady Malinda... and of Sir Edmund also. Where may he be found... that I may pay my respects to my host?"

"Hunting... a-hunting... always at the chase. While I it seems have... in my own castle... run to earth an even more magnificent creature. One who is the conqueror of all... fair damsels..."

Gadroon wasn't in the mood for a flurry of flirtatiousness; a quick shower would have more his top priority. He rather considered her ladyship could do with a cold version, the way she was carrying on.

"My lady... I beg that I am allowed to retire... besting dragons doth bring much fatigue upon a poor knight..."

Lady Malinda was all sympathy, and cooed like a cote full of doves.

"All brave knights must take rest..."

"And my fellow knight, Sir Norbert... may I know where his chamber lieth?"

Her ladyship it seemed was more than familiar with its location and guided him there. Gadroon after bidding farewell to Lady Melinda knocked in friendly fashion.

"Who is without?"

"'Tis I... Gadroon."

The door was flung open with such force that Gadroon was almost knocked over. There stood Norbert, the tufts of hair that remained to him standing out like earmuffs. His features reflected extreme anxiety and when he spoke, his voice was as a mere squeak.

"Thank the heavens it is you, Gadroon."

Gadroon was alarmed.

"What ails thee, old friend?"

The tale of Lady Malinda was swiftly related. Gadroon manfully suppressed a desire to chuckle, while Norbert could not contain himself.

"What could have been the purpose of her coming to my chamber? Why... *oddsbodkins*... I am certain she was intent upon entering my bed! For what purpose may I ask?"

Gadroon was spluttering with mirth, which he deftly turned into a fit of coughing.

"And... did she?"

Norbert was outraged.

"Nay... most certainly not! And if you mean what I think you mean and... as I know nothing of that which you might mean... I am naturally the more confused."

When put like that, Gadroon was too. He regarded Norbert for a moment or two then gave up. Short of a long dissertation on the aviary and the apiary there was little to be done. Norbert continued to wring his hands in a frenzy.

"I have not dared to venture forth into the castle corridors. I implore you Gadroon... to share my bedchamber this night... forsooth... even my bed... so there is no chance that this lady enters therein."

Gadroon was inclined to offer soothing words rather than adopt this game plan.

"Peace, my dear friend... do not be in such fear and trembling. I am sure all this is only a... um... friendly gesture of welcome on Lady Malinda's part..."

"You thinketh this to be so?"

Gadroon continued in his most casual manner.

"I have no doubt of it. Her ladyship is perchance so overwhelmed at entertaining such... distinguished guests as she perceiveth us... that she is fevered in the manner in which she showeth it. A little reflection, old friend! It is but a trifling matter."

"Perhaps you are right, Gadroon. Fie! I know nothing of women! They are but a mystery to me... one I have never sought to explore."

And if you carry on thinking like that they always will be, thought Gadroon. Norbert seeming to be to some degree placated, Gadroon went to his ablutions. Later he accompanied his fellow knight to the Great Hall. If Gadroon had thought the adulation he had received was fading, he was mistaken. Everyone wanted to shake him by the hand, the most odious hangers-on and back-slappers being stacked up like deck chairs on the prom. The feast was a succession of toasts and speeches in his honour and Gadroon was obliged to reply to each and every one. By the end of the evening he would have almost preferred to be back in Ufeltan's cave.

VII

And hedgerows swell tall,
And blossoms blow open,
And glorious woods are all
Echoing joy and hope.

Before retiring, Norbert and Gadroon discussed their situation. The next destination – the Abbey at Piedervoux – was at least a day's journey away. Norbert was adamant they must quit Charbon at dawn. Gadroon agreed to this, but was still curtly dismissive of Norbert's fears as to being ravaged in the night by Lady Malinda. The next morning when they met in the refectory to break their fast, Norbert made no mention of any illicit nocturnal visits.

Though her ladyship was not to be seen, her spouse was very much in evidence in the courtyard. When the ostlers had brought their horses, the two knights came upon this champion of the chase harrying his harriers and hounding his hounds ready for another day's sport. Sir Edmund was his usual bluff and hearty self.

"What ho, you two! Just orf? I'm so very sorry that I haven't seen a lot of either of you. True... I've not been about the place much... if I've not been seeing what's what in the kennels, I've been up to me knees in whatnot in the bally stables... eh what? Always something or other with this huntin' lark... doncha know."

Gadroon made all the right noises.

"I trust you have a fine day's sport, Sir Edmund."

This prompted the old duffer to get chatty.

"Funny... I had a bally dream last night that some damned jack-in-office stopped people doin' all this in about a thousand years hence. 'Ban hunting' he kept shouting... and they cussed well did... the pestilent knaves. I'd have had 'em all strung up from the castle walls... every manjack of 'em... if I was in charge. That'd teach 'em a lesson... eh... what?"

The Nabob of Nimrod puffed and huffed a bit more, even while Norbert and Gadroon politely thanked him for his hospitality.

"Drop by again... if you're ever over this way. Oh... and give my regards to the King and er... what's-her-face will you?"

"The Lady Guinevere, my lord?"

Sir Edmund, turning away to pat a slobbery hound, shouted at Gadroon over his shoulder.

"Damn... you're right! That's the filly! Anyhow... must be getting along... time and tide wait for no beggar... and all that... eh? Pippity-pip and pip... pip... pip."

As they were about to cross the drawbridge Gadroon spied Lady Malinda at a window. She was desperately trying to get their attention by waving some silken garment. Probably one of shocking intimacy thought Gadroon. He deliberately did not draw Norbert's attention to this display for fear he might fall off his horse.

The two knights left Charbon and rode into the Great Plain beyond. The sun bestowed little warmth on the travellers, and perhaps the elements conspired to sharpen the brain, for the two knights began to debate in earnest.

"Forsooth, Norbert... dost thou not mark well we have learned the First Wisdom?"

Norbert was as incisive as... not Bertrand Russell, more a Jack Russell.

"Certain am I that thou speakest not false, old friend. We have both been tested and tried... and each in a different manner. Methinks the wisdom we have gained is that much may be hidden behind any mask set to the world."

"Indeed. Both Lady Malinda and the Ufeltan were revealed to be much different to how they first appeared."

Gadroon had earlier given his fellow knight an edited version of the events that transpired in the dragon's cave. His conscience might have been troubled by the episode if he had not regarded these things as only part of the warp and weft of experience. The episode of the false grail had only heightened his belief that one should be wary of being deceived by appearances.

"And were not both of us true to what was in our hearts and acted according to the highest of virtues..."

Gadroon agreed and they continued on until some little time later when he spied in the distance, their goal.

"There lieth... over yon ridge... the Abbey of Piedervoux. See... we have only to cross over the River Ilyondel."

The wooden bridge that had achieved this end had seen better days. There was many a gap in the boards but, to their relief, it held fast. A gentle slope led to the edge of an expanse of moorland and beyond this, the knights could clearly see the outline of the abbey buildings. They could hear the sound of a bell echoing in the clear air, calling the pious to prayer. Soon, all manner of bells joined with this single peal, clattering in unison. This tide of sound cascaded about Norbert's ears and echoed in his very soul.

As the clouds moved in a slow procession across the towers of the abbey to Norbert, he was returning home. The knights rode beneath an archway into the paved courtyard where strode a lone figure – the abbot himself. Personal denial was obviously not a hallmark of the spiritual life for this prelate. He waddled over to greet the knights, his belly bobbing about like a balloon in a sauna.

"Welcome to Piedervoux, my noble and worthy knights!"

Gadroon was straight in with the high-octane flannel.

"My lord abbot, worthiness belongs to thee only."

Abbot Speckle hailed a passing monk, as if he were a cab.

"Brother Plume! Pray tell Brother Strudel to see to the horses... and yourself take our guests to the refectory. There they may be given refreshment after their journey."

This was all music to the ears of Norbert. Soon, strong ale, a quartern loaf, fresh cheese and a few onions were set down before them. Norbert for him to set about scoffing and quaffing like the champion trencherman he was. The replete stage had just been gained when a young monk approached their table – deferential, but still obviously keen on a pow-wow.

"Sir Knights... I am the monk Scriven. I greet thee."

The knights returned the greeting civilly enough.

"Hail to thee, Brother Scriven."

"There is some matter of import I would wish to share with you both... a great vision known only to myself. I would most earnestly entreat you to follow me to the Scriptorium."

Intrigued, Norbert and Gadroon followed this dutiful devotee as he led the way back to the courtyard. The Scriptorium lay some way from the main buildings, as if the business of art ought to be removed from the hustle and bustle of ordinary monkish pursuits. They entered, and within came upon a row of cubicles. In each of these a monk sat, perched upon a stool like a crow. A candle cast its dim light upon the page before him, and every hand laboured unceasingly to illuminate some sacred text. The iridescent blues, emerald green, and glint of gold combined to fill the place with a holy light. Here, industry had been transformed into prayer; such was the sanctified air of the Scriptorium. Scriven then led them to his own separate cell, one away from the rest.

"Our abbot desires to have a collection of books greater than any of the kings in the land... and twice as fine. He has given me the task of providing these for his library... so I spend my days copying the great treasures of wisdom that have already been set down in the past. I have a lifetime's work before me... it will be my legacy. Such things of beauty I will leave to the world after I am gone."

Upon a lectern a book lay open. The inkwell, quill and ruler next to the page indicating this was Scriven's current task. He was apparently privileged to enjoy the benefit of an oil lamp, and a sundial on the window ledge told of time's passing. Norbert took all this in. His fascination for the cloistered life was all too apparent, and growing greater by the hour.

"Ah... it is a fine calling you have Master Monk. To be surrounded by great books and the way of learning is an enviable thing. I have learned the grammar and the Latin chants, and was once taught to play the game of chess..."

Scriven pondered seriously on this.

"Then you must challenge our abbot to a game, Sir Knight. He has few enough of us brothers to play with of an evening... engaged as we are upon our devotions."

Norbert mused.

"Such dedication you must have... and you also to your work, Scriven..."

The monk was thoughtful.

"It may amuse you worldly men to know that women are quite capable of such accomplishments... and their skills are far in excess of our own humble talents. Yet... our abbot will not permit any female to enter here lest their presence tempts us with unholy thoughts."

Norbert blushed deeply, which amused Gadroon and, to a lesser degree, Scriven himself.

"These are the visions that I would wish share with you..."

Scriven retrieved a volume from a large chest where it had obviously been hidden from any prying eyes. Larger than any book they had seen thus far, this was carefully placed upon another lectern, one that stood below a small window. When the knights were invited to gaze upon the images, the effect upon Norbert was remarkable. He had hardly approached the lectern before he turned away, announcing that he felt unwell.

Scriven went to his aid and Gadroon was left to examine the painted panorama alone. As soon as his eyes fell upon the landscape he saw depicted before him it all seemed uncannily familiar. The two figures on horseback were undoubtedly Norbert and himself! Disappearing beyond the confines of the border was a most gorgeous invention. Gadroon knew it to be The Grail. This was their goal – the design was nothing less than a depiction of their Quest!

Transported to another world, Gadroon slowly turned the page. The scene was as dark as the previous one had been full of light. A figure, obviously a young maiden, was alone and hiding her face. She was intent on not looking upon the sombre land about as if it might engulf her. The knights were nowhere to be seen.

The following page showed a scene of mayhem and bloodshed. War and pestilence had cursed the land and all around the greatest suffering was inflicted upon the innocent. Gadroon could almost hear their screams as he stared at these anguished faces. If this was not enough, when he turned his attention to the image that was its companion, he saw himself! Lying upon a bier, his eyes closed, all life seeming to ebb away. Angaz – the god of death – was shown looking down at the prone body, his intention all too clear. Gadroon slammed the book shut and staggered away from the lectern. He heard the voice of Scriven as if from some great distance.

"Thy companion seems well enough now, Sir Knight... he seemed for a moment a little faint..."

One glance at Gadroon told the monk he was now the one who suffered. His features were as pale as they had been painted on the page he had just looked upon. Gadroon struggled to ask the question he knew he must, his voice almost hoarse.

"How doth the tale end, Master Monk... that I must know... and most urgently."

Scriven paused, his words were even.

"I have not completed the work... and will not do so for some time. Each episode cometh to me as a divine revelation..."

Gadroon shook his head as if in delirium.

"For me these are evil dreams thou hast made with ink and pen... they have troubled me greatly. Nay... more than anything I have ever known or seen... and it is but lines upon paper... I do not understand..."

Scriven chose his words most carefully.

"What you see there is but the truth, Sir Knight. The evil... or good... in them is seen only by men... not by the One who reveals them to me."

Gadroon took this all in, while aware he was finding it difficult to breathe.

"Nevertheless... they have brought great fear to my heart."

Scriven did not hide his concern.

"That I did not intend when I illuminated the manuscript, Sir Gadroon... I swear that did not enter my thoughts. And how was I to know that you would visit us at Piedervoux? Unless you were sent here by the divine hand that guides us all."

Gadroon sighed.

"I know not... much is a great mystery to me in this world. I wonder now whether it would have been more wise not to have looked upon what I have seen... for I am sore troubled... of that there is no doubt."

"Every man makes a choice, Sir Knight. It seems your companion was not destined to see the things that you have... but thou most certainly were."

"Aye. Fate it seems has played its own part."

At that moment Norbert appeared and looking more like old self again, which meant he was probably thinking about some more tuck. He did not offer any explanation for his sudden disappearance. During the brief hours of the day that remained, Scriven showed the knights every corner of the abbey. Gadroon attempted to banish from his mind the visions he had seen, but this was easier said than done. During the days that followed, the images would constantly return to haunt him. Alone in his chamber that very night he would be heard crying to the shadows in supplication. A voice out of the darkness then seemed to answer him saying, "Our deepest revelations make us fear most, it is then we stand naked before providence and plead for mercy."

*

After supper, Abbot Speckle invited the knights to see his library. At this, Norbert's joy rose to immeasurable heights. Observing his enthusiasm, the abbot was only too pleased to show off the ancient bibles, psalters and chronicles in his possession. In the centuries to come Gutenberg would change all this and the precious word would be handed out promiscuously to the masses. In feudal times a learned minority had a monopoly on knowledge, and were able to waffle on endlessly to each other about what they knew.

"I confess to love reading of bygone days. In those times I am certain our rulers cared more for learning. Many now cannot even read... and think only of the chase and feasting at court. Such an attachment... only to that of worldly things... brings me great sadness."

Norbert, whose commitment to The Quest had been revived by all he had seen at the abbey, could only agree.

"'Tis so... my Lord Abbot."

"Scriven may come here to my library whenever he wishes. He reveres learning and has an understanding perhaps far greater than my own. I know that some of the monks are against him... sadly the sin of envy has entered their hearts. Some believe Scriven has unwarranted privileges. I can vouch that he works twice as hard as any ploughman most days."

At the mention of Scriven's name, Gadroon recollected the images he had seen and experienced great pain once more. Norbert, however, was in the throes of bliss. His being in the abbey's surrounds had planted a seed in his soul, one that would grow within him and eventually bear spiritual fruit. In his heart he knew that only in such stillness, away from the clamour of the world, would he be content. He longed for the company of the monks, and to be permitted to worship silently and devoutly with them. Norbert pictured himself in the peaceful shadows of the chapel, obedient only to spiritual matters. All that his soul craved he saw personified in Piedervoux. Here, the individual mind did not exist; all was sacrificed to the universal.

To Norbert, the abbey was a vision of paradise, every stone part of a Divine Plan. Every arch and window had been designed to reflect some aspect of devotion. This inherent order did not permit the mind to wander; the intention was plain and simple – to be constantly at one with heaven. Within the surrounds of the abbey it was possible for the devotee to enter this heavenly kingdom as easily as to step into another chamber. Here, no barrier existed between the secular and the spiritual because none was believed to exist.

Apart from his books, Abbot Speckle had another love – caring for his nine cats. These animals, all of varying temperaments and colours, loved the prelate. It had to be so – did he not feed them and give them freedom to roam in his quarters and gardens? While fondly stroking a large marmalade version, the abbot spoke of his charges.

"What amount of affection could exceed that given by such an animal? The love attributed to man towards his fellows is made to seem meagre."

A pair of black toms rubbed themselves against his habit as he spoke.

"The king hath his hawk... the farmer his cattle and sheep... and I have my cats."

Norbert could not restrain himself from voicing the common superstition concerning the feline.

"Do not witches also foster cats?"

The abbot put his hands together in a sign of contemplation, a gesture that had the effect of disturbing Norbert's poise more than a mite.

"Therein lieth a certain wisdom. Though my sacred vows preclude me from ever taking a wife, I do not regard women as venal as... I most sorrowfully regret.... many of my fellow prelates do. Saint Gilbert welcomed women in his own order... you know... and I admire him greatly for that. Neither do I condemn those poor innocents who are accused of sorcery and... as a consequence... abused most foully. It is now a common practice in some lands and has become an evil sport for those who obtain pleasure from causing cruelty to others. I cannot approve of their misguided judgments... it is they themselves who are wicked."

Norbert might have argued the point with the abbot, but wisely held his peace. Perhaps some instinct told him the abbot would shoot him down in flames before he had time to even trim his ailerons.

"As you say, my lord..."

"Cats are also persecuted by the wanton and foolish churl. No man can force either a woman or a cat to succumb to his will. I see in both these wondrous creatures the spirit of the universe, the mirror of creation. It is said that St. Godric warmed the serpent beneath his cloak and hid the stag from the chase. An enlightened soul... he is to be blessed eternally for such selfless acts."

The holy man had become stern of countenance when he contemplated the inhumanity of man, yet this mood passed quickly enough and he smiled upon the world once more. But, sensing the lateness of the hour, and ready to be about his final rounds, Abbot Speckle bade our heroes a warm goodnight. On their way to their chambers the knights spied the rotund figure, a collection of keys dangling at his waist, disappear into the darkness of the courtyard. That same night saw Norbert sleeping as a babe, and Gadroon restless and troubled. He was also more than certain they were about to be sorely tried once more but how soon, and in what manner, he could not tell.

*

The peaceful night that Norbert enjoyed would also have been seething with nightmares had he known of the events unfolding in another kingdom not far away. One of King Arthur's Company had arrived at Malfaise Castle, lair of the infamous King Brime. Travelling under the cover of night, this mysterious visitor had on his arrival informed the castle steward that he had pressing business with this monarch. The man Mangot, after duly consulting with Brime, led Sir Wayne into the royal presence.

The King of Anghard, a brooding tyrant with twisted mouth and even more twisted brain, was conferring with his advisor, Croop. With a reputation for cruelty exceeding even that of his master, Croop gained his greatest pleasure from taunting the king's numerous victims. He delighted in jeering at them through the bars when they were incarcerated in the deepest and smelliest of the castle dungeons.

When Queen Lardiana joined the pair, a more freakish trio could not be imagined. At this moment

Brime's consort was absent from the party, greedily engaged in some debauchery that even the most ardent royalist would find difficult to condone. Brime and Croop were given to leering at their visitor when he was announced. Sir Wayne bowed low, the king acknowledging his gesture.

"Welcome, Sir Wayne! Sit thee down! It is rare indeed that a noble knight of Camelot deigns to travel in our land. Malfaise will always be in the shadow of King Arthur's court... but... in our own modest way we will do our best to honour your visit. A little wine and some sweetmeats to refresh you after your journey perhaps?"

Wayne accepted the king's offer, as Brime had anticipated. He could sense the young knight's unease and was determined to use this to his advantage as much as possible. Clearly his mission was to impart some traitorous confidence, or else why would be in the company of Arthur's sworn enemy? Brime was determined, with Croop's aid, to ensure that he revealed a lot more than he intended. After a brimming goblet of wine and a tray of delicacies had been set at his elbow, the king set up his next shot.

"Now, Sir Wayne... do tell us all news of Arthur and his kingdom. Some interesting affairs at court have transpired of late perhaps?"

Wayne related the tale of the coming of the Purple Haze, and the threat of ruin hanging over Camelot unless its demands were met. It was noticeable that his delivery became more melodramatic the more he spoke. The heady vintage had quickly taken effect and, not so much loosened his tongue as totally unscrewed it, along with his wits. Brime allowed Wayne's words to percolate for some moments before he responded. He was pleased to see that his guest continued to imbibe with abandon.

"These are most strange tidings... we are indeed amazed. Are we not, Croop?"

"Indeed, my liege... and I feel sure his majesty would wish to learn more."

The king's advisor was most skilled in the art of lying, a useful talent in his position as the royal mouthpiece. His majesty took into account Croop's inability to tell the truth when personally assessing anything he said. His policy was simple – never to trust Croop a fraction of a fraction of an inch – ever.

"Indeed I do most desire to do so. But first... what are we to make of this incredible tale of the *Purple Haze*? Is not all this talk of visions and ghostly demands brought about by the fruits of the vine?"

Wayne, a little over-refreshed himself by these same fruits, hastened to defend the veracity of his tale.

"I know this to be so, your majesty... for also do I know that the Purple Haze was evoked by the darkest necromancy..."

The king and his advisor exchanged glances of the nudge, nudge, wink, wink, variety.

"How very interesting... do tell us more, Sir Wayne. In my humble experience, the magical fraternity are renowned for using their powers only for some significant purpose..."

Wayne played what he believed to be his trump card.

"The sorceress who wove the spell dearly wishes to bring ruin to Camelot... thus hath she set a trap for the Company. It is an impossible task they face."

"A sorceress you say? And the name of this foul witch? Pray do enlighten us..."

A sudden fear wiped the cheery grin off Wayne's previously triumphant chops.

"I cannot say."

Brime then played one of his own cards – a joker.

"I see. And if The Quest failed... and the Round Table was then no more... how would you feel then, Sir Wayne?"

The ensuing outburst of passion nearly caused Wayne to spill the contents of the goblet into his lap.

"Why... I would greatly rejoice! I have no love for those fools that make up the Company! I wish them to grovel in the mire where they belong! Let Camelot fall and my ridiculous uncle with it."

Brime feigned surprise and alarm, in equal measure. He then started fishing in earnest, his hook well-baited.

"You have no love for your own king... Arthur... it seems..."

"He hath wronged me greatly..."

"How so?"

Wayne's expression changed, as if he had been recently snogging a waffle iron.

"I have been sorely insulted. The king regards certain knights of the Company as being superior to me."

Croop's voice was as slippery as an oil slick.

"Who can these poltroons be who could possibly assume a higher rank than the king's nephew?"

Wayne spat out his reply.

"The two knights who I most despise are soon to arrive here... in your own kingdom... in Malfaise... of that I am certain."

The king's eyes narrowed until they resembled a pair of fresh oysters.

"And their names?"

"Sir Norbert and Sir Gadroon."

The king and Croop exchanged yet another glance, this time of a more sinister nature.

"I am sure we will make their stay at Malfaise long and most eventful... eh, Croop?"

As soon as Wayne heard these words he nearly retched. The effect of too much wine combined with the sickness of betrayal suddenly contrived to produce a foul mixture in him. By giving vent to his jealousy, and speaking foolishly, he had condemned two of the Company into the hands of King Brime, a man known for his merciless ways. Treachery, as Wayne would discover, has a bitter taste and inevitably brings its own harsh reward.

VIII

And others led Gawain to a glorious bed
In a noble room, hung with strips
Of shining, silk, trimmed with gold,
With a bedspread sewn in the softest fur,
Gleaming ermine, and around him curtains
On red-gold rings...

In the light of dawn, a mist could be seen to lie in swathes of translucent grey upon the land – a robe Venus had carelessly thrown over her naked beauty. Eostur was long gone, now the time of Sol was coming and the ancient rites of Beltane would soon be enacted. Dancing and feasting would abound, honouring the time of new fertility in the earth. A bit of rumpty-pumpty among the youthful element would doubtless be part of the celebrations too.

Abbot Speckle had bade the knights farewell, assuring Norbert and Gadroon that their next destination – The Castle of Malfaise – lay less than a day's journey from the border of Longres. Norbert and Gadroon sensed that once they entered the land of Anghard, The Quest for the Grail would begin in earnest. They looked out over the land before them. The way seemed fair and, as the sun ascended in the sky, their spirits rose with it, Gadroon proposing that they had undoubtedly encountered the Second Wisdom.

"Chance meetings bring revelation in their wake, Norbert... that now seems certain. Piedervoux... Scriven and the good abbot hath brought much to reflect upon."

Norbert sighed, as if pining for an old girlfriend – an unlikely event in his case.

"I have vowed that once our Quest is over I will return to savour again such repose as I did find there at the abbey. I believe it will be a glorious hour for me."

Gadroon, sensitive to Norbert's blissed-out state, said nothing. Secretly, he wondered if that time would ever come to pass, for he could feel great changes coming. Then, every kingdom would be affected in some manner – great or small.

*

In the early evening the two companions came to Malfaise. The sun painted the walls of the town with a pleasing orange glow, but the sharply pointed turrets of the castle had a forbidding presence. Both sensed that to enter such a place was to venture willingly into danger, yet Norbert and Gadroon knew it was their fate to do so.

They urged their horses towards the town gate. Carts, horses and many on foot thronged the way and an ochre cloud of dust hung over all. From a niche in the wall of the gatehouse, a painted statue of King Brime stared at them. Barefoot urchins surrounded their mounts and assailed them with offers of inns and rooms to stay. Everywhere too were vendors of pasties and other dubious-looking delicacies. Gadroon brushed them all aside with a word, and the two knights continued towards the castle.

Norbert was unfamiliar with town life and its sights. He marvelled at the densely packed houses with their steeply angled roofs almost reaching down to the ground. Merchants and tradesmen occupied all the streets that led from the main thoroughfare, and folk of every rank and calling mingled in a sea of humanity. Clerks, clergymen, messengers, spicemongers and apothecaries jostled the esquires and their wives, in rich crimson silks and blue velvet, their cloaks trimmed with fur.

86

Through an archway Norbert could glimpse many a mean and narrow alley, no more than a muddy path a few feet wide. All manner of rubbish was piled everywhere, and the stench was unbearable even from some distance away. Norbert could not imagine what it would be like to exist in such a confined space, squeezed in among the warrens of tiny rooms. Because the upper storeys of the houses almost touched, little light was able to permeate down to street level.

Occasionally, a face would emerge from some dank crevice, a grotesque mask with empty eyes, set to gawking at those who passed. A figure would suddenly appear from some mean window, or dart round a corner. Groups of slouching youths went shoeless in the mire, tumbling against the crippled beggars who squatted in the doorways. The poor in their uniformly dun-coloured clothes were everywhere. Many of the women looked particularly destitute, their clothes no more than rags, and often they held an equally wretched infants in their arms.

When the two companions approached the castle it became apparent how much its sombre presence dominated the town. Every street converged on this cobbled yard and here was much activity. Carts and carriages were being unloaded and affluent folk and their servants were everywhere. All seemed anxious to leave the hustle and bustle of the town to gain the safety of the castle. The line of those crossing over the drawbridge seemed unending. Norbert and Gadroon urged their horses onward with a view to joining them.

*

If evil has a pervasive odour, then Malfaise Castle gave off a pong worse than any to be found in the rankest alley of the town. Entering the courtyard, the knights were hailed by a most unctuous steward.

"I am Mangot, sirs. Malfaise welcomes the noble knights of Camelot; we are indeed honoured by your presence here."

Gadroon bowed slightly, but was not taken in one jot by such ripe twot. The carefully choreographed team of ostlers did not impress him either. As their horses were led to the stables, Norbert noticed a figure skulking in the shadows – had they known it, Croop spying on the newcomers. Our heroes were shown to their quarters by yet more obsequious lackeys.

At the obligatory banquet that night, The Hall at Malfaise was stuffed to bursting point with guests. None of them however, seemed inclined to extend the hand of friendship, or any other limb, towards our heroes. Thus, they were more than relieved to encounter Lapin. He performed a passable *pas de deux* before them, at the same time introducing his friend, Hendrique the Minstrel. Clutching his lute, the singer/songwriter was a rising star in the Dark Ages.

The warmth of their reunion evaporated as soon as King Brime approached with his retinue. Lapin and Hendrique immediately became part of the aether also.

"Sir Norbert, Sir Gadroon, welcome to Malfaise."

The voice was like a rusty grating being forced open with a crowbar. The two knights made a passable show of respect to the king, at the same time being in no doubt he was a psychotic berk.

"Sire."

"Sire."

"Queen Lardiana will join us ere long... and this... is my most loyal advisor, Croop..."

The cove, who had been lurking in the bushes, was brought forward.

"Such an honour is it not, my liege... to entertain such renowned members of the Company of the Round Table."

Gadroon regarded Croop as if he were something he would carefully avoid stepping in. Lock and stock having being presented, here came the barrel.

"Where are these fair knights? Show them to me!"

The piercing tones cut through the air like a scalpel while something resembling a demonic dumpling advanced towards them. Queen Lardiana had hips like a hippo, the rest of her looking like five dogs fighting in a sack.

"Where have you been hiding, you gorgeous gentlemen? Now... do not stay too long at table this eve for I shall want to see you dance a carol."

Gadroon kept his cool and bowed low once more, Norbert following suit. King Brime beamed upon them like a Halloween lantern.

"I have ordered that you are to be served only the most succulent of meats and the finest wines. You are my most honoured guests."

This all sounded about as kosher as Herod announcing he was starting up a crèche. Gadroon bowed once more, but drew the line at any more scraping. Brime bore the queen away as if he were towing a heavily laden galleon. As soon as they were out of hearing, Lardiana started quizzing her husband.

"Why are those knights of Arthur's here? Are they spying on us? There was another one of them snooping about some days ago..."

Brime was perfunctory.

"That was Sir Wayne. He still remains here in the castle as my guest... he is a weak fool who cannot hold his liquor..."

Lardiana licked her lips.

"...a pretty little thing though."

Brime ignored her.

"Sir Wayne confided certain most interesting matters to me about Sir Gadroon and Sir Norbert... they are engaged upon a Quest."

"What do you mean? What *quest?*"

"Capital letters, my dear... they seek out the Holy Grail."

Lardiana sneered, making deep valleys in her fleshy face.

"Those ridiculous old tales! My old nurse used to read them to me when I was a child... in a bound parchment... written by Crusty White... a foolish monk from across the waters. Such nonsense they were!"

"That may be true... but I certainly intend to prevent these two from continuing on their journey."

"Why? Are they to be playthings for me? The tall one is certainly handsome..."

"I had it in mind to let them *be my guests* in another sense... I shall ensure they rot in the depths of the castle for some years."

The king could see Lardiana was up for more quizzing. He raised a restraining hand.

"...I have my own reasons for ensuring that they do not find the Grail... whether that *Holy Vessel* exists or not. I am given to understand that Camelot could well be destroyed if these knights do not succeed upon their Quest. The garrulous Wayne mentioned a sorceress whose very name caused him to shake in his boots. I am certain that is Morgan le Fay... only one such as her she would cause such fear in his miserable little heart."

"Ah... yes... Morgan has that affect on lesser souls..."

Brime made swift enquiries.

"And are you still on good terms with that belle of the black arts or have you two quarreled of late?"

Lardiana was haughty.

"Morgan and I have always been as close as if we were sisters..."

Brime knew how Cinderella must have felt.

"Then I would wish you to invite her to the castle as soon as you may. There are matters I would wish to discuss with her. I am certain she is as desirous to bring about the fall of Arthur as I am."

Lardiana tried being coy, but ended up only being fubsy.

"I would still like one of those knights to play with before you lock them up... I find young men wear out so quickly these days."

Brime regarded his queen with more than a modicum of distaste, a look he had been honing since the day after their wedding. He had certainly not married for love, not an emotion the king had ever experienced. As for Lardiana, some might have regarded her as a harmless eccentric. Beneath the potty persona was a nasty bundle of barbed wire.

The festivities about to begin, the king took his place at the banqueting table, Lardiana beside him. The servants began to put a great variety of dishes before the guests. When a boar's head was placed near Croop the difference in their features was barely noticeable. As the evening progressed, Norbert and Gadroon felt they were not just on the outside looking in, but were totally invisible. Neither did the spectacle of Croop watching them like an ardent vulture make them feel any more at ease. It was little wonder that, in such a hostile atmosphere, they had no appetite for the spiced delicacies and perfumed vintages on offer.

The feasting done, the guests were spellbound by the spectacle of Queen Lardiana dancing. An elephant on roller blades would have displayed more grace, yet the entire court applauded in suitably sycophantic fashion. The hours dragged by unmercifully and the only oasis in this desert of despair was Hendrique performing his lilting ballads. Every air he played upon the lute had the magic of romance and the soft words of his songs enchanted Gadroon. The knight closed his eyes the better to let the melody take him where it would.

One poignant melody had just ended when he opened his eyes to see a serving maid at his side offering him a jug of mulled wine. She smiled at him shyly as she set it down, and for a moment they looked upon each other. Gadroon, his heart caressed by the minstrel's echoing chords, felt a tremor of emotion he had not known for many a long year. The maid hurried away to answer the demands of other guests, and disappeared among the throng. Just after midnight the two knights bade good evening to the king and queen. A totally tipsy Lardiana joshed them incoherently, while Brime seemed at his most sinister. With many courtly bows, they exited to their quarters.

Not long after he had retired, Gadroon was woken by the sound of his door being slowly opened. If the elm boards had not creaked he might not have heard. In the darkness he slowly eased his arm out from the coverlet and felt for the haft of his sword, the weapon never being far from his grasp even when he slept. The door opened a little more and a figure was dimly lit in the threshold. Slim and too slight for a man, Gadroon realised it was the serving maid. She came into the chamber and silently closed the door. Gadroon spoke, in a not unfriendly manner

"Ho... my little one. What canst thou want?"

The maid started slightly but continued to walk towards the bed.

"Oh, brave Master Knight... will thou comfort me?"

"What ails thee, little maid?"

She kneeled by the bed, almost touching him.

"I am little afeared tonight, sir. I know not why."

The maid came closer and in the half-light Gadroon could see the outline of her firm breasts.

"I see."

"I beg you... please protect me, sir."

For Gadroon certain stirrings beneath the coverlet occurred, sensations that were familiar, but not of late. He eased back the sheets in invitation.

"Yea, sweet maid... I will surely look after thee."

"Shall I cast aside my shift, sir? The better for you to warm me."

"Perchance that would be wise."

The garment flung hither, the maid then nestled contentedly in Gadroon's arms. The heat beneath the coverlet could have melted a large part of the Arctic Circle. To put his lust into abeyance, Gadroon launched into some small talk.

"What is your name?"

"I am Willowpetal, sir."

"A pretty name for a pretty maid."

Corny, but then compliments often are when written down.

"Oh, thank thee sir. Thou art such a kind and gentle knight... so well dost thou guard me."

She moved even closer, stroking his chest softly. Inevitably one part of Gadroon responded more than any other and Willowpetal could not help but be aware of this.

"Oh, sir... doth that mighty wand belong to you?"

"Certainly it doth, and becoming more mighty by the minute methinks."

The maid was all enthusiasm.

"Oh... let me to touch it, sir... if thou will. Oh... by all nature...it is magnificent! Like a great oak in the forest! Its girth is wondrous!"

Gadroon thought precious time was now being wasted. His entreaties began to assume a certain urgency.

"And will thou feel its power, Willowpetal?"

"Oh, sir... what doth thou you mean? Within me? Oh... but, sir... perchance it will be too much for such a little maid as I..."

"I will be gentle with thee..."

"...I have never known a man before..."

No time like the present.

"Thou shall, my sweet maid... thou shall."

Gadroon put his lips upon hers and cupped his hand over her breast. He felt it swell under his palm and next he turned his attention to where the landscape was soft and wet. The maid's tender thighs willingly parted.

"Oh, sir... I know now I do so wish to give myself to thee. Never before have I desired to know man as now."

And she undeniably did, as proved by her commentary during the knowing.

"Oh, sir... that is wonderful. I am in heaven now I know. Oh, how I have waited so long for this moment. Oh, beautiful, gentle knight. I do love this so... it is a gift of the divine..."

Gadroon had to admit he agreed. If God had created anything more delightful than this he had yet to discover what it might be. Norbert might well have defined ecstasy to be found in denial but Gadroon at that moment would not have agreed. He plunged and thrusted, slowed and quickened and the maid encouraged him in all he did. All good things must come to an end, and this did – in the usual way – with satisfaction all round.

Of course, it was unlikely to end there. Having sampled the first chapter of *The Joy of Sex*, Willowpetal was eager to get on to the next, including the footnotes. That night they worked steadily, right through to the index. From a rank amateur Willowpetal became a mistress of her craft in one night, even suggesting a few variations herself. Gadroon was a willing teacher and Willowpetal a model student. At dawn they reached for each other once more, and then the maid fled back to her quarters.

Gadroon dozed in an aura of delight. When the door was opened again he half-imagined Willowpetal returning. But no shy and gentle maid was upon the threshold on this occasion. Half a dozen of the burliest palace guards filled the chamber. As Gadroon reached for his sword one of the guards kicked it away.

"Get up, you dog!"

The same oaf threw the knight's hose onto the coverlet.

"Gird thyself."

To Gadroon, dressing himself before an audience of grinning Gumbies was not how he would have chosen to begin the day.

"A nice way to be greeted of a morning! Does your king always have such fine manners?"

The Captain of the Guard thrust his coarse features in the knight's direction.

"Take care, knight... King Brine has ways of dealing with those who displease him."

Gadroon considered. With a bunch of thugs whose recreation probably included G.B.H., he ought to be circumspect. Gadroon donned his doublet with as much dignity as he could muster in the circumstances.

IX

***Until they knew he was trapped, the beast
That bloodhounds had run to the ground.***

The sun was just peeking over the castle walls when Norbert and Gadroon were marched into the courtyard. The nature of that great golden orb being to shine upon good and evil alike, Croop was getting his fair share of the beaming stuff. In outstanding form as he strutted in front of his audience, the brainless riff-raff that made up the castle soldiery. More than willing to applaud (they liked nothing better than kicking up a row) Croop was encouraged to ham it up more than the finest Parma.

"Traitors! Enemies of the kingdom! Spies! Poisonous vipers in the bosom of our noble kingdom!"

Norbert and Gadroon watched this rank performance with indifference.

"No punishment would be too harsh... no death too slow and painful for those such as you... vermin who would threaten the sanctity of the realm. What shall be done? You shall be hanged..."

On cue, grubby hands reached out to seize the two knights. The prospect of manhandling their betters always appealed to them.

"...on the morrow!"

Grunting with disappointment, the ranks of ruffians retreated, though Croop's next command pleased them.

"Take them to the dungeons!"

This was more to their taste – there would be ample opportunities to hurl the prisoners down flights of steps and other simple delights. Croop however could read everything in their nasty minds – an experience similar to perusing the *Daily Mail*.

"Do not harm them! I wish them to savour fully their last hours in this world..."

Norbert and Gadroon were led away.

*

The stone seats set into the wall of the tiny cell were about as comfortable as a cheap flight to Corfu. Norbert reviewed their situation gloomily – literally so. The window in the dungeon let in about as much light as the candles on a birthday cake for a two-year old.

"What is to be done? What crime have we committed? Yet it seems we are still judged... and condemned also."

Gadroon was equally melancholy.

"It matters not to the tyrant... in his eyes all men are guilty and must therefore perish."

Our heroes could not have been aware of the events that had brought about their arrest. In the small hours Brime had suddenly felt acutely bilious, and had summoned Croop. The king was certain he had been poisoned – an outrageous attempt had been made on his life. Already intent on confining Norbert and Gadroon the next morning, Croop now even had a real reason to lock them in the dungeons.

It was not, however, the real reason. Lardiana had, during the previous evening, added a lethal draught to the king's pigeon pie. The decision to murder her husband had been prompted by the threat of one of her lubricious escapades being exposed to the court. Enamoured with a potboy in the kitchens, the queen had been discovered in a compromising position by a keen-eyed courtier. The sneak was Wignob, the king's food taster.

The plan to poison the king had failed. In a moment of random paranoia, Brime had summoned Wignob to taste the various dishes offered to him. The food taster having been ordered to remove the said pie had done so. Deciding there was nothing amiss and unable to resist such a delicious morsel, he had scoffed the lot. Moments later he keeled over in the clerestory, to be pronounced a stiff by the steward who discovered the corpse. Lardiana was quite satisfied with the way things had turned out – her peccadillo with the potboy would forever remain undiscovered. The way in which this turn of events determined the fate of Norbert and Gadroon, she neither knew nor cared.

Norbert was at this moment reflecting moodily on the nature of kingship, while Gadroon was becoming more and more cynical about life in general.

"How will the Spirit of the Grail help us now?"

Norbert was sanguine.

"This is the trial we must face... one to show we are worthy of our divine calling. To be sorely tried is part of such a venture as The Quest."

Gadroon responded with a wry laugh.

"I warrant a sore neck will be ours upon the morrow."

A sound of rusty keys and a bolt being shot back announced the arrival of a visitor – of the unwanted variety. Croop – grinning like a mad gerbil – entered their cell.

 "I come with word from the king that will secure your release... if you are prepared to agree to his wishes."

If Croop had expected this to prompt the prisoners into doing high-fives, he was mistaken. Gadroon eyed him with some disdain.

"So... the king's lackey wishes to strike a bargain..."

Ignoring this, Croop continued.

"If you swear to abandon your foolish quest for *The Grail* then you will be freed and may return to Camelot. The king gives his solemn oath you will not be harmed."

Gadroon roared with laughter.

"*Solemn Oath...* you say! Has it not been shown... on many an occasion... that King Brine's word is worth less than a swineherd's curse?"

After the bouncer, Norbert lobbed up a googly from the other end.

"Neither thou... *or thy infamous monarch...* are worthy even to speak of the Holy Quest. Heaven smileth upon our venture... no mortal may dissuade us from our sacred task!"

Croop sneered.

"As you desire... your foolish words have sealed your own fate. The king in his infinite mercy... thought to spare your lives. You have refused... and in doing so have woven a noose about your own necks. In addition, the torturers will be ordered to discuss ways of ensuring that you both undergo a prolonged and painful death."

Croop turned on his heel in authentic villain's style and the dungeon door closed behind him. Norbert fizzed with indignation.

"Is there no justice in this world?"

Gadroon did not offer much hope in this department.

"In my knowing of this earthly realm... there is not. The wolf taketh the sheep whenever he wisheth."

"What is to be done, Gadroon? Apart from offering up to my maker as many prayers as I know in my heart..."

Gadroon looked thoughtful.

"I am a great believer in ways and means, Norbert. Always there lieth an answer to even the deepest puzzle. I also suspect at the root of all this infamy is much that we do not know."

"And we may in some way find this out?"

Gadroon pondered the more.

"Consider... it seemeth certain Sir Wayne hath betrayed us. We went as fowl into the net when we came to Malfaise... for King Brime was told of our coming. If Wayne persuaded King Brime to be the instrument of his revenge against us then this could have been brought about in countless ways. No... there is another reason why we are kept here. You heard the words of Croop... King Brime is intent on preventing us from continuing upon The Quest. Why is that?"

"He is a godless knave."

"I agree... but I suspect Wayne's own knavery has more of a practical turn. Is it that... if we succeed in our mission, he fears the future will go badly with him? How can this be? If we fail... The Purple Haze will exact what is due from Camelot with Wayne among the number who suffer. This bond made at Yule was known only to those of the Company. Thus it seems Wayne informed Brime of all that had taken place that night also."

Norbert nodded dejectedly.

"That now seems clear."

Gadroon continued with his speculations.

"Yet... I am certain Wayne knows of some other matter concerning The Purple Haze. Its presence bodes yet more ill for Camelot than that which is already known. Can it be that another power doth direct its ways?"

Norbert looked afeared.

"What can it be, Gadroon... this greater evil?"

"I can only believe that it is one who hath a desire for revenge against Arthur himself... not Camelot... though I know they may be considered one and the same. I do not believe Wayne has this much hatred for the king. He sought to punish us because he believed we made him look a lesser man before the Company. His pride hath made his heart black. I believe he has sought to seek aid from one whose heart is blacker still."

"Brime... then?"

Gadroon shook his head.

"Nay... he hath not the wit for this venture. There is another much more cunning... and merciless than he. It seems Brime would have to make an ally of them also if he wishes to take the greatest advantage of Longres' misfortune."

Norbert was in despair.

"A tale of deceit and ill-will..."

Gadroon could only agree.

"Indeed... yet I sense the fox will outwit its hunters. Wayne is at the mercy of Brime and the king in turn will be beggared also."

Norbert was the most outraged by the thought of Wayne's treachery.

"Wayne's betrayal is a crime unpardonable... he deserves to be..."

Gadroon cut him short.

"Yet more revenge is not the answer here, Norbert."

"How so? I swear... if they knew... any of the Company would say he deserves to be skewered like a roasted fowl."

"Well, old friend... you may comfort yourself to know that Wayne may well have evoked forces that will bring about his undoing anyway."

Gadroon's surmising would have done credit to Sherlock Holmes, but it brought little aid to their current plight. Norbert, like Dr. Watson, was baffled by much of his companion's reasoning. He also suspected things of which he most certainly did not approve were involved. But in the circumstances he thought it best to be like Dad, and keep Mum.

And so the dreary day drew to a close and night took over. Just down the corridor, other unfortunates began to make the darkness even more stygian with endless cries and moans. A CD of James Last would have been as choirs of angels compared to such endless howls of despair.

*

A new day began. A beam of light was falling across the wall, opposite where the knights lay dozing. To accompany this unexpected beauty came a lilting air that told of noble deeds and fair days, the latter bursting with birdsong and bumblebees. A chord of such sweetness melted in the air, its echoes purging every speck of melancholy from the hearts of those who heard it. The knights were awakened from their slumbers... listened... and held their breath. Could such a sound be created by the hand of man... or minstrel? Hendrique!

Some yearn for riches, gold and precious things
Some wish for power, and the throne of kings
Some do love to labour, others just to dream
But I knoweth of another way, so it doth seem,
To be like wind and water, and precious moonly light
Be always as the minstrel, and sing always of delight.

The notes of the lute hung in the air and gradually dwindling away. Another melody started up and Norbert would have drifted further into a land of bliss had not Gadroon urgently spoken.

"Hark, Norbert... to the words he singeth! Now! This moment!"

Soon you must
Make ready, and trust
For lock and key
Will ease for thee.

While Gadroon and Norbert waited to see what would unfold for them, in the outside world, the life of the castle was gradually stirring. The hour had arrived when the guards changed watch and the new contingent were late to arrive at their posts. The previous night's festivities had taken their toll. An hour before midnight, a barrel of strong ale, surplus to the festivities, had been assigned to the guardroom. Inevitably, a certain amount of tippling had taken place during the watches, and it was a groggy pair that Lapin encountered when he peered around the door of the guardroom. One of them opened a jaundiced eye, almost shutting it straight away.

"What ails thee, jester?"

"What *ales* thee it would seem more to be..."

The guard who answered to the name Navet, grunted.

"Be off with thee! I would sleep awhile afore our watch is relieved... after that... to slumber more."

"Would that thou could be able to do that, O guard of generous girth! But I do know that those who should come will not... for they have fallen into a drunken drowse. So much so that... even the moon after midnight mocked their muddled minds. Drunk deep they have and thus deeply drunk they be. Neither a-waking up nor a-walking upright may they do this morn. They lieth still... and still they lieth... where they fell... last eve."

Navet opened the other eye, one bilious and accusing.

"Eh? What meaneth thou with all this? They cometh not? How know ye of this, jester?"

Lapin was as light as the guard was all heaviness.

"Why... I passed their quarters but a little time ago and their snores made such noise as could be heard in the next kingdom methinks."

The guard reluctantly opened both eyes.

"Bah! A plague upon the idle churls!"

"The knaves deserveth thy wrathful words, O worthy watchman. Thou and thy companion have been treated ill by such comrades as these."

A full minute passed before Navet's brain lurched into gear. A few neurons fired up with the result that the guard was inclined to be a mite suspicious.

" 'Tis better if this be not one of thy accursed jests, thou fool... or it will be the worse for thee."

Lapin was innocence personified.

"Methinks it is not I who deserveth thy curses, Master Navet... but thy fellow guards..."

Rousing himself, Navet roughly shook his companion slumped over the guardroom table, dead to the world.

"Gimp, ye knave! Wake... I tell thee!"

The other's response was to slide off the table and onto the floor. There he lay, and probably would have continued to do so for an unaccountable time, had not Navet proceeded to prod him with the toe of his boot.

"Up, thou nincompoop! Curse thee! We shall have no more rest this day if thou dost not stir!"

Whether his companion's prodding or some other inner prompting, moved him was uncertain, but Gimp staggered to his feet. Together he and Navet stumbled out into the courtyard in search of their errant fellows. They were not so completely witless as to forget their charges in the dungeon below. Navet ordered Lapin to remain in the doorway of the guardroom while he and Gimp went upon their errand.

"Stand there! Let none enter or leave! We shall not tarry long I trow."

Lapin bowed most obligingly.

"Fear not! None shall come or go without me seeing."

And that was exactly what the jester meant when, as soon as the guards were out of sight, he signaled to Hendrique who was hiding in the stables across the way. The minstrel led the knights' horses into the courtyard where he tethered them loosely to a post. He then sprinted across the courtyard, entered the guardroom and took the cell keys from where they hung invitingly on the wall. The sharp click of the cell door meant the knights were of a sudden at liberty. Norbert could not contain himself.

"Hendrique! A miracle..."

With a firm gesture, the minstrel bade him be silent. They followed their rescuer up the stone steps into the guardroom. Lapin was still keeping a close eye on that part of the courtyard from where he anticipated the guards would eventually emerge. As it was, Navet and Gimp were much delayed. If they had believed waking the other guards was to be a simple task they were sorely mistaken. They found them prostrate upon the earth floor in their quarters, the empty ale barrel between them and no amount of cajoling, and outright bellowing could rouse the drunken miscreants.

Hendrique, while replacing the keys in the guardroom, perceived a flash of steel from behind a screen set in a corner. Gadroon and Norbert were overjoyed to find their swords hidden there. Lapin then slowly sidled into the courtyard while the others waited in the shadows. At an imperious wave from the jester, they ran to their horses and jumped into the saddle.

"Ride! Like the wind! I will delay the dozy dolts further if need be."

The knights needed no encouragement, and swiftly spurred their horses towards the gatehouse. If the guards there had been swift enough, they might have raised the drawbridge, or lowered the portcullis, but it was not to be. They rode helter-skelter through the town, out through the city arch and into the land beyond, careless of any that might be in their way. After a few hundred yards, Norbert was surprised to see Gadroon suddenly rein in his horse. He had espied a figure by the way slowly waving.

"Willowpetal!"

The little maid, her eyes as bright as her smile looked up at Gadroon.

"My noble knight... you are free..."

Gadroon suddenly realised it was she who, having heard about their plight, had informed Lapin and Hendrique. He also knew instinctively that Willowpetal had cajoled the pair into bringing about the knights' rescue. Gadroon's heart was almost breaking within him for he knew that now he must part once more from the little maid. And who knew for how long, or what might transpire, in the meanwhile?

"Willowpetal... thou hast brought about a miracle... we owe you our lives..."

The maid looked up at him her eyes glistening. Her face shone with the light of love.

"Thy life is from this moment on the most precious thing in the world to me... more than anything... I love thee... I cannot hold from saying this thing because it is true... I knew as soon as I first saw thee..."

"And I love thee too, my Willowpetal..."

The maid handed two tightly-wrapped packets to Gadroon

"Here... these are for you and your faithful companion. This will sustain you upon your journey."

Gadroon took these almost absently for his gaze was fixed upon Willowpetal.

"I thank you for your kindness, my sweet one... but it is the thought of thee that will give me all the strength I need in coming days."

At his words, the maiden's countenance shone once more with the greatest affection.

"And I shall keep you in my heart... every moment of the day and night and think of thee constantly. In that way we shall never be parted."

Gadroon bent down and kissed her. The maid's arms went about him and she wished never to release him, for her longing was great.

"We shall be together again... that I promise... and before we both know any time has passed."

"Oh, sir knight... I do believe this to be true... but..."

Gadroon could see tears coming to her eyes, and he grasped both her hands, looking upon her most devotedly.

"Have faith, my Willowpetal. Believe always in our love."

She agreed silently, but could not hold back her tears any longer and wept. Gently Gadroon released her, as he knew he must, for he knew it was not wise to tarry any longer. With one more glance at the maid he set his steed onward. Willowpetal watched until she could see the riders no more but Gadroon dared not look back, for fear his heart would break.

The two knights rode swiftly for some hours until they had put many miles between themselves and Malfaise Castle. The possibility of being pursued was foremost in their minds and onward they went, deeper and deeper into the kingdom of Anghard. After some leagues, they reached the edge of a forest, one known in the old tongue as the Dark Woodland, to others as Twypren.

When they finally stopped to rest the horses, Norbert, though puzzled by what had occurred, made no mention of the maid. Willowpetal's unexpected appearance by the wayside had naturally surprised him, as had Gadroon's response. The book of love would always remain sealed for Norbert – that was to be his fate. Yet to see how preoccupied was his friend showed Norbert how great were the deeps from where true affection springs.

Had the knights but known it, today was the longest of the year. The sky was streaked with a candy floss pink, gradually fading into the clay coloured clouds beneath. Never had the world looked so magnificent as it did to Norbert and Gadroon at that moment. Liberty nourishes the spirit, and they believed freedom was truly theirs. As the sun was setting, they set about finding shelter for the coming night, brief as it would be.

Many leagues away, in Malfaise Castle, the quick-witted Lapin had been well aware that awkward questions about the prisoners' escape would soon be asked of him. As soon as Norbert and Gadroon departed, he and Hendrique let it be known they had been by requested by King Tirhadeth of Tomberg to appear at the Windleroot Music Fair. Willowpetal told all she would accompany the pair as their dancer.

X

Then the drawbridge came down, and the thick gates
Drew back, swung open, unbarred. And the knight
Crossed himself and rode across

High Summer came upon the land in the days that followed. Norbert and Gadroon avoided the open road and dared not venture into any hamlet. They hid in the forest during the long, sweltering hours of day, concealing any part of their dress that would mark them as knights. The provisions Willowpetal had provided were long gone, and they were obliged to skulk about in the darkest hours like vagabonds foraging for food.

The heat continued unabated and Gadroon knew they must debate their next move. No longer could they exist in the forest in a half-starved state. He was also concerned over time that should have been devoted to The Quest, being wasted. At the end of yet another sultry day, he and Norbert discussed all this.

"I do not believe that Brime and his men are searching for us. If they are... then we have either been most fortunate... or they have been more than blind. I suspect Brime has other fish to fry and he cannot be bothered with chasing us."

"Perhaps my prayers have protected us from the stings of iniquity."

Gadroon was in no mood to dispute the point.

"Perchance that is true, Norbert... and if they continue to do so... then there is no reason why we should not venture into the world of men once more. "

Given that various sort of beetles had been their only company of late, the prospect was attractive to Norbert.

"I would welcome that, Gadroon... with all my heart."

"Good... then we are agreed. We will make our way towards the border with the Kingdom of Tomberg. The

Grail resides in the Land of Dolfay, which adjoins it. We must first ride some way further west into Anghard... then turn south... below the Hills of Gawel."

"How long will be our journey?"

"It will be more than a day before we come upon the river Dwylon... there we must follow its course south until we reach the Goffrow Bridge. It is said to be the tallest bridge in all the kingdoms..."

Realising he was coming on like the Rough Guide, Gadroon quickly returned to his usual bluff self.

"...and we should not tarry there too long, either... gazing upon its magnificence."

Norbert agreed easily enough. He did not have the taste for Gothic architecture that scholars of the future would have – going into raptures about lancets and mullions.

*

Norbert would long remember the journey through Anghard, and with little affection. The glaring presence of the mountains of Drenost seemed to bear down interminably. Was it possible the friendly peaks of Feilach in the north of Longres were part of this same range of mountains? Norbert kept gazing into the landscape, searching in vain for the smallest cottage. Within these, he imagined roast boar, venison pasties and jugs of ale, all arrayed on the festive board. These images filled his mind, but not his belly.

Eventually Norbert became doleful and his spirit waned, so much so that he could hardly keep himself upright in the saddle. Gadroon, happening to turn about, stared at the flagging figure of his companion and drew his mount up to him.

"What ails thee, old friend? Come... we must traverse a few more leagues 'ere nightfall. Art thou sick?"

Norbert hardly had hardly the strength to reply and, realising this, Gadroon quickly reined in his horse. A copse of trees lay ahead, and he urged his companion to gain the shade of the overhanging boughs. This Norbert did, and promptly fell off his horse. Luckily, he was only winded. Gadroon, while helping Norbert to his feet, was alarmed by the sight of his companion's pale features. He bade that he rest against the trunk of an elm.

"Don't stir, old fellow... not that you are likely to... I shall return."

Gadroon had espied through the trees a cow, her udder swollen with milk. Knowing an everyday story of country folk, he was certain a pail and a stool would be hidden somewhere in the hedge nearby. There – in the hedge! Beckoning the cow, and then balancing himself on the stool, Gadroon set to work. Before long he had filled half a pail and, returning to the still supine Norbert, set the warm frothing milk this before him. Norbert grabbed the pail and would have spilt all upon himself had not Gadroon prevented him.

"Easy, old friend... slow is the way. The wise-woman in the village used to say that milk was a food... so eat slowly."

Norbert did as he was bid and steadily drank until not a drop of the milk remained. His colour returned almost immediately, and he even managed half a smile.

"That was most excellent... I have never drunk better."

"And probably never will again. Now take your ease... while I return the good farmer's pail."

Gadroon, shortly returning, regarded Norbert.

"Dost thou feel hale enough to ride?"

"Aye... I do."

And so they continued and by noon the next day were within sight of the River Dwylon. As they passed through a secluded hamlet, a cottager rushed out from his door and, without a word, pressed bread and bacon upon them. Gadroon was now quite as ready to believe in miracles as his companion.

The Dwylon valley, a deep crevasse with sheer sides leading down to the rushing waters far below, tried them greatly. The path was narrow, the wall of rock above forcing them nearly to the edge of the gorge. They crawled along, making slow progress and finally halting at a cleft in the rock ahead of them. They found this to be a low-ceilinged cave and decided to make camp there for the night. The next morning, they resumed their journey, discovering the path gradually ascended to emerge on a broad plain. Not only was a more hospitable landscape a welcome sight, but before them was a clump of fruit trees! Norbert spurred his horse towards them.

"Apples!"

Gadroon quickly drew up beside him.

"Pears also... and plums!"

They picked the trees' offerings from where they sat, reaching up and stuffing themselves with ripe pippins and soft damsons. They remained beneath the laden boughs until they were satisfied. Now when they rode, a warm wind was behind them. Gadroon was anxious to gain the Goffrow Bridge before nightfall. He reasoned that even though any shelter they might find would be no better than the cave they had just left behind, at least they would have crossed into the kingdom of Tomberg.

Eventually the great bridge stood before them. Two immense turrets, of a ruddy-coloured stone, flanked the arches that spanned the gorge. The knights stared up at the domed gables high above them as they crossed. Norbert wondered darkly how many of those who had helped to build this great edifice had plunged to their deaths onto the rocks below. The muted tones of the sunset echoed such melancholy reflections.

*

111

At first the kingdom of Tomberg seemed to be little different from the land they had left behind. As dusk approached, the companions found shelter in a ruined barn. Although part of the roof had collapsed, the place offered enough dry straw in one corner to lie upon. By searching about they even found a quantity of hay for the horses in a shed nearby. The knights then settled down to sleep, trusting the morrow would bring them good fortune.

The view the next morning suggested that Lady Luck had taken a long vacation. An air of desolation was everywhere and it seemed likely that in the distance a storm was about to break. Black specks that were birds appeared and reappeared against the billowing grey and white clouds. No other creature seemed curious enough to peer at them in this lifeless land.

The town of Meutreville, where they intended to find lodgings, lay many leagues distant. After some hours Norbert and Gadroon finally came upon a pair of rude huts, a stone-built shelter next to them, beside the way. The sound of several dogs barking indicated that their presence had not gone unnoticed. Smoke was issuing from the doorway of the nearest hut and from this emerged an old woman. She stood, arms akimbo, and regarded them sourly, while the dogs continued to howl furiously. As they drew up beside her, Gadroon smiled in greeting.

"I bid thee good morn, mistress."

The woman continued to stare and eventually she spoke, though not words of good cheer.

"No welcome there is for strangers here."

Gadroon was not disconcerted, by either the sentiments or the convoluted grammar.

"We have travelled far and would wish to sup. Dost thou have any fayre? It matters not how simple."

The old woman eyed them, taking in their demeanour and knightly trappings. She retreated into the hut and returned with something wrapped in her apron.

"Half a quartern loaf..."

Norbert went to take it. As he did so she regarded him slyly.

"'Twill cost 'ee a silver penny."

Norbert was outraged.

"How so? Such a coin would buy a week's provision of bread in any market in the land."

The woman made to snatch back the loaf.

"Then find such a place if 'ee can..."

Gadroon reached in his purse and tossed her a coin.

"Here... and given willingly."

The woman caught the coin in one hand and thrust the loaf at Norbert with the other. She then retreated once more into the smoky interior as the dogs took up their yapping once more. The two knights coaxed their mounts back along the way. After another mile or so they found a stream where they let the horses drink, and themselves partook of their rude meal.

Gadroon waited for his steed to drink its fill before he took any of the water himself. He splashed his face and hands and felt refreshed. Norbert did the same but was still smarting over their treatment by the old woman.

"That impudent crone... no better than any common thief..."

Gadroon was inclined to be philosophical – being one of the privileged classes, he could afford to be.

"Come... forgive her, Norbert. She has done us no harm... in truth she has given us what we asked... thou canst not quarrel with that. Neither can thou eat silver or gold... so which is worth the more? That or the bread, which thou holdest at this moment?"

Norbert continued to grumble.

"It be half stale as well..."

Gadroon was consoling.

"Dear old friend... thou shalt have feasts aplenty in the days to come I do not doubt. Now be of good cheer! We may reach Meutreville ere long."

Norbert humphed a good deal, but it was noticeable that when he had a full belly his temper improved. They had better fortune on the morning of the morrow when they came upon a peddler of pies – both sweet and savoury. The pieman – obviously a keen follower of folk rhymes – was off to the fair.

A procession of days and nights followed as they travelled on. The wastes of Anghard were but a memory, the way they followed being lined with trees in full leaf. When an errant wind ruffled the topmost branches, the sound was as pebbles shifting with the tide. At night, the stars could be seen from one horizon to the other, pressed into the black velvet sky as if by an invisible hand. At noon on the fourth day of their journey, a cluster of cottages and other buildings came into view. Their assuming they had come upon a friendly village was to prove as sensible as having a bonfire in a firework factory.

*

Had Norbert and Gadroon known of the current woes besetting the kingdom of Tomberg, they might well have taken a long detour. A series of poor harvests had brought starvation and beggardom to the peasantry. The usual helping of superstition being added to this woeful mix, a belief they had been cursed by the gods, was currently rife among the populace.

As in previous years, and the years before that, when the rain did not come, they watched the wheat wither in the ground. And, as if heaven were set upon mocking them further, one dawn a storm came. The downpour was so heavy it was impossible to walk a few yards without being drenched. As the menfolk took shelter in the village square the irony of their plight was not lost upon them.

They grouped together disconsolately beneath the canopied tomb of Sir Eustace Bladding. The effigy of this knight, who had been the lord to previous generations, seemed almost to mock them from beyond the grave. And what did this gross monument truly commemorate? Naught but a life of gluttony and cruelty.

The ornate filigrees of its design seemed to mock the very souls of the peasants now clustered about the knight's resting place. Prayers had been said for more than two thousand days by the priests in the great chapel at Valentin when Sir Bladding died. Among the peasants none mourned his passing. They had tilled his land, toiling so their lord might grow fat from the corn they harvested. The fathers and grandfathers of the men who now stood about so forlornly had at the knight's funeral been obliged to file past the coffin as it lay in honour before the altar.

Thus it was little wonder that the men of Tomberg had little regard for nobles, knights and their ways. Majestic upon their fine steeds they might appear to others – figures of legend, with shining armour and lances held high. The common folk knew these fine gentlemen would ride them down without a qualm. There is no guarantee that chivalry resides with he who carries a sword and shield, whether it boast a gold pentacle upon it or not.

We are informed that the policeman's lot is not a happy one. In the time in which our tale is set, the lot of the peasant was not a bowl of cherries either. On the economic ladder he was but one rung above the serf, who got no wages at all. The peasant was unlikely to be familiar with jangling a pocket full of change either. His landlord took a fifth of his earnings, the priest a tenth, leaving him – and the family he was obliged to support – with little enough. During a harsh winter they might survive or they might not. Even when men first settled in one place, the notion that a community always helps its members has always been a nebulous one. A hungry man is an angry man.

And not for the peasant the niceties of court dress either. He had two sets of clothes – and every night he slept in them. Thus he was guaranteed to stink all year round. Because the women stayed all day in the hut spinning, they smelled of woodsmoke, hence they were infinitely more attractive. To add to the stench of her spouse was that of his animals, often kept inside the hut for fear of them being stolen.

Of such ilk were those Norbert and Gadroon came upon as they entered the village. Such an aura of hostility greeted them that, almost involuntarily, the knights halted their horses.

"What make you of them, Gadroon? I fear we are not among friends."

"There you speak most wisely, Norbert... but it is our duty to be courteous to all... and without favour."

"Rank means but little when we are called by the divine power at our end."

"Quite. But that said, old friend... it may also be wise to rest a hand lightly upon one's sword as we approach these new acquaintances..."

Norbert was understandably somewhat perturbed.

"Think you they wish to enter into combat with us?"

"A drunken man believes he may rout an entire army..."

"Are they drunk then?"

"If you cut any peasant... ale will flow from the wound. I blame them not... take away his liquor... and what little comfort has he in his hovel?"

"Perchance thou art too harsh concerning his lowly station..."

"As a boy I knew an old woodsman who I delighted to talk with and who would enthrall me by the hour with his tales. My father told me years later his lips were scarce ever wiped before his next draught."

The crowd continued to stare at Norbert and Gadroon. Most were in grimy doublet and hose, among them youths as thin as yarrow stalks who muttered to themselves. What it was that filled their minds except fear and superstition? They were the kind who always looked about desperately for the second magpie. Gadroon urged his horse towards a one-eyed varlet. Within his remaining orb a look of malevolence simmered like a witch's cauldron.

"What name has this place, my friend?"

The peasant stared dumbly at him. Gadroon was determined that he should reply.

"The name... if you please!"

The man spat vehemently onto the ground.

"It hath no name... and never will."

And with that Gadroon had to be content, and the two knights turned their horses and took their leave. Their dealings with the denizens of Tomberg were not at an end, however. A trio of rascals – Staple, Tight and Bate by name – were that day established on the path of wrong-doing. Unfortunately for them, it would cross the way taken by our heroes.

The Widow Athilde resided in a cottage on the other side of the village. Surrounded by elder and myrtle trees, roses and lupins arched above her door and all was fair. She tended burdock, fennel and leeks and a great many herbs also. Known as a woman of ancient lore, Athilde kept in health ailing peasants and helped bring many a babe into this world for many a year.

Staple and his knavish confederates had no mind to share her arcane knowledge; they were solely intent on stealing anything from her they could find. Rogues they were, and there is no such thing as a 'loveable rogue' except between the pages of Mills and Boon. And if the widow resisted their robbing, they would not hesitate to

117

beat her senseless with the ugly-looking clubs they carried.

Within her cottage, and engrossed upon blending a healing potion, Athilde did not hear their approach. But a sixth sense alerted her that all was not well. She left the potion where it was and crept outside to the back of the cottage to hide behind an old willow that stood there. The sound of someone attempting to force the front door came to her ears. Athilde stayed still, invisible in the shadows, waiting. At that precise moment, Norbert and Gadroon rode into view.

Bate, the most witless of the three vagabonds, cried out in alarm. Immediately alerted of something untoward, the knights approached the cottage. The battering of the door timbers ceased and Staple confronted the knights.

"Be off with you, *cursed knights*... this is no affair of yours."

Gadroon was inclined to disagree and said so.

"When I come upon thieving rascals I am inclined to teach them a lesson not to go a-robbing..."

Bate faltered, ready to flee, while Tight, holding his club in both hands, advanced towards Gadroon. The knight dismounted and Staple wrenched a dagger from beneath his doublet. Just as swiftly, Gadroon drew his sword. Staple was inclined to sneer.

"You cannot better us... with all your finery..."

Gadroon was as the serpent about to strike.

"I have felled a few score of men in my time... three more will make but little difference..."

Hearing these words, Tight halted where he was. Staple, however, kept on coming. Norbert, still in the saddle, shouted out to him.

"Put up the blade, you fool... or it will be the worse for you."

Ignoring the warning, Staple lunged at Gadroon who, with one stroke of his sword, cut two fingers from his hand. At the sight of this, and Staple's subsequent screams, Bate went running off like the wind. Tight, flinging aside his club, fled after him. Blood poured from Staple's wound falling onto the ground, while Gadroon slowly sheathed his sword. The would-be thief clutched his hand and stared at Gadroon.

"What have you done to me?"

Gadroon was stony.

"The same that you would have done to another if I had not come upon you... and worse."

At that moment Athilde appeared from behind her dwelling. She carried a cloth and handed it to the wounded man.

"Here tie that about you... it may stop the bleeding."

Staple seized the makeshift bandage and, without a word stumbled off. He could be heard cursing the companions who had abandoned him until eventually the distance swallowed them all up. Athilde turned and curtseyed to Gadroon.

"I am the Mistress Athilde... and I have both of you noble knights to thank for my life."

"Mistress, I am Sir Gadroon and this is my companion Sir Norbert."

"The angels have sent me protectors... that I am not harmed by likely evil."

Gadroon sighed.

"Aye. That kind of vermin do not stop at murder."

Athilde looked away for a moment.

"And is it not a tragedy that times have come upon us when men think nothing of doing these things?"

Gadroon nodded slowly.

"It is, most truly. Men so easily become as unthinking beasts."

Athilde turned back to gaze at him.

"You have seen much darkness in the souls of others, I perceive."

"I have, mistress... but I still embrace the light."

She laid a hand on his arm.

"I know this. Despite the hatred and cruelty you have witnessed you still have great love in your heart."

Gadroon bowed his head.

"I do that... and long may it remain there. For this I am grateful to those who protect me... the ancestors... and perhaps even those spirits I do not see... but I know are there."

Athilde, her hair glistening like snow in sunlight, reached out to grasp the hands of Gadroon in her own.

"And with these great gifts of light and love you will always be sustained, Sir Knight. For heaven and earth are but filled with these things if only we know where to seek them... and I know you have discovered that for yourself."

Gadroon felt a strange sadness come upon him. Athilde looked deep into his eyes.

"Fear not, O great one! You have far to go upon your journey... but you will be at peace when it is over... that I truly promise."

Norbert could not stop himself.

"And how *will* we fare, lady... upon our Quest? For it seems that you know of these things... though I confess I do not know how."

Athilde looked up at Norbert's anxious features. She smiled upon him with such kindness that for the moment much of the care he owned seemed to flee from him.

"Though I *do* know of your Quest... how it will be, that I cannot tell... for much is hidden... even from me. Though I have been given the gift of secret sight, I cannot see all. That is the way of things and humbly do I accept it."

A silence, broken only by the sigh of the wind, came upon the three who stood there. None seemingly dared to speak. At last Gadroon went to mount his horse once more.

"We must continue our journey..."

Athilde, as if waking from some deep slumber, held up her hand.

"But... you must take refreshment... it is the least I can offer the brave men who have saved me..."

Norbert immediately brightened up – several kilowatts.

"We cannot presume upon you, mistress..."

"Nay! You must do so... and perhaps it would be wise for you take your ease here... then resume your journey with the morrow."

One glance at Norbert told Gadroon that to disappoint his companion would be a callous act. He also felt it would do no harm to be there in the cottage to guard Athilde that night. Gadroon knew it was unlikely her assailants would return, but it would be as well to make certain. Thus he agreed they would remain, much to Norbert's delight.

"You are most generous... and we thank you, Mistress Athilde."

Athilde's eyes sparkled, brighter than precious stones.

"It is my duty... and my pleasure to be hospitable to all travellers."

And she bade Norbert and Gadroon enter her home.

*

Norbert popped a ripe strawberry in his mouth. He thought he had never felt so content or satisfied in his entire life, as he did at that moment. Gadroon, long since replete, eyed him with some amusement.

"Well, old friend... I have never seen you sup so well... and not a scrap of meat or fish there was in sight..."

Athilde laughed knowingly.

"Does it not show how we may be satisfied... and with full bellies... without bringing any harm to our fellow creatures..."

Norbert, repressing a belch, had to agree.

"Indeed... that was the most toothsome supper I have enjoyed for many a day..."

Gadroon looked about him. The dwelling was small, yet there was a feeling of airiness and space all around. It was as if the world beyond was the same as that within. This became more marked as the day drew to an end and the moon rose, casting her light into that singular interior. So bright and full she was, the lit candle almost wished it might flee from the scene. Unprompted, Athilde spoke of her life, and her two listeners took in all that she said. Did they but know it, The Goddess herself addressed them, for she had been chosen at birth as one of her blessed handmaidens.

"My husband Herian was as good a man as any woman could wish for. I wept when he was taken from me... he went to fight what he believed was a just war... if there ever can be such a thing... and never returned. For long days I waited to hear his voice once more... and then I knew all hope had gone. Many a year has now passed since then..."

Athilde then took up a small harp and ran her fingers across the strings. Immediately the very air sang with the sound, and when she picked out the notes of a melody they came as droplets of water splashing upon a stone. Norbert closed his eyes such was the effect upon him, while Gadroon could only look on and marvel. In that moment Athilde truly became the Moon and, when she sang softly to the harp chorus it was as if she had summoned all the stars in the night sky to be round about her. She sang these simple lines, over and over.

Those who seek shall find
Heaven shares this mind
Treasure awaits you there
Fairer than all that is fair...

The music faded with the stars, and Athilde laid her harp aside. She smiled upon Gadroon, and he knew that the words she had sung were meant for him and his companion, who now slept peacefully. Before he also rested Gadroon knew there was one question he must ask of Athilde.

"Our journey will take us to the town of Meutreville... thereafter we cross the Bridge of Amuthdel and pass into the kingdom of Dolfay. I have a great fear of what will come to pass in Meutreville... a darkness seizes me... even at the mention of that name..."

Athilde closed her eyes. Her words came as if from a great distance.

"The greatest fear is of the land of fear itself. You, sir knight... and your companion also... must walk alone... in that world. The place of terror... where you will believe for a time that hope is no more... there you must venture. It is your fate. Only then will you see the light that lies beyond... that blessed ray that will guide you to your goal. That light, when you finally come upon it, will shine upon you with a brightness you cannot at this moment know. It is the light that you... and no other mortal... have ever seen."

Gadroon sighed.

"I knew this. In my heart I was always certain the path to the Chapel of Glainseg would be painful and difficult."

Athilde's tone was now clear and strong. Never loud, it still filled the room.

"Take courage, my noble one. That path is the only one that leads to the truth! You must leave all the shadows that still linger within yourself... and there are many... behind you. It is the pure alone who behold the pure."

"Aye. That is so. A knight must always strive for the highest and the greatest good..."

Athilde smiled.

"And that you do already. But to gain the greatest prize... the one you seek... you must enter that holy place with only holiness in your heart. Glainseg is not of this world, I assure you..."

"But I believe it will be there for Norbert and myself..."

Athilde hastened to reassure him.

"Indeed it will... but only because you are of the chosen ones. To any others passing there... nothing of Glainseg can ever be seen. Those who are the guardians of the Chapel await you... and patiently... for time means but nothing in that place... that I know too."

Gadroon was filled with wonder at Athilde's words.

"You tell me that Norbert and I are *chosen*?"

It was Athilde's turn to be wondrous.

"You did not think so? Indeed you are... I assure you of that. What great power was it brought you here to my dwelling this day? Who decided you were to shield me from harm? And this same power made it so that I would tell you of all these things you wished to know."

At that moment the Moon, who had been hidden for some moments by the clouds, reappeared and all was swept with an ocean of silver. Gadroon bowed his head and, in that instant, felt all the power of The Goddess to the very core of his being. It was as if heaven had gathered him to its bosom and he was assured a part in that kingdom – one invisible and eternal. He nearly fell prostrate at Athilde's feet but, with the invisible power that she owned, Gadroon was held upright. He whispered of all that he saw.

"The Goddess! Loenel herself... she is with me! I know this! I am able to behold her!"

Athilde smiled upon him.

"It is Loenel who is the great spirit of The Grail! This you must know... she will be with you until the end of time. The Goddess smiles upon you, fair Gadroon."

Gadroon raised his eyes and saw deeper into the mysteries. The eternal beauty of The Goddess was there before him!

"Athilde... my lady..."

"Yes, Gadroon... I am The Goddess also.... as all women are... and may be more so if they only wish. This we know and I was most fortunate to have been chosen as her handmaiden. I knew this was so as a child... my dear mother only lived long enough to tell me this... but I vowed to follow Loenel always... and she has ever protected me..."

At that moment the Moon withdrew once more behind a veil of cloud. Norbert stirred from his slumber and, in that instant, Gadroon returned once more to the ordinary world. There would be other moments when he would know The Goddess, when she would look long and deeply upon him and with great mercy, but these times were yet to come.

"Ho... Gadroon! Have I slept long?"

"Nay, my friend... but a trice. Perhaps it is time we wished our hostess goodnight and sought greater slumber ourselves."

Without a word, but with many a smile, Athilde led them to a chamber where two down-filled couches awaited them. The air was filled with the scent of lavender, and indeed bunches of that soothing plant hung from the low rafters. Gratefully the two travellers lay down, within moments to fall into a deep and untroubled sleep. Gadroon was to dream also, not of the commonplace reveries of the night, but visions from the world that lies always but a brief distance from our own.

There, Athilde appeared to him as a young woman, beautiful and enchanting, her eyes even more bright than in the present world. Beside her stood the beloved, a fearless warrior but one who owned a sensitive manner, not common among men of war. A certain sadness was about him also, and he was

125

troubled, perhaps by knowing that he could longer be with Athilde. In this dream Gadroon spoke, showing his concern for her.

"And what will happen to you alone in these wild and troubled times?"

She answered calmly, and without fear.

"It is so that folks hereabout say I am a sorceress and would use that as a reason to do me harm. Some swear there is a great treasure hidden here... 'fairy gold' they say. I know heaven watches over me and nothing may harm me... and I also have many enchantments that I employ. Not to be seen by any mortal eye is no great task for me to bring about."

She smiled upon Gadroon and in his dream he saw himself floating through an endless rose-coloured dawn into the heart of the sun. He heard Athilde's words from afar.

"And always there will be those who are sent by Loenel to protect me."

With that, Athilde was no longer there and neither was her companion. In his dream state Gadroon suddenly felt alone and most vulnerable, more so than he had ever felt, even in battle. When he looked down at his sword the weapon turned to mist. To his amazement all the rest of him turned to nothing also.

*

When the knights resumed their journey the next morning all seemed to promise well. The clouds lay comfortably above the horizon, and swallows flew higher and higher searching the skyways. Wild roses grew beside the way and their sweet fragrance was everywhere as they bade farewell to Athilde.

"Go well upon your journey... and return to Valentin another day."

"Ah! *Valentin!* They said this place hath no name... now I know that is not so."

126

"Indeed... it is a fair name... and all will be well... of that I am sure. Now go thee in peace both of you... O brave and noble knights."

Athilde insisted they take as much as they could safely carry in the way of provisions and, for this they were more than grateful. Experience had now taught them they could not rely upon foraging for food in arid lands. At this moment, all owned a stillness, profound enough to cause Gadroon to ponder once more their situation, and to share such thoughts as he had with Norbert.

"I swear that as soon as we crossed the Goffrow Bridge I never once believed we were in any further danger. Yet my unease as to what is happening in the world beyond us has grown. I am certain much wickedness is at this moment brewing... I can feel it in the wind."

Norbert shuddered to think that more trials would be theirs in the days to come. The Quest had taught him one thing about himself, that he was most certainly a man of regular habits. The unpredictable way in which supping occurred had proved to be most vexing. Others troubles of a more dramatic kind were very soon about to make themselves felt, and very soon.

XI

She bent to his face
And kissed him well,
Then they argued sadness and grace,
Love's heavens and hells.

As Gadroon had foreseen, malice was bubbling away in Malfaise castle. Croop was at this moment ladling out a portion regarding Sir Wayne's shortcomings.

"He hath a maiden's way about him, Sire... and will not take up arms against his king... of that I am certain. The heat of his anger hath already cooled. Passion cannot be kept alive with fire... it is ice that sustaineth it."

Brime deliberated, rolling a baleful eye.

"I had already thought much the same. He is weak... as many of Arthur's followers... with all their talk of chivalry and noble deeds. But *we* know the ways of the world do we not, Croop?"

"Indeed we do, my lord..."

Brime was as dry as Tio Pepe.

"I am of a mind that Wayne hath been useful to us, but now he is no longer. He hath nothing more of import to tell us and must be cast aside like some soiled hose..."

Croop was as oily as can be.

"And your plans, my liege?"

Brime was brief – as a thong on the beach at St. Tropez.

"We shall summon the armies of Anghard and march into the kingdom of Tomberg. Those there who will join us against Longres... let them. If any chose not to do so... they shall be put to the sword... it matters but little either way. After that we shall lay waste Arthur's land. The time has come to defeat Camelot... of that I am certain."

"Yes, your majesty."

Croop was silent for the moment. He had long awaited the blow to fall, now that moment had arrived he was more than alarmed. It would be unwise to question the royal will, and thus he remained silent. Inwardly, he knew Brime was most unwise to act so. The people of Tomberg were nothing but half-starved peasants, what kind of soldiery would they make even if they joined the men of Anghard? To slaughter them – seemingly inevitable – would evoke anger in Longres and that was no small thing. Despite Brime's sneers, if it came to battle, Arthur would be a formidable adversary. For more than a century, Longres had been the victor in every campaign they had fought. The art of war had been passed down from generation to generation, and the warrior tradition had grown by the year. With some trepidation Croop waited to hear what the king might have to say next.

"At this moment the Queen has a formidable ally... and their schemes are more subtle than one could ever imagine. When a woman is so inclined she may obtain any end she wishes. Is that not so, Croop?"

Rather absently, Croop agreed. Like Norbert, he had never quite seen the point of women. What was it about the fairer sex that was so *fascinating*? During his time at Malfaise it had been a continuing mystery to the king's advisor as to why *the ladies* were so feted at court. At Camelot the esteem in which they were held was beyond belief. Arthur's knights made so much of pledging fidelity to these exotic creatures, that Croop was convinced they were all touched with madness. With such a myriad of thoughts in his mind he followed Brime to the Queen's Chamber.

*

If Morgan le Fay always took the sexy role that Barbara Windsor played, Queen Lardiana would have to be

Hattie Jacques minus the sweetness. Neither appreciated being thwarted in their desires and they both worked double shifts in order to get their way. Lardiana had a temper like a volcano with heartburn, and Morgan was the Daughter of Darkness, which has to be ultra-scary in anybody's book.

Morgan le Fay's malicious moods were spurred on by her ongoing grudge against Arthur. As the legends relate, she had never forgiven the king for chucking her after their hot date all those semesters ago. Arthur going steady with Guinevere guaranteed the Queen got permanent bad vibes as well. Morgan was in the same bag as *the knights sans piete*, the bad guys who had sworn to destroy Arthur and the Round Table. That dreary old bore Spenser mentions this bunch of ASBOs in *The Faerie Queene*. Morgan didn't read books anyway, apart from ones with really nasty spells in them.

Lardiana had the problem of suffering from a dose of unrequited love. She had the hots for Gadroon, but knew he fancied her as about as much as a plate of cold cabbage. Suspecting this, she got uptight – there being no fury like a woman scorned, so they say – and persuaded Morgan to put a curse on the noble knight. The plot got a bit thicker at this point because Morgan fancied Gadroon herself, but she wasn't going to let on to the randy royal about that, no sirree.

So what kind of spell did she cook up? This one was right out of the Bumper Book of Necromancy for Neophytes, and no mistake. A Hammer Horror Midnight Special – to bring about the death of Gadroon and bind him to her in the underworld. There he would remain for all eternity, or even longer – as her lover and pet wraith. Only a super-sorceress could dream up spooky stuff like that.

As we know, Brime's plans for Norbert and Gadroon had been more mundane – slamming the pair in the pokey. Their subsequent escape had evoked the royal wrath, so much so that Croop had – literally – almost lost his head. When Croop had informed the king his prize birds had flown, the old custom of executing the messenger had nearly enjoyed a sudden revival.

By the time Brime had calmed down a bit and reprieved his advisor, the king had other things on his mind. Bringing down Camelot by nobbling the Grail hunters having been Plan A, he now switched to Plan B – the invasion of Tomberg. Somewhere in his folio of schemes was also Plan Z – employing Morgan le Fay's magical powers. Brime was willing to try anything, though secretly he regarded Morgan as a cut-price Mystic Meg.

Neither did Morgan attempt to disguise her contempt for Brime. In her view he was a tosspot rather than a despot. Nevertheless, when Lardiana and Morgan entered the Great Hall to inform Brime they were preparing a spell to curse Gadroon, the king congratulated her, and Morgan accepted the compliment with good grace. Brime felt confident that with Gadroon out of the way, The Quest would be abandoned. Norbert he regarded as not even worth considering in any way. This morning His Majesty was inclined to strut about and make speeches while the two women yawned, his consort discreetly behind her hand, Morgan more openly.

"I shall be master of every kingdom in the land! All shall now feel my power and tremble! My glorious armies shall show none the slightest mercy! I shall bring Arthur to his knees... and the glory of Camelot will be no more! My enemies will be as dust... whirled into oblivion by the winds of fate..."

And so it went on – interminably – more hot air than in a Turkish Bath. Croop knew it would all end in tears, his own probably. Morgan le Fay and King Brine in cahoots meant double-trouble squared whatever happened.

*

The sorceress was most busy in her Temple that evening. Out came the black candles, the ripest, most pongy incense and the deadly sacrificial blade. Incantations that would have been 'R' rated filled the air and the performance got under way.

"Angaz! God of Death! Hear my summons! I command thee to appear before me!"

Interrupted from a nap, this particular deity was not in the best of tempers when evoked. He even yawned a couple of times, which just goes to show that even a god who dispenses the endless sleep, has his own little foibles.

"I come in answer to thy summons, O Mistress of The Dark Ways. Why dost thou evoke Angaz? What wouldst thou desire of me?"

Angaz yawned once more. Formal exchanges with necromancers and the like always tired him out.

"I desire that thy icy breath shall be upon one mortal! He who I shall name."

Angaz knew the drill; he had done this stuff enough times.

"Name him!"

"Sir Gadroon de Montaigne!"

Despite his usual imperturbable countenance, Angaz clocked in as fazed.

"He floweth with great power... as a mighty stream doth. Why wouldst thou wish the waters of life within him to run no more, O Follower of the Path of Shadows?"

"Mmmff."

"Thy silence speaketh of nameless and ghoulish things..."

Morgan wasn't letting on, not even to The Grim Reaper himself. All this Q & A might have gone on unto eternity, or even longer, had not another divine presence appeared. This one needed no introduction but she went through the usual formalities.

"I am Loenel... The Great Goddess! I wouldst command that thou hearken to my words!"

Morgan wasn't sure she wanted to hear any of these particular sentiments, but knew she had no choice.

"I am thy servant, O Queen of Heaven... as all upon this Earth. What wouldst thou with me?"

Being a goddess, Loenel never bothered with small talk – not even any waffle about the weather.

"The noble knight whose life thou wishest to end... is this why thou hath summoned the Lord of The Underworld?"

Morgan had made her mind up, and said so.

"He shall die!"

Loenel was of a different view.

"Know ye that Gadroon hath been ordained by Nen – Chief among all gods – to be the protector of those who are appointed as my handmaidens! Gadroon has already proved thus by defending and protecting one of my chosen band... Athilde..."

Morgan was a feisty dame, as legend always tells, and she was inclined to do a spot of talking back.

"*I* have no need of a protector! No mortal man shall ever come to my aid! I am that face of the cold and dark moon that despiseth men! Knights... with their child's games... and their *chivalry!*"

Even Angaz was amazed at her nerve. Having a barney with the top-gun goddess had to be a dodgy move in any universe. Loenel was not best pleased either, you could tell that without too much close reading.

"Take care, thou Daughter of Doomsday! The Queen of Heaven is not to be questioned as to how she may order the universe. Know ye not that of *every face* that The Moon hath... each one of them is my beloved sister?"

Morgan was smart enough to avoid any backchat this time. Loenel gave her a final look, and an even more final word.

"Harm him not... this knight Gadroon! I have spoken!"

Loenel departed to dispatch other heavenly errands. Morgan addressed Angaz once more.

"I have summoned thee, Bringer of Death! Thou *shalt* do my bidding..."

Angaz was, not surprisingly, aware of certain metaphysical principles.

"I *shalt* do thy bidding, O Darkest Damsel of the Dark... but the Laws of Creation will... as always... decide the outcome."

Morgan was quite equal to that particular thesis.

"Do you think I am foolish enough not to know that I too must abide by these laws? Though my will is known to be more mighty than the oceans... and more resolute than the mountains... I obey that power which commands me. Loenel hath perhaps forgotten that I too am the handmaiden of a great deity... *The Dark Goddess*... is that not so?"

Angaz wasn't going to argue the point; he also had pressing business to attend to. Gods and goddesses have a busy old life, and have to keep to a tight schedule, what with deciding the fate of mortals and all that. That was particularly relevant if you were the God of Death. When your *time has come*, he is always prompt about keeping the appointment. That was in the rules too, as well as him being very polite.

"I acknowledge your exalted rank, Morgan le Fay. Now... if you don't mind... I would appreciate you deconsecrating the circle... closing the four gates... and dismissing me... or I shall be late for a rather important meeting..."

The sorceress obliged and the Grim Reaper popped off, so to speak. While returning her magical paraphernalia to the iron chest beneath the altar, doubt kept intruding into her mind. She had a niggling feeling that the spell wouldn't work – at least not completely to her satisfaction. There was not much point in putting a curse on anybody that only worked in a half-assed fashion. You might as well save your energy and go on a day-trip to Bognor instead.

Away from all this darkness, Loenel reflected upon her confrontation with Morgan le Fay. The Goddess had every reason to protect and nurture Norbert and Gadroon, for she wished most earnestly for The Quest to succeed. Only this way would the power of The Goddess be maintained in the universe – the feminine element must always equal the masculine, down to the last microgram. Maintaining the balance of yin and yang required almost constant attention. Loenel was heartened by the feeling she had a staunch ally somewhere in the mortal realm. This magus had been assigned by the great power of magic to also sustain and protect Norbert and Gadroon. She was not yet aware of his identity but knew she soon would be.

During her ritual, Morgan also had felt acutely the presence of another unfamiliar force. Her formidable will had been deliberately challenged and, more remarkably, made weaker. The flow of her power was not as intense as it usually was – its constancy had faltered and even ceased on occasions. The source of this disruption to Morgan's intent was, of course, Edrith, Merlin's pupil. He had honed his skills enough to believe he was capable of disrupting any magical practices the sorcerers might undertake. During her summoning of Angaz he had been able to successfully divert much of her magical energy. While all this tricky stuff had been going on, Gadroon felt as if someone was walking over his grave, wearing size 13 rugby boots.

*

The Summer was its highest, ever about to tumble into those blowsy months that follow its glory. The rains of many weeks before had swollen the waterways, but the constant attention of the sun had returned them to their usual course. Gadroon was in good spirits, feeling that any delays had now been accounted for.

"As soon as we cross the River Perogel we will be set upon the way to Meutreville. Let us hope we may find there enough provisions for the journey to Dolfay."

"Indeed, Gadroon. This is the finest news we could ask for."

Any mention of fodder tended to liven up Norbert.

"Soon we shall be in sight of our prize. Think on that, my friend."

The knights were taking their ease, resting against a haystack. Wild roses and honeysuckle covered the hedgerows and all was fair. Gadroon closed his eyes and Norbert, not wishing to disturb him, retired to the other side of the haystack. He eventually fell to slumbering himself. Although aware that he was dreaming, Norbert was suddenly convinced that he had woken in another world – a paradise filled with countless platters of venison pasties. Why, he only had to reach out and...

Norbert opened his eyes. He could not believe this was indeed so! There before him was that dainty, and literally on a plate! He was about to avail himself of the said offering when something or other caused him to hesitate. Lady Malinda! There she sat before him – a basket of good things before her. Norbert could not help to also notice she was wearing a bodice that was cut extremely low.

"Sir Knight, you must take your fill... until you are satisfied..."

To Norbert any *double-entrendre* made as much sense as double-entry bookkeeping.

"It seems I have no appetite for..."

"Not even for love, sweet Norbert?"

136

Whereupon Lady Melinda sidled up closer to him, and Norbert was in a pickle bigger than a jar of Branston's. When she began to caress his thigh, our gentle knight turned pinker than a prawn sizzling on a Bondi Beach barbie. Just at that moment Gadroon, refreshed from his nap, appeared from behind the haystack. Lady Malinda was aghast.

"Sir Gadroon... how you did surprise me!"

"And thy presence is also one that brings astonishment to me, my lady. What brings thee to here, pray? So far from Charbon..."

Her ladyship nearly muffed her lines.

"I... I... came to give thee sustenance upon thy journey, O noble knights."

Gadroon bowed low.

"I thank thee for thy kindness, my lady..."

Norbert recovered somewhat.

"Most kind..."

Gadroon was puzzled by one feature of the tableau before him.

"I perceive a pasty... untouched..."

Lady Melinda took a turn at colouring up a bit and, to avoid further embarrassment, opted to scratch the fixture. Smoothing down her vampish velour, she jumped on her horse and headed for the hills. To be strictly accurate, she went in the general direction of the Kingdom of Dolfay, though the knights were not to be aware of that. Gadroon helped himself to a ripe pippin and bit into it reflectively.

"Methinks, some strange and wyrd tale this be, Norbert. Why doth Lady Malinda pursue thee with such ardour... for this must be the only reason for her travelling so far from Charbon? Perhaps it is part of some riddlesome legend that will be puzzled over endlessly by scholars in some far-off time. I know not..."

Norbert, braving the pasty now it was no longer spiced with amorous overtones, said nothing. What could he possibly venture to say about matters with which he was not familiar? Gadroon continued to idly speculate upon the marital arrangements of the Wooslak-Bascoombes. Gothic good-timers, perhaps?

XII

Where war and marvels
Take turns with peace,
Where sometimes lightning trouble
Has struck, and sometimes soft ease.

On the first day of the following month – Tornith in the old calendar – King Brime and his army struck at an unsuspecting Tomberg. This marked the first blow of what would be recorded in *The Great Chronicles*, as *The Unjust War*. The king insisted that 'vicious bandits' were to blame for his decision to invade. It need hardly be said this was untrue. A few folk may have occasionally crossed the border into Anghard in search of forage for their animals and food for their families, but that was all. Crimson with rage, Brime addressed his court with the ripest rhetoric.

"We shall no longer tolerate such open thievery... these vagabonds must be taught a sharp lesson... and a sure one... at the point of a sword."

Whether any of those farmers who held land near the border of his kingdom had openly complained about these supposed iniquities was most unlikely. A wiser and more munificent monarch would have known that with the coming of a good harvest in Tomberg, any such incursions would cease. Unfortunately, the bullies and oafs who made up Brime's court welcomed this unjust act of aggression. The scum who served in the ranks of the army were also ready to delight in any licensed rape and pillage.

Brime had decided that his troops would strike at the heart of the neighbouring kingdom. They would enter Tomberg, cross the Great Bridge at Goffrow and march upon Meutreville to lay the town waste. The outlying hamlets were to be ignored; the might of Anghard would be best demonstrated by shedding as much blood as possible at one time. Brime was a tyrant and a murderer who took pleasure in treating others as if their lives were of no account. Carnage was about to be unleashed that even Angaz might turn away from such a sight.

It was fortunate that the town of Meutreville lay some leagues away from where Norbert and Gadroon were camped. Having once forded the River Perogel, they had turned off the principle way through the kingdom, preferring instead to take to the pathways. Waking with the dawn the next day, the companions broke their fast and took their ease, unaware of the relentless advance of Brime and his army some leagues distant.

Nightly Gadroon saw Willowpetal in his dreams and her fate weighed heavily upon his heart. He did not so much fear that she would be dallying with some young swain, as carried off by plague or pestilence. If Norbert knew nothing of making love, Gadroon knew, as yet, little about the eternal power of love. A maiden's yearning, a poet's pleas, the shared joys of lovers, these were emotions unfamiliar to a knight. All women – whether country wenches or ladies of the court – were creatures of another world, ones who exercised a fascination upon Gadroon, but of their true nature he knew little. Willowpetal had cast a spell on him, one he had been powerless to resist. But this was no sinister enchantment, the knight fervently wished to be bound to her.

This unexpected devotion had also made him question, not only the nature of The Quest, but that of knighthood as well. If The Grail was the epitome of purity and compassion, then its nature must surely not embrace the dealing out of death – as Gadroon had done on many an occasion. He might well claim he had been defending the weak or fighting injustice, though this was not always so. In war, often there was ultimately no right or wrong. Gadroon did not think of himself as a good man, or even a bad man – just a man.

The courage he owned was of the sullen sort that warriors often possess – a determination to survive. Gadroon confided these and other such sentiments to his companion that morning.

"If I continue in knighthood... some battlefield will claim me and the ravens feast upon my flesh. The old women who scour among the corpses upon the battlefield will take this silver ring from my fingers. So Sir Biston will have his way... curse him! Of kin I have none... so none will remember me. This journey of life leads only to one end, old friend... into the unknown. And so our Quest is as the same... is it not?"

"With one great difference... whatever may happen to either of us in the coming years... I have faith that we shall succeed upon our Quest."

Gadroon pondered, if briefly.

"Indeed, Norbert. In my heart I believe that also. But as for the rest of our lives... to win or to lose... what matter it? Our own small fate means but little. The sun will still rise in the heavens... whether we be there to gaze upon it or not. Neither will the stars fall from the sky at our passing."

Norbert had that light in his eyes that Gadroon now knew well.

"Your soul will light you to a better world, Gadroon."

"Perhaps that may be... I will not deny it... and I thank thee. But what mean these things while we are still on the earth? 'Tis also true a lover's lament will mean nothing when he is but dust... like the minstrel's song... a mere whisper upon the wind. Yet I cannot help but feel my heart warmed by such things."

Norbert was inclined to be a tad cynical.

"I have observed that the attentions of Lady Malinda are bounded on every side with words of deceit. They mean nothing... counters in some game where hideous desire is the only winner."

Gadroon rose to his feet.

"Maybe hers are the false words of love, Norbert... but love cannot be played false."

Norbert lightened up.

"Those could be the words of Lapin..."

Gadroon smiled but was determined to continue with his discourse.

"Does the promise given of a moment mean any the less than any other? Let us not be harsh upon our fellows! We call upon such dreams to cherish us in times when there seems to be but little hope. And those days come to us all we may be certain of that... and when we least expect them. In truth... I feel that we two shall soon encounter more terrors than we have ever known before."

"None can know..."

"Aye... and I will cease to speak of such... for one may bring misfortune to bear merely by dwelling too long upon dark thoughts. That is the way of heaven and earth methinks."

As the sun rose higher the two knights contemplated the next part of their journey. If they had known what lay ahead they might well have changed their plans, but Destiny guides with an invisible hand. By the time dusk fell they had joined the old highway once more. Here, Gadroon was puzzled by the telltale signs that a great host had passed along the same way, and only the previous day. They could not have been aware how close they were following in the wake of Brime's army, but some instinct made Gadroon decide to slow their pace. They would arrive in Meutreville a day later than they had planned.

*

The face of war always remains the same, and before that fearsome look we remain helpless. We witness the crime of life being needlessly and callously destroyed and are impotent before it. When Norbert and Gadroon came eventually to Meutreville it was nothing but a smoking ruin. The stench of death grew more as they came closer to the town. Shattered dwellings were all around, and countless fires lit the sky. Everywhere, what had once been a home was now a few charred embers.

They rode on, through streets where corpses lay sprawled out amidst the destruction. Those who had survived this holocaust – youths with chiseled cheekbones, women huddling in shawls – peered from the shadows, their eyes filled with terror. Children, wailing and bereft, clutched at those nearest them while unceasingly, there came the sound of yelping dogs. The two knights moved slowly, as if they were the only constant in this seething chaos. The face of Gadroon was as stone; if he faltered, he knew, all was lost. More than once the horses' hooves slithered in pools of blood. An old man blundered across their path and, breathing his last, fell dying against the wall of a house.

Brime's army had seen to it that his ruthless will was served. Their savage work done, they had been herded back to the highway by their leaders. All that remained for them was the march back to Anghard. A few stragglers remained, pillaging and looting where they might. The knights came upon a small knot of soldiery in the town's centre where the daily market was held. The coarse shouts and staggering gait meant they had found a store of liquor in some merchant's house. A scream from a building nearby rent the air.

"Come Norbert, we have business here."

"Think thee it is the soldiers up to some devilment?"

"Aye... if one may give these stable sweepings such an honourable title."

A louder scream rent the air, unmistakably female and vibrant with terror. Gadroon swiftly moved his horse in the direction of the sound, Norbert following.

"Are the scoundrels intent on harming her... whoever she may be?"

Gadroon dismounted, next to a building where the door had been torn from its hinges. His face was set and grim.

"Norbert, if I were to be given a silver shilling for every wench I have saved from being ravaged by soldiery... I would be one of the richest men in the land. Come... I'll warrant we have some vermin to dispatch here."

In the back room of the house they came upon a sorry scene. A band of soldiers had trapped a young girl and were flinging her from one to the other like a rag doll. In her terrified features Gadroon could see a flickering vision of Willowpetal. His cry was wrathful and commanding.

"Leave the maid be!"

The brute that held the girl lurched round, seeming to see nothing that warranted any pause in what he was engaged upon.

"She's mine! You can have her when I've taken my fill if there is anything left to sport with. Now begone! Captain Crimp does not give up his prize to any."

Gadroon could see they were outnumbered, but not for a moment was he pricked by the goad of fear. He drew his sword and, seeing Norbert hesitate, called out to him.

"That one nearest you! Take him first!"

Another of the four immediately rushed at Gadroon who side-stepping neatly, slashed at the back of his attacker's neck as he passed. He tumbled into the opposite wall and breathed no more. Norbert was equal to his own man and stabbed him fiercely in the belly. Blood was everywhere and he fell back, clutching the wound. Crimp realising the attack was more formidable than he had realised, reluctantly loosed the girl. He and his remaining companion now faced the knights. Gadroon called to the maid, now trembling in the shadows.

"Run! Run! As fast as ye may! Now!"

She came to her senses and made for the door. Gadroon then turned his attention to dealing with his adversary. Whatever vileness dominated his nature, Crimp was most certainly a formidable fighter. Norbert too was hard pressed and fell back against the onslaught of his own foe. Hard they fought side by side until Crimp slid on a patch of blood on the floor and over-balanced. The moment Gadroon needed! He thrust as hard as he might and cut through chain mail and sinew alike through Crimp's throat. The weight of his falling body nearly took Gadroon's sword arm down with it. So intent was he on retrieving his blade he left himself open to the cowardly, but telling stab from the other soldier. In horror and rage Norbert slashed at the assailant with all his strength and took the man's head from off his shoulders.

Gadroon, swaying as soon as felt the blow, tried to keep his balance but could not. He fell to the floor and as he did so, realised he had never speculated upon death until this moment. That time had always been in another day and in a place far away. What Gadroon did not know was this evil moment had been brought about by one who was determined that Angaz would take him. With unholy glee did Morgan le Fay stare at a vision of the blade as it plunged into the knight's undefended side.

"That be a poisoned blade, my Gadroon. It will not heal in an instant... if at all! Such a potion goeth deep into the heart... I know full well for I have used the same brew myself many a time. It took all my cunning and more to conjure the bane upon that blade."

Her features darkened as she felt, even in herself, the venom seep into the blood of Gadroon and begin to freeze the very marrow in his bones. She smiled at her success. Soon the soul of the knight would be hers! The beauteous Gadroon would be locked with her in a ghostly embrace forever!

Norbert, breathing heavily and stumbling amid the carnage, acted as quickly as he could. He dragged the limp form of Gadroon out into the street and laid him across his horse. Then mounting his own steed, he slowly led Gadroon's steed back along the way they had come. He had no thought but to return to Valentin where he prayed Edrith would aid them. Norbert also fervently hoped he would meet no one on the road. Between the desperate desire to find aid for his companion and a fear for his own safety, his journey seemed interminable.

We hover in a state of death every moment of our lives, our demise tacit in the very fabric of our existence. If we could predict every peril we might encounter then we would pass through all unscathed. A hero is naught but a lucky fool. Norbert was now relying upon every speck of good fortune to sustain him in his purpose – his own, and any that Heaven could provide.

XIII

His strength saved him, and his courage, and his
faith
In God: he could have died a dozen times
Over.

After some nights of hearing the tramp of the retreating army, all sound had now ceased. In Athilde's cottage, Norbert slept but fitfully, constantly leaving his bed in the small hours to gaze upon his friend. He prayed to God, not only for Gadroon's recovery, but for all those who suffered from the scourge of oppression. The sights he had seen at Meutreville had sorely tried his faith, and his store of compassion for a great number of his fellow men had dwindled greatly. For the victims of such wanton cruelty he could do nothing. Norbert believed that mercy had to be evoked to relieve these ills from the world. But, closer to his own heart, would this be enough to save his dear friend?

Gadroon had only been dimly aware of what had occurred since his wounding. From that moment on he had felt distanced from all. He could not discern the procession of the hours, tell day from night, nor if he was asleep or awake. Drifting upon a black and endless sea, Gadroon wondered if he would ever see the shore again. He was beyond all power of reason and all that remained for him was a surrendering to the forces that were loose in the unknown. All had become without meaning. Sometimes he cried out at phantasms he believed were crouching about his bedside. When this happened he trembled unceasingly. To Norbert, this was a harrowing sight, his noble companion reduced to the state of a gibbering simpleton.

Athilde, who had willingly offered aid to Norbert's sick charge when he arrived at the cottage door, unceasingly prepared potions to relieve Gadroon's sufferings. These concoctions she stirred in an iron pot suspended over the fire and encouraged Gadroon, in his rare waking moments, to sip them from a wooden cup. She brought all her herb lore to bear upon finding a cure for him. Leek, nettle, fennel and radish went into brews designed to bring out the poisons in sweats. This treatment was alternated with cooling draughts of burdock, apple, and myrtle berries.

Norbert feared for the life of his friend and spent many an hour pacing the tiny cottage in his anxiety. His sojourn went unrelieved also, for he dare not leave the cottage knowing that Brime's troops might still be abroad. The days passed and, rather than show any signs of recovery, Gadroon seemed to grow continually weaker. His face grew paler and he now rarely opened his eyes.

Athilde continued to gather herbs, venturing deep into the forest under a full moon for this purpose. Lupin, basil, gentian, rue and mallow... willow bark and ivy berries – all these things she employed, but to no avail. Gadroon slipped further and further into unconsciousness. Eventually Norbert's efforts to remain calm failed him and he loudly voiced his despair.

"What is there to be done? Is my dear friend to die? Can you do nothing for him with your endless slops?"

Athilde sat on a stool, her hands clasped together, her eyes to the floor saying nothing. Her silence caused Norbert to vent his anger further upon the world and the injustice of fate, as he saw it.

"Gadroon has saved others from death and dishonour and this is God's reward... to let him die..."

At last Athilde spoke, her voice cracked with the effort.

"All of my knowing... alone this cannot help him..."

Norbert raised his hands to heaven in supplication.

"So he will die... is that all you have to say?"

Athilde raised her eyes to Norbert and looked upon him.

"There is one who may bring life back to him... yet I do not know if he will come..."

Norbert almost shouted in his desperation.

"Who is this? How may he be summoned... how soon?"

"There is still danger abroad... I do not know if he has survived the attack upon the town... nor even if he would be willing to venture here..."

Norbert was pleading.

"But surely you may try... you must!"

"I will do all that I am able... to summon him."

Norbert waited but as Athilde did not seem inclined to move, he grew more impatient.

"Do you tarry?"

Athilde raised tired eyes to the knight.

"Leave me be, that I may summon him in my own way."

Norbert was suddenly fearful.

"Not by sorcery?"

Athilde was as patient as she could be. Her words came quietly and simply.

"I know not what you mean by that..."

Norbert suddenly grew suspicious, as he was wont to do.

"Is he a wizard then... this... healer?"

"He calls himself by no name... he is but a man..."

Norbert grew even more agitated.

"And what is he called?"

Athilde offered Norbert a face as bland as the Moon.

"Why do ye ask me that? Surely it is enough that one may come to your friend's aid... even if he may be *The Prince of All Devils himself...*"

The power in Athilde's words struck at Norbert, almost as a blow. He knew he had said too much, but so troubled was he in his heart he could not bring himself to ask her to forgive his own anger. He went to a corner of the room and remained there in silence. The ashen countenance of Gadroon upon his pillow was now strangely similar to the still features of Athilde, apparently in some kind of trance. Both seemed to be denizens of another world, one where death was no stranger.

Norbert realised he should not interfere in the ways of this world, one of which he knew nothing. He fell into an uneasy doze, one ended by a sudden knocking at the door. Afeared, he almost dared not move, but Athilde ran to answer the summons. There stood Edrith, in his familiar cloak and hat. Athilde almost wept with joy and relief.

"Thank Loenel and all her daughters that she has sent you, O blessed friend. Come! Come! I bid you the greatest welcome I am able!"

"I come in answer to your call, fair Athilde... moon maiden of the starry night."

The wizard stepped inside, whereupon his whole presence seemed to fill the cottage. Norbert rose, somewhat awkwardly, to greet him.

"Edrith..."

"Good Norbert... I greet thee once more."

"My Greetings to you... and I pray that..."

"Your companion? Without doubt... or delay... we must make him whole once more."

Norbert humbly spoke.

"Can you aid him?"

"That is my purpose and my desire, Master Norbert..."

Edrith beamed upon him encouragingly before turning to Athilde.

"Are there blackberries yet growing in the hedgerow?"

"Yes... I'm sure there are... I saw the first few yester'een... most are still green... not ripe..."

Edrith, now inspecting the places where Athilde stored her herbs was, as always, encouraging.

"They may be still efficacious... I pray thee fetch some... and dandelion heads also... all else I need is here methinks."

The obedient woman was almost out of the door.

"I go forthwith."

"My protection is with thee... and my will also goeth alongside to aid thee."

Norbert could only marvel at the turn events had taken. He thought it wise to retire to his corner and keep out of the way. The sound of Edrith grinding various herbs with the pestle reached his ears, but he preferred not to enquire as to the wizard's intentions. He could hear Gadroon's shallow breathing and wondered what passed through his friend's mind at this moment, if anything at all.

Norbert could not know through how many a dark mists had Gadroon wandered. He had known the wraiths of the ancestors, some acknowledging him, others turning away. He had fought yet again a thousand battles, standing with companions against his enemies, till he left the field weary of spirit. At other times always was he falling, through endless space, in limbo, until he came to a place where the darkness was most opaque. Dimly did a light shine in the distance, and he tried to force himself to go there.

Edrith, after administering to Gadroon the draught he had prepared, swallowed a goodly amount himself. His purpose was to enter into the same world the knight occupied. It did not take long before the magician saw before him the figure of death standing over Gadroon's form – and far too attentive for Edrith's liking. He hailed him, as any wizard would – boldly.

"Angaz! Exterminating angel! Mighty god of the great void of emptiness! What dost thou?"

The figure of Death never spoke to any mortal. When his icy breath crackled in the air, thoughts appeared in the mind of those who might address him. Edrith felt as if he was wearing an igloo on his head.

"You would dare to ask of my business? 'Tis no affair of thine, thou foolish and insignificant wizard!

Dost not know that the Lord of The Underworld conquereth all... and none may be spared?"

Edrith was looking pretty cool during all this, it must have been the spiritual snow goggles he had manifested for the arctic conditions.

"This I do know, O mighty Angaz. There be times when even Death does not win the game... the coin falls another way and all changeth."

"You dare to bandy words with me, sorcerer! Know ye that my power cannot be overthrown. If death is the lot of any man... then no mortal may save him.... this cannot be."

"Then *I* shall save him!" a voice said.

Edrith looked towards source of this new voice. Clear, like the peal of a mighty bell, rich, sonorous and promising always life and hope. The Moon, in all her glory, had risen in the East. Her arm was draped in sisterly fashion across the Sun. The Goddess had no fear of Angaz, as he knew only too well. Was she not also of heaven? Only mortals fear death, and among them are those who span the two worlds of here and there – the wizard and the High Priestess. Loenel knew not a day passed when Edrith would not offer devotion to The Goddess – as all true men and women of magic do. Without hesitation, she lent every speck of her power to him. Together, they would prevent the march of death upon the soul of Gadroon. Loenel addressed Angaz, and her words were now as the endless, rushing stream of light that flows eternally through all creation.

"I have decreed that this knight is forever under my protection! Those of a pure and honest heart always will be! Athilde has he saved... now the maiden of the town also... whence he sustained his wounds. Gadroon is of true courage and would give his life willingly to save any and all of my daughters from harm. He doth also love another of my handmaidens... with all his heart... and this doth please me greatly. All joy there is in the truest love among mortals!"

Angaz merely stared. Expressionless, unmoving, and nine below zero.

"These things mean nothing to the One at the End of Life!"

Loenel summoned all the powers she could command, every one.

"Cease your deadly mission, Lord of the Underworld! Let this mortal return to live once more..."

Angaz did not stir, merely gave his rejoinder to the words of Loenel.

"He is mortal and... as you say... must die. What matter if it be now or later?"

The eyes of the Goddess flashed, as does the heavenly light upon all oceans in day or night.

"Morgan le Fay hath cursed him, this I know..."

Angaz shrugged a gesture that was never encouraging in his case.

"The sorceress will prevail... none can prevent her. Deep is the desire in her heart for him also."

The light of Loenel was bright the more, so that even Edrith looked away.

"Aye! So that she might bind herself to him in the Underworld. A foul and wicked desire! This shall not be... I swear it!"

Angaz remained as heartless as the frozen wastes.

"Why care ye so much concerning this mortal, O Goddess?"

"Those who follow me I succour. This knight is blessed because he knoweth the ways of the Moon... this Athilde hath told me. The maid Willowpetal has shown him the ways of love and that wonder of heaven is mine also. He shall live so that the one who is in his heart will be reunited with him once more."

Quicker than quicksilver did Edrith then stand between Angaz and the figure of Gadroon lying motionless before them. The wizard then spoke his piece.

"The wizard cares naught whether 'tis dark or light... for he knoweth all that belong to all worlds. Sir Gadroon shall be in the light from this moment on!"

He raised his right arm, and with that a glimmer of light broke in the East. As the words of Edrith still echoed, Loenel gave to the wizard the gift of The Sun. Edrith took the golden disc that she had presented to him and held it. A Phoebus Frisbee! The wizard knew all the tricks of the art and threw it first then high and low. He caught it neatly over and over again, making it spin upon the palm of his hand. So intense was the light of the Sun that now even Angaz must shield his eyes from its divine illumination. Loenel looked upon this scene and smiled, and her voice now had even greater power as if she was herself now as all the heavens and all the gods and goddesses within it.

"Behold the Searcher upon the Quest! He who will find the spirit of The Goddess within The Holy Grail! He is now ordained by the Mistress of The Moon for this task! The wizard hath protected him... and his loyal companion Norbert also! Restore the chosen one to this life! So be it!"

At this, the glorious skies became so bright that Edrith could no longer see. In the cottage of Athilde gold and silver blazed in every corner. At that moment Norbert felt he was being lifted into the air upon beams of light and, when he looked at Gadroon, soft rainbows shimmered all about him. Athilde raised her arms in the air with such joy upon her features, and she danced slowly in the celestial light, turning round and round with the utmost grace, her beauty awesome to behold. Truly the light of the Sun and the moon were in that place. Together they had been commanded to bring healing to the body and soul of Gadroon.

Morgan le Fay, when she perceived all this in a vision, was wroth. Her anger was like the chill of Winter, her heart cold as stone. Once more her plans had been thwarted and she cursed them all – Loenel, the wizard Edrith, Athilde, and even Angaz the god of death.

*

Norbert rarely dreamed and when he did, it was usually of feasting. That night it was all very different. He saw flocks of birds rising high into the sky and with this vision came an uncanny sense of peace and contentment. When he woke it was to the sound of birdsong, and never had he heard that chorus so sweet and melodious. Somehow he knew that all was well once more, and when he saw his companion, knew indeed it was so.

Gadroon was sitting up on his couch, a flush upon his cheeks, and one that was not from fever. His brow was clear, his eyes bright and there was even the trace of a smile upon his face. He supped at a bowl of broth, the first sustenance he had taken for many days. Norbert was overjoyed, and looked upon his friend with the greatest affection, mixed with not a little wonder. Words formed upon the lips of Gadroon and he began to speak. Strange it was to hear his voice after so long.

"Hail, Norbert! I feel as if I have been far from you in some strange land... but now I have returned. I am much pleased to see you once more."

Norbert could not help but clasp his friend's hands, and stare at the features, every detail of which he now knew so well.

"And I am much pleased to see thou also. Our faithful friends have been tireless in their efforts to bring the return of thy health and strength once more. They have been as saints in their devotion to finding cures for your ills..."

"I live only because of them... that I know. And you, old fellow... how art thou?"

"I admit I did despair on occasion... but let us not speak of it... as thou once said. It is such a great joy to see you smile once more."

Gadroon, somewhat unwillingly, closed his eyes.

"I must rest the more before I can continue to take part in our Quest... but that day will come soon I know..."

"Truly. Even now you must embark upon that of which you speak..."

Gadroon smiled upon Norbert, and fell into sleep once more, a sublime peace upon his features. Norbert saw the sun upon the wall of the cottage and remembered the moment when all was filled with light, the sign that Gadroon had returned from the darkness. To those who had not seen these things it might have seemed as lunacy. But what is madness if it is not simply another view of the world?

*

The next day Athilde had risen at dawn to gather nuts and berries. Norbert was alone in the cottage when Edrith appeared, in that mysterious way he did – silently, invisibly and with absolutely no warning. Norbert lost no time in thanking him once more.

"I am in thy debt more than to any other man I have ever known. My great friend has been rescued from the jaws of death..."

Edrith would have preferred not to have been reminded of Angaz at that moment, even in passing, but he took it in his stride.

"Aye... 'tis true... he doth have fearsome jaws."

Norbert shuddered.

"I cannot believe a wound such as that could nearly cause Gadroon to die..."

Edrith looked fixedly at Norbert.

"Any warrior would expect to take a cut like that at some time. This was no ordinary blow..."

"How mean you?"

"The power of malice was in that blade... such as would cause any other man to die instantly. Sir Gadroon hath the good fortune to be protected by..."

"God?"

"*Goddess*, Sir Norbert! Loenel... The Goddess. It is she who saved Sir Gadroon... I may vouch for that. All I did was to use the power she bestowed upon me."

Norbert, in his way, was inclined to be theological, ontological even.

"But there can be no *Goddess*... that is impossible. It is *men* who have power upon this Earth that is plain to see... so there must be a *God* in heaven."

Only having only one deity in charge of the cosmos was not to Edrith's liking. It sounded too much like having some headmaster constantly ranting in the Prep Room.

"I have never journeyed in Heaven, Sir Norbert... so I cannot say. But here upon the Earth... where does the power that sustains life come from? Why... from the earth and sky and all that is around us... the domain of the Goddess... all creation. The Earth plays host to man... and much do men abuse her hospitality methinks."

Norbert took this as a condemnation.

"You dislike your fellow man?"

"I cannot hate that which for the most part I do not see..."

Norbert was perplexed, and not surprisingly.

"But you are in the world... part of it... I perceive you before me..."

Edrith said nothing, merely smiled, and Norbert at that moment experienced a strange feeling. Did his eyes deceive him? So much so that the wizard was not there before him? Before, he had might have feared some foul wickedness was afoot, but now he began to realise there was much about the ways of the universe he simply did not know. When Edrith spoke once more, his voice seemed full of great wisdom.

"I care but little for the ways of the world or man, Sir Knight... they are of little concern to me. I do not yearn for earthly riches... neither gold... silver or the favour of kings. All things must pass... as the great sage Gorgius Harriosus once said. I seek other riches... those invisible and on high... the Heaven you spoke of just now..."

"You have spurned the company of your fellow man then?"

Edrith shook his head.

"Nay... I would never turn my back upon any who seek out my help... as thou hast seen. But consider this...not all goodness is prompted by the highest ideals... but is it worth any less?"

Norbert was acutely aware that he and Gadroon had been saved twice over by the wizard.

"Then you are a good friend to all men..."

Edrith smiled at that.

"Nay, Sir Norbert... you bestow too much praise upon my humble self. Once I grew most impatient and vexed with the ways of men... anger I showed too often... a vexed wizard is not a pretty sight. But with time I learned those lessons I was in need of knowing."

"But seek you not common friendship ever?"

"The wizard is always alone and must be so. He has few friends amongst ordinary men because he knows there are none he may truly trust... even other wizards. He chooses his enemies well also... as all must... for they may be just as useful to him in his journey."

"How so?"

"They show a man where his weaknesses lie."

"Why should this be of benefit to him?"

"To test his courage and his faith... that is the way of the knight also is it not?"

"Aye... in that you are right. It seems that I was as strongly drawn to the world of chivalry as much as you to the world of wizardry."

Edrith smiled.

"We each have our destiny. Magic is a strange and secret calling. I stand at the centre of my own universe... as do you. I cannot ever be part of your world, Sir Norbert... yet you are part of mine if I wish it to be so. That is the difference between us. I have power over you... yet I choose not to use it."

Norbert was somewhat perturbed.

"That is not a pretty thought..."

"Nay... rather be thankful that you and I are of the same mind."

Norbert was then inclined to retreat behind the biblical barricades.

"But none may have power over Creation..."

"Indeed. The magician is as bound by the ways of the universe as any other mortal. He cannot suit himself always, and he is unable to determine the outcome of events. Yet the talent hath been bestowed upon him to increase the likelihood of a particular one... of many possibilities... coming to pass."

"But perchance... he may choose one that is evil."

"And who is to decide that? Every man has his shadow, Sir Knight... a part of every soul is not in the light – that must be so. We must acknowledge such in ourselves and also in others. If a man is all darkness then perhaps he should be pitied not condemned... denied the sun... the light of heaven that bringeth joy."

Norbert reflected upon this, as Edrith wished him to do. He recognised in Norbert a man who was intrinsically good, but one in constant terror of discovering any evil within himself. Norbert's next remark was absolutely Q.E.D.

"But I believe the god whom I praise rewards good and punishes evil."

"And it is for your god to do so if he wishes. But do not thyself be too hasty in appointing sin to others. It is never wise to judge... even if thou believest one serveth thy god in doing so... and thy praise to him be most fulsome."

Norbert got into shirty mode.

"Dost say my prayers are false?"

"Indeed not, Sir Norbert. Surely they are most sincere... but good fortune cometh from will and providence as well as prayer. If this was not so then priests would rule the world... which they most certainly do not... and methinks it is fortunate that is so."

"But is not the spiritual path the most blessed?"

"Every path leads eventually to the place that was intended for the traveller when he started upon his journey."

Norbert thought that was a bit too cute and said so.

"Thou spinnest words as doth Lapin..."

Edrith turned to leave.

"You will learn much upon The Quest, Sir Knight... more than it is possible for me to say. Many truths that are beyond words will you know... those perhaps even beyond understanding. I bid thee farewell... we shall meet again... for you will have need of my powers ere long... that I know also."

Norbert watched Edrith depart, a little sullenly. He dreaded any changes in his well-ordered life. When they inevitably came they gave him pain. There were certainly to be many unexpected changes upon The Quest! His deliberations were brought to an end when he saw that Gadroon was now awake. Norbert, like the good fellow he was, showed him all attention.

"How art thou?"

"So much stronger, old friend. So much so and the power to reason has returned to me at last. Well and truly have I known the Third Lesson. Quite simply... all is not as it seems. We must be careful not to believe we

160

know the truth when it is more likely we see only a part of what is there. Lady Melinda and Edrith have both shown you that good was there when you thought it not so. Is that not true?"

"Aye... maybe it is."

"I too have seen the world anew, old fellow. By being so close to death, I have known life..."

Gadroon said no more and, as he gained in strength, the more he found that his mind dwelt upon the fate of others dear to him. Willowpetal was foremost in his thoughts, but also Lapin and Hendrique. He consoled himself with the belief that Lapin had the luck of a fool, and Hendrique following in his wake would thus share his good fortune. Gadroon doubted the three had remained in Anghard. But whither had they gone, and wherever that might be, were they safe?

A time of waiting was at hand, one forced upon him. But all has purpose – even delays. The Grail would remain patiently for the moment that was assigned for the knights and the symbol of the Goddess to encounter one another. Gadroon continued to reflect on all, while Norbert spent his time becoming great friends with Athilde's cat, Cadolew. Now that Gadroon was out of danger, a certain domesticity reigned in Athilde's cottage.

XIV

***But the lord dressed
Early, he had tricks to try.***

The time of harvest was nearly over. Tranquil days,
those that came before Autumn approached, were upon
them. Gadroon had recovered enough to ride his
mount and the knights were now making ready to
resume their journey. The day before their leaving
there came a knocking at the cottage door which
caused both knights some alarm. Gadroon was about
to reach for his sword when without, a familiar voice
was heard.

"It is Nouvin, good sirs. I am far abroad from
Charbon and bring news of happenings in all the world
..."

There stood the page – cheery of countenance – as
they remembered him. His mud stained garments told
of much travelling, and over many miles. Athilde
smiled in welcome at their visitor.

"Welcome, ye who from afar. Come hither and take
refreshment... it seems you have much to tell..."

Nouvin bowed low as he entered.

"I have that, fair mistress... and not a little. But
indeed I will take some little sustenance before I begin
my tale... as thou art so kind to offer it."

Like the tireless host she was, Athilde set out some
simple fayre, as much as she could furnish at such
short notice. What was provided pleased Nouvin so
much he was not willing to speak until he had
consumed the best part of a quartern loaf and many
pats of butter. All this time Gadroon was looking him
over with great interest.

"I swear thou art inches taller... and broader also...
since I last set eyes upon thee, Nouvin. Then... thou
wert a youth... one who has now become a man."

He who was addressed smiled, knowingly.

"Ah, good Sir Gadroon... I have seen many things that would account for my sudden gaining of years..."

"Tell all, Nouvin! It will be as well... for we are about to travel into the world once more and would prefer to know how its countenance has changed since we last set eyes upon it."

The page bit heartily into an apple and surveyed the company. His eye fell upon Athilde. She smiled upon him, with more than a little tenderness so that Nouvin, despite his newly found maturity, involuntarily blushed. His account of all that had transpired within The Kingdoms of The West began with telling of being woken one morning to see King Arthur and a great army approaching Chateau Charbon. Nouvin had decided destiny was calling him and that most insistently. He hurriedly gathered together those things he considered were necessary and joined their ranks. As they marched westward he soon discovered their purpose.

"King Tirhadeth's castle at Diohan lies to the south of Meutreville. When he heard that this villain Brime had sacked the town and slaughtered many therein... the king sent messengers to Camelot. Arthur did not hesitate... he summoned all his knights and those who were willing to accompany him as foot-soldiers... and rode out the next morn to aid the aid of Tomberg."

From the moment Nouvin had begun his tale, Norbert and Gadroon were stunned and silent. They knew not to make comment, and spoil the flow of the telling.

"We crossed the River Ilyondel then left the way to march across country... thus we would not be in sight of the town of Malfaise. Two days had passed since we crossed the border into Anghard. Now we set up camp upon The Plain of Wythlon. The next day King Tirhadeth joined us with his knights and as many men as he could muster. We were right glad to see him and his army for we could not know what number of the enemy there would be."

Gadroon could not hold himself back.

"And the battle was fought there upon The Plain?"

"Aye it was. I had no soldiering in me so I served as a herald... but I saw much of the fighting. 'Tis true we *were* outnumbered... but the enemy were a rabble... *and* we had right upon our side. Our cavalry went forward and the rest arranged themselves in ranks. We gathered at the top of a slope and they arrived below us... a sorry sight I must say. Arthur lost no time in giving his orders... the day could only end one way... defeat for our enemies..."

Brime, being told of Arthur marching into Anghard, had no choice but to engage his own troops with Arthur's forces. A weary and spiritless company it was that engaged with Arthur, also one lacking in any discipline or leadership. It is one thing for armed men to terrorize civilians, another to face crack troops.

"Arthur led the first charge... his knights with him. Never have I seen such a glorious sight! No army could ever hope to stand against them! They would have followed Arthur into hell and back such was their courage and loyalty to their king and. I swear the lion upon Arthur's shield came alive and roared... such was his might!"

Norbert and Gadroon had fallen silent. They could see the scene vividly and part of them wondered why fate had robbed them of the chance to ride into battle with their monarch. Gadroon felt this acutely, as if he had somehow betrayed the Company.

"Brime and his men were no match for the heroes of Camelot. Like wheat falling to the reaper were they. Then Arthur went at them again, and our knights had destroyed all of Brime's cavalry within the hour... as well as hacking down all but a few of his foot soldiers. Only one or two of our cavalry fell."

Any clash of arms had been the same for centuries. Cavalry ruled the field, for the mounted knight was the scourge of the foot soldier. A few score of horsemen could cut down any opposition on the ground in a very short time. Occasionally a knight would be unhorsed, his armour then sending him to his doom. His hauberk – a knee-length coat of mail – would weigh him down, and the helm and visor made him almost blind.

It seemed that Arthur, in one blow, had avenged the people of Tomberg and wreaked a terrible justice upon Anghard. Many of Brime's men had turned tail and fled and Arthur let them go, but he showed no mercy upon those who remained. Such was his anger and loathing for King Brime he was determined to rid the world of a tyrant, one he had always considered a dangerous neighbour also. Neither after his corpse had been found after the battle, hacked unmercifully by Arthur's knights, was his memory ever honoured. Faggots were gathered and his body burned where it lay, along with those of his court who had perished with him. Croop somehow escaped from the field, slipping away into the forest, never to be seen again.

Arthur mourned the death of his nephew Wayne, even though his treachery was known by all at Camelot. He had stood with Brime and his men, and many a knight wished to close with him. But it was for Lancelot to dispatch him, and that with a single blow. Arthur ordered Wayne's body be taken back to Camelot and buried there, for he insisted Sir Wayne had once been a noble knight. Neither Gadroon nor Norbert shed any tears over the end of Wayne, but one part of the tale mystified Gadroon still.

"We are sure Wayne told Brime of the curse The Purple Haze had put upon Camelot... but how did Arthur know that Wayne had done this? "

Nouvin shrugged.

"I confess I do not know... though when it was seen Sir Wayne was not riding with them... and then all saw him among the enemy... the Company knew he must be a traitor."

Gadroon pressed home his point – Perry Mason style.

"Yet... they were before unaware of his crime. And why did Wayne ride into battle alongside King Brime... knowing it would mean his certain death?"

"Once more, Sir Knight... I confess I do not know. A further puzzle there is also... another rode with me when I left Charbon to join Arthur..."

"And know ye who that might be?"

"Well-hooded were they and I did not find out until we crossed the border into Anghard... then I looked upon... *Lady Malinda... in disguise... as a man.*"

Norbert was inclined to scoff.

"You jest, Master Page..."

Gadroon was not of the same mind.

"I do not believe Nouvin was mistaken. 'Twould explain why Lady Malinda was but a few leagues from Meutreville when we came upon her... would it not?"

Norbert agreed absently.

"That may be so."

"I do not doubt we shall meet Lady Malinda once more before our Quest is over, Norbert. I sense she still holds the keys to this mystery."

Nouvin, who had taken to glancing in Athilde's direction more than once, could not help but remark upon her melancholy.

"What ails thee, mistress?"

"You will forgive me, Nouvin. I am a woman and I cannot rejoice in tales of war... and the suffering that always comes with that accursed happening. A cause may be just and right may even prevail... but I cannot forget the widows and mothers whose menfolk have perished in battle. I believe there is only one victor in war and that is Angaz himself."

*

The knights were making ready to leave. The rich gold and brown of all about, more than hinted at Autumn's coming. Nouvin was standing at the cottage door with Athilde and felt explanations were necessary.

"It is my duty to remain here for some little time and protect Mistress Athilde...."

Gadroon nodded, almost vehemently.

"A wise decision. There may be..."

"...some wanderings in the night."

Nouvin blushed when he said this and Athilde tried her best not to giggle. Norbert and Gadroon thanked their host most profusely and many assurances were made of returning. Nouvin helped them load the horses with the provisions that Athilde had provided. Gadroon bestowed a little advice upon the page, *sotto voce.*

"Now as thou art approaching manhood, Nouvin... 'tis a perfect time for thee to learn something of woman..."

"My intentions are honourable..."

Gadroon hastened to reassure the page.

"I doubt it not... and Athilde will welcome your *attentions* as well. Go to it, lad... she is still comely... and if thou hast aspirations to *ride as well as a knight* she will teach thee much concerning the proper handling of a lance..."

To calm his further blushes, Nouvin gave all attention to directing the knights upon the way they must follow.

"The road to Dolfay lies over yonder... go ye not near the town of Windleroot... 'tis but a broken-down place. Once the jewel of the sacred Isle of Teflon... now naught remains of it but a wasteland. Even the Minstrels Fayre at Tableton is no more."

By the time the knights left Valentin the sky had turned a charcoal grey. Miniature diamonds of dew hung from the branches of the trees. A few leagues further upon the way they met those who had fled from Meutreville when the town had been sacked. From the country round about where they had been hiding, they now slowly returned to their homes. What awaited them there? Even those who were fortunate enough to have their dwelling not left a smoking ruin still faced the prospect of all within being desecrated.

By noon Norbert and Gadroon had reached the ford over the river Perogel – the name meant 'Dream of Water' in the old tongue. From there they rode north to the River Amuthdel, the westerly arm of the Dwylon, its course widening on the way to the sea. They were to cross the great bridge into the kingdom of Dolfay and, an hour before sunset; Norbert and Gadroon were looking upon this great oak structure. To the common folk it was known as Iswell's Bridge – legends insisting it had been built by Iswell the Giant, aided by the Devil. It was said Iswell laboured for thirty years while the bridge was completed and on that day, he died. His lifeless body fell into the torrent below and was washed out to sea, to be consumed by the fishes.

They tethered the horses and made their way down a steep path that led to the beach that ran below the bridge. Gadroon had been told of a friendly community who lived in huts upon the shore, and he was of a mind to seek them out. A night in the open was not a welcome prospect in the chill month of Gwalwyn, now fast approaching.

Rocks and pebbles made up much of the shore. Gadroon had expected to find fishermen trudging up and down in the shallows scooping flatfish into their nets. On the isolated patches of flat sand – the colour of overripe barley – they found no one. After walking some way among the endless heaps of sea wrack, the two knights rested on an ivory-coloured log, one stripped of its bark. The rocks were now in deep shadow and crows hopped from one to the other, their blackness contrasting with the milky wings of the gulls swooping and twisting in the air above them.

All around were warped shapes of wood thrown onto the shore by Winter storms, some resembling creatures from the darkling deeps. The surface of the river glistened with a silver haze, and the creeks that wandered across the mud flats seemed to have been traced there by an invisible finger. Norbert stared long at the horizon, believing he saw a wooden ship with furled sails. Was she drifting with the current hoping eventually to find some safe haven? Norbert continued to gaze into the distance, wondering if his own soul was held in this mysterious vessel endlessly adrift in that mighty swell.

Forbidding clouds began to gather and, as fickle as a country wench, the mood of the river changed. The wind chivvied the water until fractious wavelets ran to the shore, tumbling over and over in disarray. The call of a curlew sounded a melancholy warning as the sun finally fell behind the hills and the air grew chill. The companions set off to walk further into this unknown world until Gadroon halted, the wind blowing strands of hair across his face.

"It is no use! I believed we would find the dwellings with ease... we cannot remain here... to the Bridge of Amuthdel we must return."

The night posed questions the daylight could never answer and, at Gadroon's words, Norbert felt his heart fill with dread. Why he knew not, but fear gripped the inside of him, tighter and tighter. But he knew they dare not linger, and he followed Gadroon, crawling over the rocks in the half-dark. As they ascended the path, a lone crow cackled somewhere nearby. When the great bridge loomed out of the darkness all Norbert's worst terrors came rushing to meet him. He stared into the very centre of the walkway where sinister shapes seemed to play in the shadows.

"For certain this is a foul and evil place, Gadroon. I feel as if I may meet The Devil himself at any moment."

Gadroon put his finger to his lips in some alarm.

"Take care, Norbert... or that extraordinary nobleman may appear to you sooner than you might wish..."

On cue Norbert screamed as if he had been seized by the jaws of Hell. What he saw, advancing slowly but purposefully over the bridge towards him was a monstrous creature. Norbert was frozen with horror and as this thing drew near, the whole of its dread appearance became only too clear. Its eyes, as if from the depths from the Pit, glared at him and the fiend – with tongues of fire and teeth of iron – was swathed in black, darker than black could ever possibly be.

"By all angels above! It is Satan himself! May every saint in Heaven protect me!"

In his panic Norbert had lost even the will to flee. He looked about for Gadroon and found he was nowhere to be seen. His companion had deserted him! He was alone to face... The Destroyer! The Greatest Enemy man could ever know! Norbert could feel his whole being, within and without begin to tremble, in the utmost dread. Pleas for deliverance were torn from him, as if his heart were being wrung by the merciless claws of the creature he saw so vividly before him.

"Have mercy! I cannot die! Do not take my life from me!"

Norbert felt his knees quiver as the awesome figure continued its slow tramp towards him. A hellish glee played about its features, as if the seemingly inevitable end of Norbert was some infernal jest. As he was about to surrender all hope, a voice came from somewhere near, so commanding that it was within him.

"Stand, Norbert! Do not falter! Behold The Watcher at The Gate is before you! He is sworn to try all upon The Quest! To prevent you from fulfilling your task he will if you allow him! Then... never will you enter the Sacred Kingdom. Are you worthy to set foot within that holy place, Sir Norbert? Where is your courage? Where doth it lie deep in your heart? Speak! Now!"

Norbert suddenly found his voice, though it was no more than a frightened squeak.

"But I see The Devil before me..."

The sweat poured into Norbert's eyes, blinding him. The voice within his breast resumed, louder and suddenly familiar.

"Better the Devil you know, Norbert... rather than the many thousand you do not!"

Edrith! Norbert looked about him. Where was the wizard? His voice had truly been inside Norbert's head. As soon as this thought came to Norbert, a vibrancy entered his body. He could be mighty also! And he was so! Now gradually the knight could feel the presence of magic about him, though he would not have said as such. A reassuring, powerful force it was, one that for the first time in his life, he would willingly embrace. The thing of terror, which was now but a few paces away, had halted in its stride. All of a sudden it seemed to doubt its own being – its very existence. Norbert drew his sword and raised it high, his voice no longer feeble and weak, but one that must be obeyed!

"Begone! Thou wraith of nothing... empty thou art... and of no substance! Vanish into the void! Return to the land of nightmare from where thou comest!"

The creature seemed to stare unseeing at Norbert. Before, when its eyes glistened with that infernal light, it had seemed ready to crush all that stood in its way. Now it was no more than a lifeless shadow, one that soon faded into the darkness around it. In a few moments all trace of the creature was gone. The knight stood and stared, anxious the nightmare would not return. Then he realised the presence of two he knew about him – Gadroon on one side, Edrith the other. They smiled upon Norbert in a way that made his heart swell with pride, and the love that he felt for them knew no bounds. Gadroon put his arm about his companion's shoulder.

171

"Thou hast banished thy demons, Norbert! Only a true warrior hath the power to bring about such a thing."

"Nay... Nay... 'twas Edrith..."

Edrith spoke quietly.

"The wizard takes his own magical world with him all the time... wherever he may be. He journeys far... and often bestows his power upon others. You found your own inner strength, Sir Knight... by owning that power... for even a moment... you perceived demons as they really are... mere phantoms."

Norbert shook involuntarily.

"I cannot believe *how real* that fiend appeared to be."

"The Devil is merely one of the many faces of your God, my old Norbert. How you saw the Prince of Demons was in the fashion of your own creation... how you believed him to be."

"Yes... that was so... he appeared to me at the same moment I was aware of his terrible countenance. You are right... it was I who manifested this thing. So it seems The Devil is just another part of Creation..."

"Part of *you*, Norbert."

"Indeed. That I now realise... my task was to stand and regard myself... with all honesty... and without fear."

Gadroon beamed upon him.

"And most well you did that... like a true knight..."

Norbert was still pondering.

"How didst thou know The Devil would appear before me at that moment, Edrith? And also that I might need thy aid to overcome him?"

Edrith smiled in his wizardly way.

"Merlin schooled me well in the art of entering the soul of another... namely thine. As to demons... I have also some wit of their ways. I have oft ventured forth into those domains where no light enters.... that world you have known yourself, but a few moments ago."

Norbert paled once more.

172

"And thou hast been there *willingly*, Edrith... into this place?"

"That is so. Lately, my mission was to learn what secrets lay in the soul of Morgan le Fay. Deep I journeyed into caverns below and beyond the deepest places anyone could imagine... far beyond where even the soul of the universe resides. A world Morgan owns... known to none save herself..."

Edrith smiled once more.

"...but now known to me."

Despite his lingering fears, Norbert's curiosity got the better of him.

"And pray tell us what did you find there?"

"I learned much Master Knight of the past and the future... how 'twas Morgan herself who manifested The Purple Haze."

Norbert was aghast.

"I cannot believe it! Then in some uncanny way it is her doing that Gadroon and myself have embarked upon The Quest?"

"Indeed so... even though she then strove to bring death to Gadroon... so that the Quest would be abandoned."

Norbert put two and two together, and got his sums right.

"Then The Purple Haze could claim its prize, as The Grail would not be brought back to Camelot..."

"Aye... 'tis true. Morgan hateth Arthur and the Company enough to want this to come to pass... and she was willing to weave any spell she might to bring that about. It also seems that she had enchanted Sir Wayne also..."

Gadroon stared a little at that.

"Sir Wayne's treachery was not of his own doing?"

"Morgan chose her victim well when she ensnared him. He was weak enough to fall under her spell and it was he who summoned The Purple Haze to enter the

Great Hall... with many an incantation she had schooled him to recite."

Gadroon almost whistled down the wind.

"You spoke of the future, Edrith. Canst thou tell what the sorceress intends shall come to pass next?"

"Morgan believeth the Round Table will soon be no more and the Company dispersed..."

Norbert was inclined to protest.

"That cannot be..."

Edrith remained as cool as The Fonz.

"'Tis not as unlikely as all that. Merlin knew this was to be so also. Thus it was that he left Camelot..."

Norbert got his synapses up and sparking.

"But if Morgan's desire was to destroy Camelot... why did she not strike down both Gadroon and myself from the beginning?"

Edrith frowned.

"That is one riddle to which I have no answer. Morgan is the reflection of Winter and Death... and she knows that with the finding of The Grail new life will come to the world. That will mark the coming of an Eternal Spring. This she cannot prevent... but even so she has sworn to see Longres destroyed and Arthur with it."

Norbert thought for a moment and then came up with something that could have won him a pub-quiz all on his own.

"So Morgan le Fay still desires to thwart us even though she knows she cannot succeed?"

Edrith nodded.

"Aye."

"And it all matters but little in any account... if Camelot is to perish as thou and Merlin do believe. This is all the greatest of madnesses."

Edrith was cool once more, as the cucumber.

"I can only tell thee what I know, Sir Norbert... and the wisdom of Morgan may be greater than mine. She may see what I cannot. I am a mere man... it is The

Goddess who holds all things in her palm. She may do with creation as she wisheth."

Norbert shook his head in disbelief.

"How can it be this Morgan is part of your Goddess? She is both evil and stricken with unreason..."

Edrith was straight down the line.

"She is The Dark Goddess, Norbert. All things have light and dark within them... as I have told thee. This must be so or naught would change... as night becometh day... then to return to night once more."

Norbert gave up.

"I confess I can see neither see sense nor nonsense in this tale..."

"Well, Norbert... you will soon have the chance to talk of these things with the lady of whom thou speaketh."

"What mean you?"

"You will soon meet Morgan herself upon the way... that I know... and you will need all your wits about you in that hour."

Gadroon had kept his own counsel while all this was said. Now he desired to hear of other matters.

"We will see what that meeting brings when it come to pass. But what news dost thou bring of the jester Lapin... the minstrel Hendrique... and... Willowpetal?"

"All are safe..."

Gadroon sighed with great relief.

"And when shall I be reunited with..."

"The maid? Soon... and most assuredly... but..."

"But?"

"Many a twist and turn there will be in the plot before you two are reunited, Sir Knight..."

Gadroon silently cursed all authors.

"Forsooth! I doubt it not."

Edrith clapped his hands together.

"Come... now is the time for celebration! I have made plans for you to meet one whose ancestor was none other than The Giant Iswell himself!"

They dutifully followed the wizard, once more taking the path that led to the beach. Though the night was now pitch black, Edrith did not once make a false step. They followed the line of the shore once again and suddenly a sizeable dwelling appeared in front of them. The door of the hut flew open to reveal a huge man clad in what looked like the skins of various animals, a cloak flowing behind him. On his head was what looked like a purple turban, and in his fist he gripped a thick staff.

"Ho! Ho! Ah! Ha! Be these thy friends... and also now my honoured guests, O wondrous wizard? I bid thee welcome noble knights! I am Pengrym... he who liveth here upon the wild shore... and also knoweth the name of every creature of the air and of the land also. Any that hath life and moveth I do embrace. Pray gather about the fire! I and my trusty companions did fetch faggots and tinder while 'twas still light. Refreshment too you will soon have... and we shall have great celebration. Is that not to be so, Edrith?"

The wizard smiled, almost capering about among the rocks in his joy.

"Indeed we shall... and all may be amazed later also... after the feasting..."

Pengrym laughed – a sound like rolling thunder.

"Ho! Thy tricks are always worth waiting for, O man of magic! Now... we need helpers here... *Yarooiiioh!*"

Pengrym had cupped his hands about his lips and made a deafening cry which brought several figures – some dressed as exotically as Pengrym himself – from out of the night.

"Ha! There thou be, my stout fellows! Gather ye more faggots... so we shall have a truly fine blaze! Know ye not we have exalted company? Two knights who have seen the Devil himself I vow."

Norbert was incredulous.

"How didst thou know that?"

Pengrym laughed once more, and slapped his thighs in merriment.

"Know ye... I have looked into the eyes of many who have met that same fellow upon the Bridge at Amuthdel. They do always tell the same tale..."

A rude table was soon set upon its legs, and a great cheese, quartern loaves, raw onions and pickled cucumber were set out upon it. Soused gurnets and herring were also there to tempt any of the revelers and, as if this was not enough, Pengrym set two of his helpers to roasting a fat rabbit over the fire. A barrel containing the oldest ale was set upon a rock, tapped and many a stoup sampled. Thick, rich and sweet, it was mellow to the tongue and, before long, warmed every heart. Pengrym, discovering a fresh audience in Norbert and Gadroon, regaled the pair with memories of his childhood days. Long gone, but every recollection as clear as if it was yesterday.

"I would lie awake and listen to the waves coming closer and closer to the shore... sometimes I wondered if those wild waters would not carry me away forever. The slap and slough of the tide was not the only wonder to me. There were many leagues of sand dunes here at one time and every day they changed shape. The wind cut and carved them, then the waves smoothed and sculpted them also until both had made for me mountains and valleys... caves and pinnacles... and every spiral of wonder."

As if complementing these tales of enchantment, the night sky was of a sudden filled with coloured lights of every hue. The brightest vermillion, the most transparent blue, blankets of emerald and gold – all crackled above the party below. Edrith had indeed provided the magnificent display of fireworks he had promised, one worthy of his calling. After the final thunderclap, Norbert was moved to congratulate the magician but it was not to be. Edrith's finale had featured his own disappearance, fittingly in a puff of smoke.

Mellow with old ale Norbert sought out Gadroon, who was occupying a moderately comfortable log, and perched down beside him. Both were inclined to indulge in a knightly chat. Norbert kicked off proceedings with a medium-sized confession.

"There were moments when... as I saw The Devil... all my courage seemed gone... I wondered if I was truly worthy to be a knight at all."

Gadroon was comforting, as always.

"Nay... doubt thyself not, Norbert. The rank of knight is bestowed upon a man long before he is given the accolade. His noble deeds may have been done perhaps hundreds of years before... or they may even be known to the world at some time in the future. Knighthood is eternal... and know ye that those who protect the defenceless and right all injustice may not always be known by the name of knights. The spirit of righteousness and good is bestowed upon the humblest, and sometime in secret. That I know to be certain."

Though slightly foggy with ale, Norbert was still capable of setting a course from one thought to another.

"And we have learned the Fourth Lesson, I believe..."

"How that is so, Norbert... and much more! Surely it is that what one sees in the world is truly what is inside one's own self. Would you not agree?"

Norbert did not immediately reply, content as he was at that moment to stare at the sky overhead. Darkness – the absence of light – he now knew was always present to some degree in the heart of man. If that was the way it was, he considered himself fortunate. He had survived more than a glimpse of the Pit.

XV

Morgana the goddess she's called,
And no one in all
The world could resist her call
If she bade him come –

With the following dawn, the companions bade a fond farewell to Pengrym and his companions. Weighed down with gifts of loaves and fishes, they set out once more. Norbert was feeling a little fuzzy from quaffing strong ale, but after a league or two of riding in the fresh air his brain began to clear.

Anghard and Tomberg left far behind, the knights quickly realised that Dolfay was a very different land. If they had expected the kingdom that hosted The Grail to flow with milk and honey, this was most definitely not so. A bleak, inhospitable landscape greeted them after they had crossed the Amuthdel Bridge, offering no apology for being the whitened bones of a long forgotten world. More ancient than Longres, the land spoke of the presence of gods. The towering mountains had once echoed to the footfall of heroes and in the mist-filled the valleys, the spirits of mighty warriors could be felt, even if they were not to be seen. Soon the knights found themselves in the very midst of this singular land.

Dolfay was also a place of forest and moors, containing the great sweep of trees and coarse grass that eventually became The Great Marshes bordering The Southern Seas. There, everywhere was naught but a maze of exhausted creeks and barrenness. The roads in this kingdom were few, and finding any who travelled upon them even more rare. Wild boar and cattle abounded, and occasionally bears were to be seen. The ruins of buildings all to show a people once lived here, in the peaks above, a castle stood like a lonely sentinel – it too abandoned.

The knights spent a night beneath the shelter of a great rock, one that made an awning over them. In the dawn they were obliged to shake themselves in order to bring some warmth to their frozen limbs. The dawn light had streaked the turquoise sky above the peaks, but by noon the sky was grey once more. Winter, and thus Yule, was fast approaching. The knights were all too aware that only a few days were left for them to fulfill their Quest.

While following a narrow path into a valley, they could see at its end a coming storm, one that was soon to be upon them. When this came, the fur caps they had taken from their packs quickly became sodden and heavy. Gadroon's hair was matted into a single flap across his brow. Eventually they sought shelter in a dell, much filled with water, but they now had little choice. The rain hurtled out of the sky – seeming to have no end. The hills around were covered in mist and the trees sombre, as if in mourning. They waited in some discomfort until the rain began to leave off and they could move on. The moor was so sodden the horses' hooves sank deep into the earth. Fording a stream, the water plashed about them, rising high in the air. The way, now lined with tall ash and thorn, led to higher ground. As the rain had finally decided to cease, the companions halted, tethering the horses to an overhanging branch.

The air had become cold and stung their eyes, and the light had an unreal luminosity. A profound stillness heralded the sky once more turning a darkening grey, then rapidly to black. This was no earthly weather! Lightning crackled in the air and a whiff of something charred came to Gadroon's nostrils. Most acute was a sense of approaching danger – then *she* appeared.

Only partly visible in the fevered flashes of the lightning, tall and moving with great purpose, this female figure approached. Gadroon could not turn away; the eyes alone would have cowed a multitude. As he regarded that face, with a beauty beyond doubt magnificent, there lurked within it an air of menace. Gadroon attempted to reconcile what he was seeing with the vision that enveloped him. Reason ceased to serve him, his whole being obstinately insisted that before him was none other than Morgan le Fay.

*

Who is given to speak when in the presence of the Dark Goddess? Does the mere mortal, overwhelmed by her presence straightway proffer obeisance? Or does he wait, silent and trembling, for the deity to deign to make an utterance? Gadroon bowed to none on Earth save his king, who he believed to be ordained by Heaven. Thus when he stood before Morgan le Fay his features were set, as stern and unmoving as the rocks about him. She stood but a few paces from him – her eyes caves of crystal. Her gaze was fixed upon Gadroon, and she smiled. In that smile was all that ever is and all that ever will be. The knight was in the presence of the void of infinity.

"O noble and wondrous, Gadroon! How long have I waited for this moment..."

Gadroon's features stayed unaltered.

"You seek me out here? In a land where none rule? A place where there is no king... no lord? There is no law here save that of the sword, Morgan le Fay. Any may court danger who approacheth another in such a land. State your business... and that most speedily. I know not whether thou mean to do me ill... thou hast once already..."

She held up a delicate hand.

"Peace, brave warrior! I do not come with hatred in my heart. Nay, that is not so. It is *love* only that I bring thee... pure love... sweet... devotion..."

Gadroon turned away, desperate not to stare into the glinting jewels of her eyes. If for one moment he succumbed to the fascination of Morgan he would be lost forever. This he knew. An enchantress is always most proficient at her task.

"Why speak you of love to me, Morgan? It is not for my ears to hear these things. Take your blandishments elsewhere... I beg of you..."

Morgan laughed at that, and it was the sound of the glistening torrent upon frozen rock, that most haunting of music – sadness mixed with yearning. Gadroon put his hands over his ears so as not to hear those enticing tones, once heard they would remain with him forever.

"But am I not the one you love?"

Morgan took a pace forward, and when Gadroon looked again, before him was now Willowpetal. For an instant he was deceived and went to take her in his arms but the next moment, the realisation came.

"Ah! Your cursed spells! 'Tis nothing but a wraith before me!"

Morgan's voice was hard.

"Maybe she *is* at this moment, Gadroon! Your little maid may no longer be of this world! Think on that!"

Gadroon's features could not help but betray his pain.

"No! No! This cannot be! My heart is full of the dream that Willowpetal and I will be joined once more! Nothing... no one may take that vision of hope from me... not even thee."

The look of Morgan was as fire and ice.

"And if this is not so... what opportunity will you have lost, Gadroon? Your maiden cannot possess anything of my beauty... that is impossible. My perfect brilliance which sets precious stones to shame... is this not so? Look upon me, Gadroon! What do you see?"

"No... I must not..."

But it was useless to resist. Gadroon felt his gaze being drawn to Morgan. The lustre of her hair, the lips

– vermillion against her pale skin – all were gorgeous and sublime. The slightest movement of her body made the air about her tremble.

"Think of the pleasure that awaits you at my touch, Gadroon... nothing of me will I deny to you. I will arouse you to such passion... one so intense... so much greater than you have ever dreamed. Do you not wish to be loved by the Dark Goddess? To know you have the most intense love any mortal can ever possess... is that not so fine? I have all the endless joys of the night within me! And you, sweet Gadroon... may join with me in that eternal delight... with ways of love unknown to any man. But they will be yours only... yours only... of that you have my promise. Will you not kiss my honeyed lips? Will you not be mine... that we may be always together in eternity?"

Gadroon was in torment, his heart racked and twisted by these words. He cried out in his anguish.

"Because I am in thrall of The Goddess... I love all women... I nurture and protect them... that is all I can vow."

Morgan in that instant became even more overwhelming, as one who could so easily be worshipped. She began to purr.

"I know this, O fabulous man. And I am yours... the most beautiful creature... the most desirable woman in all eternity... I am yours..."

Gadroon felt his words wrung from him.

"Cease! My heart is promised to another! Why do you pain me so?"

Morgan drew even nearer so that she was almost touching him. Gadroon felt powerless to retreat.

"Because I *want you*, Gadroon! Nothing may prevent the Dark Goddess from taking that which she desires. Do you not know how great is my power? I am the mighty seas... the darkest night... the deepest cavern... the brightest star in the heavens. All that has meaning... all that is secret is known to me... I am the very soul of Creation... all is in my thrall and bows to me. I think you will do so also..."

Unsought, a vision of Willowpetal came to Gadroon. The face of the little maid was troubled, a doubting look about her. She was lost and he must search for her! In the instant Morgan reached out to touch him, to draw him to her, Gadroon suddenly fell back. For an instant Morgan was dismayed. The words the knight then spoke startled her the more.

"What of Sir Wayne? Did you not bind him to you also?"

The eyes instantly lost their brightness, Morgan sneered in contempt.

"That weak fool! I had only to look upon him for the merest moment and he swore to do my bidding. Everything I asked him to undertake he was only too grateful to do. He even swore that he would bring The Holy Grail to me...."

Gadroon's eyes lit with anger.

"But wait... I have told too much..."

Gadroon had regained his quietude and now regarded Morgan with nothing of the awe he had previously felt.

"You have revealed enough for me..."

"That I have..."

Gadroon was as steel.

"I would ask that you consider one more matter."

"And pray what be that, Sir Knight?"

Gadroon gathered all his inner strength to say the words he knew he must.

"If we succeed in Our Quest..."

"Yes..."

"Then I wish you to swear to me The Purple Haze will be no more and thus can never harm Camelot now or ever again."

Morgan le Fay was silent for a long moment. When she spoke it was the sound made by the serpent as it lies in wait.

"Rarely do any make demands of me, Sir Gadroon... and live."

Gadroon was motionless.

"I dare to do so... because I know full well what fate will eventually befall Longres... and I wish that no other evil... of thy making... come upon Camelot before that time."

Gadroon waited. After a little while Morgan le Fay smiled.

"No mortal man has ever made me give my oath before, Sir Gadroon. Truly thou art as one above all."

"Wilt thou do this?"

"I do grant thy wish."

"Then I have served the world as best I may in fulfilling this."

Morgan smiled once more.

"Indeed and the world should be grateful to thee..."

The knight lost none of his composure.

"And now... begone! For now you must know you have not triumphed over me."

Morgan lowered her eyes for an instant. Was there now not a hint of sadness in her voice?

"You are right. I cannot own you... another does. Perhaps I will dream of what might have been... but dreams are not so satisfying as..."

"Say no more!"

Morgan stepped back and looked upon Gadroon once more. Unmistakably, she had regained her pride.

"All men are feeble... pathetic creatures. Most are like Wayne... who now is forever condemned to wander the void... a just reward for his cowardly ways. Do you not agree?"

"I speak my own counsel, Morgan... but it is not my way to judge."

Morgan began to walk away, then turned for an instant.

"It is impossible for me to find a man who I desire. Yet... you I did want, Gadroon. Fate has decreed that we shall not be united it seems..."

Gadroon was terse.

"Aye. That is the way it seems."

"Then... farewell, O brave knight. May your maid only realise with every moment of the time she is in your company that she is so very fortunate to have come upon you."

"And I am fortunate to have found her."

"Indeed."

Gadroon watched in silence as the figure of Morgan le Fay faded into the blackness around her. He closed his eyes then opened them again warily. To his relief, the enchantress was nowhere to be seen. Truly she had departed, no one could possibly have known where. For some little time Gadroon could not bring himself to move but a pace, and remained staring at the place where Morgan had been. He drew out of his trance when he suddenly recalled Norbert, and began to look around for him, but he was nowhere to be seen. After some searching he was discovered curled up inside a hollow tree, asleep and apparently oblivious to thunder, lightning and the incantations of any sorceress. Gadroon felt light of heart at the thought and laughed to himself. He left Norbert to his snoring.

XVI

And their talk was of joyful things, they spoke only
Of bliss.
Words came flowing free,
Each was pleased
With the other...

The knights journeyed deeper into the Kingdom of Dolfay. The coldest month of the year had come, and the Gaefyd winds that arrived unwelcome from the north, bit into their flesh. The trees were naked of leaves and crows whirled on high against the murky skies. The surrounding land showed even less evidence of life – a cattle bier, a field from where wheat had been harvested decades before – but of peasant or traveller none. As the day wore on and the light began to fade, Norbert and Gadroon yet again sought shelter for the night.

The moon had risen in the East – a silver globe over the silhouettes of the trees. Gadroon looked about him. At that moment a stable would have been as a palace.

"Canst see aught that will do for us, Norbert?"

"Nay... not even a fox's burrow."

Gadroon stared into the pale moonlight. From out of the shadows something loomed, but not a creature of menace as the demon at the Bridge of Amuthdel, but a formless shape. Gradually, lines appeared that seemed to hint at a building, these grew the greater in height the more they looked on. Gadroon was amazed.

"What can that be? I would swear they be castle walls before us..."

"In such a land as this?"

"Methinks we must find out if 'tis so..."

The knights rode towards an arch that gaped in the walls and, to their surprise, found themselves in a courtyard of no mean size.

"Some great lord must abide here..."

Gadroon did not respond, only looked about him.

"Didst thou notice...?"

"What... pray?"

"The hooves of the horses make no sound upon the paving beneath us..."

Norbert tensed.

"Wizardry?"

Gadroon could not help but chuckle.

"Do not such things seem commonplace in our lives now, old fellow? Let us see what doth transpire... as we have learned to do... it seems."

A shaft of light was issuing from the keep of the castle, rivalling the moonbeams above in its intensity. Dismounting, and tethering their steeds to something that felt solid, the two companions made their way along an ethereal path that led they knew not where. Soon all around possessed a more comforting reality and all might have continued to be reassuring had Norbert not seen a familiar figure approaching – Lady Malinda herself!

"My noble knights, I greet thee both!"

One glance at her ladyship was nearly enough to send him screaming for the exit, but Gadroon had other ideas. He whispered urgently to his companion.

"Wait, Norbert! Recall thy vows of chivalry I beg of you!"

So low and humble was the bowing of the errant knight that he almost split his hose. Lady Malinda, throwing wide her arms, was all hospitality.

"Welcome to the *Castle of Comforts*, Sir Norbert and Sir Gadroon. Know ye... that here you may rest before you continue upon your journey..."

Norbert was still as alarmed as a 4x4 on double-yellow lines. Gadroon sensed he was understandably wary at the prospect of any *tête-à-tête* with her ladyship and hastened to reassure his companion once more.

"This is all meant to be... I am certain Lady Malinda has much of import to tell us..."

"Come... refreshment awaits..."

Lady Malinda bade them follow her to an inner chamber where they sat upon couches of silver and blue, as if floating upon clouds. Gadroon, aware this house of cards might collapse at any moment, was determined to speak his piece.

"My lady... if I may be bold..."

The irony was not lost on Lady Malinda.

"I beg you to be so, Sir Gadroon."

"What know ye of Sir Wayne... he once of King Arthur's Court?"

Her ladyship smiled knowingly, not for the first time in her chequered career.

"Ah... thou hast asked a question most sensible, Sir Gadroon... for a tale doth hang upon all that..."

"I would feign know all, my lady..."

"And you shall. When Sir Wayne came to Charbon some little time ago he sought an audience with Sir Edmund and then remained in his company for a goodly time. My spouse then came to my bower to tell me that... no matter how hard he tried... he could make not one grain of sense out any of that which the youth sayeth to him. He had spoken much in riddles... of how The Purple Haze and Sir Edmund were one and the same... and how the Round Table would soon be wrapped in Mellow Yellow! Much he did say to myself later was the stuff of fireside tales and the ramblings of ancient scholars who have lost their wits."

Gadroon was most intrigued.

"Fie! What canst we make of this?"

"What could I do but assure Sir Edmund that I would speak with the young knight... thus Sir Wayne was shown to a private chamber. Certain books are kept there... and straightway of these he seemed much afeared as if the books... those very things resting upon a shelf... might somehow bring him ill."

At this revelation, Gadroon was most curious.

"What did thou make of all that, my lady?"

"I confess I knew not what to think. Sir Wayne told me he had spent some time at Piedervoux... riding there in some haste from Malfaise. He had arrived at the monastery in the middle of the night... only one monk was awake in the small hours... one Scriven..."

Gadroon could not help exclaiming.

"Scriven!"

"This monk took him to one of the small side chapels in the abbey and there Wayne confessed all. Of his tryst with Morgan le Fay... how together they had sent The Purple Haze to threaten Camelot... of his treachery to both of thee..."

Norbert was more than astonished; his whole head began to go up and down like a yo-yo.

"Sir Wayne begged Scriven to pray for his soul... which... naturally... the monk agreed to do. He then told Scriven he was certain if he returned to Malfaise then death would be his lot. Scriven then apparently took him to the Scriptorium..."

"...and showed him a certain book perhaps?"

Lady Malinda nodded.

"...thus it was so. There upon the page his fate was pictured... in terrible detail... he confided to me... his own death upon the battlefield. As soon as he beheld this he left the Abbey and had ridden through the night to Charbon and thus we received him."

Gadroon was on the case straightway.

"But this cannot be all to the tale..."

"Nay... indeed not.... for Scriven went to the Abbot as soon as he was able and told him all. Word was then sent to King Arthur..."

Gadroon slapped his thigh triumphantly.

"And thus our king was in readiness for war..."

"As you say..."

The two knights sat in silence for a time and reflected long and hard upon what they had heard. Lady Melinda toyed with an apple, but not in any meaningful way, Norbert was relieved to see. At last Gadroon spoke, and his words were measured, almost with a slide-rule.

"Did Sir Wayne speak of any other things that he might have seen in the book of Scriven?"

"He did so. Doubtless you wish to hear of the fate of yourselves?"

Gadroon was staunch, as ever.

"My Lady, the final part of our journey beckons... the end of The Quest is in sight. All truths will soon be ours... this can only be one more that we must own."

Lady Malinda agreed.

"Very well. It is all most simple... you, Sir Gadroon will be given joy... and Sir Norbert will gain the fulfillment for which his soul yearns."

Silence fell once more in The Castle of Comforts. Considering the surroundings, the peace that reigned in the hearts of the two knights might have been unreal, but it was still most profound.

*

Norbert and Gadroon left the castle in the early hours, almost at the moment the Moon was setting. Fitting it was that when they rode, Norbert should choose to recall his dreams. These had come to him whilst Gadroon was experiencing his encounter with Morgan le Fay. As Norbert embarked on his recollections, the Moon faded into nothingness.

"I saw most plainly the Holiest of Holies before me... so much so that I believed I could reach out and touch this most heavenly thing."

Gadroon was impressed.

"That is the great power of the Cup of Fioleth... that it may manifest itself wheresoe'er it wisheth. It is a good omen thou hast encountered the most precious Grail, Norbert. I believe the sacred vessel is bidding us well."

Norbert continued.

"The light that sprang from within the Cup was beyond all understanding. Doth this vision foretell more, Gadroon? Thou art wiser than I... concerning all matters..."

"Wiser than thou? Methinks there is only one who is truly wise..."

"God."

"*Goddess*... if you please, Norbert! Did Edrith the wizard teach you nothing?"

"My dear Gadroon..."

"Enough, Norbert! We are but a few leagues from the Sanctuary of Light... the Temple of *The Queen of Heaven*! It is only through the munificence of The Goddess that we are permitted to behold The Mysteries at all."

Norbert thought it wise to change the subject.

"And is Lady Malinda part of the Fifth Wisdom? This I wonder... as she too has told us much to lift the veil upon the mysteries that have surrounded us..."

Gadroon, relieved that any theological debate was not in the programme, thought about this.

"I believe her to be a Guardian of the Grail... as I believe Morgan le Fay may be also..."

At this, Norbert nearly fell off his horse.

"You jest... surely?"

"Nay... I do not... we have both been tested Norbert... to see whether our resolve be strong enough and if we are worthy... and indeed wise enough... to behold the truth. The five lessons we have been taught are all one..."

"That... all is never as it seems?"

"In truth, my friend."

Thus the two knights continued once more on their journey into an unknown and often hostile world. Pumpkin-faced Norbert – staunch and simple, the cream of peasant stock – and Gadroon – gaunt, determined and of noble lineage. Together they made a curious pair, yet, a deep loyalty and affection had grown up between them, qualities that stood apart in any era. In The Dark Ages – most precious indeed.

XVII

Gawain's path
Wound through dreary scenes,
And his head leaned
First this way, then that, as he hunted
That chapel.

Gadroon spurred his horse onward, Norbert following in his wake. Glainseg lay before them. The Quest was about to be fulfilled. The Chapel was but a few leagues away and Norbert could feel the power of The Grail urging them onward. Hidden from the profane, preserved in a timeless state, The Holy Vessel would soon be revealed to them! A pair of deer ahead of them kicked up their hind legs and went scampering into the undergrowth. Shadows flitted in and out the trees and at last, the way led out into the open. The sight which greeted the knights could not have been more sublime.

Before them was the Lake of Fioleth. Swans glided upon the water while ducks and other wildfowl clustered by its banks. The knights crossed over a wooden walk onto a small islet. Hid from view, here lay the holy place. Out of the shadows suddenly appeared a form, and Gadroon's hand went to the hilt of his sword. The figure that fell on the ground before them was quickly revealed as being more pathetic than threatening.

"Mercy, good sirs! Would you harm a poor beggar who doth kneel before you?"

Gadroon sheathed his sword.

"Indeed I would not! But strangers who come upon one another should announce their presence... lest one or other think they may be enemies."

"Forgive me, Sir Knight... forgive me... indeed I was foolish. 'Tis little wonder I am called by some... *The Wild Man of The Wild Wood.*"

"I greet thee... whatever thou may be called...."

He knelt before them once more, this time with his head almost touching the ground. Gadroon would have none of it.

"Come... stand before us I beg you! Be as an equal... not as a cringing cur."

When he did they saw the full extent of his unkempt appearance and the paucity of the rags that he wore.

"Great blessings be upon you, fair knight... the Goddess will reward you a hundred fold for your compassion."

Norbert took this in.

"Would you take bread and water? Perhaps you are hungry and thirsty?

Tears sprang to the withered features and the beggar wrung his hands in supplication.

"I live only through the generosity of my fellow man... devout pilgrims... as yourselves... blessedly chosen to be in this sacred place. Good knights... ye have fulfilled my wish to remain in this world to see but one more dawn."

Norbert unbuckled one of the saddlebags and promptly presented the beggar with half a quartern loaf and a flask of spring water. The beggar took these gifts, bowing as he did so.

"A miracle... a miracle..."

Norbert reflected it was also a miracle how quickly these offerings were devoured. Gadroon was inclined to make after-dinner conversation.

"Now... Wild Man of The Woods... what is thy true name..."

"I am Sir Percy Duval..."

Was there a hint of pride hidden amongst all that humility?

"So... thou wert once a knight... forgive me... I mean to say that thou art still..."

"No longer am I horsed or squired, 'tis true... but I retain my oath of chivalry. For... *chivalry... is... devotion...*"

At these words Norbert felt a strange sensation, as if he was being watched by someone or something. The ragged knight sensed this too and spoke urgently in a faraway voice, as if he were singing.

"It is the spirit of the woods calling to you that you hear, Sir Knight. Listen closely for you may here wisdom from him for *Gensith* is the great and true friend of all woodland creatures."

Norbert heard the voice quite clearly in his mind and marvelled.

"You will return... return... to the Abbey... that is your true home... Camelot will be forsaken forever."

Norbert closed his eyes and Gadroon saw he was swaying, overcome by a kind of ecstasy.

"Thy words are of great comfort... it is all I would wish for... I thank thee..."

Gadroon, curious, quizzed Sir Percy the more.

"And you have remained about here for some time..."

"I cannot remember when I first came... only that I saw a vision of The Goddess and swore a sacred oath that I would never leave her side. I have spent the days and nights here in great devotion since that time."

"Do you pray daily in the chapel?"

"Nay, Sir Knight... I am not worthy. I know that I would perish if I was ever to rest my eyes upon such holiness that is to be found within."

Gadroon bowed his head slightly, as if it was he who was paying obeisance to the other. The two knights stood together, creation making no distinction between their appearance or circumstances. From the folds of his ragged doublet Sir Percy took something that he passed to Gadroon. The knight stared at what he now held in the palm of his hand. Glistening with its own light, its beauty and design were unsurpassed.

"A ring... a silver ring... two hearts are worked upon it. It is most fine."

"It is a gift for thee... or rather for thou to bestow upon another..."

Gadroon could only stare in wonder.

"Do you mean to give me this?"

The other nodded gravely, and before Gadroon was a vision of a smiling Willowpetal. He now knew in his heart they were to be united once more! Turning to thank his benefactor, Gadroon looked about him, but of Sir Percy there was no sign. Norbert was also staring at where the ragged figure had been but a moment before. Gadroon stared at the ring still clutched in his palm. That was certainly still there and real enough, the morning sunlight mirrored upon it. The knight looked at it once more then secreted it deep in an inner pocket of his tunic. He addressed Norbert.

"Glainseg has several guardians... and Sir Percy will not be the only one we shall meet, I feel sure. If we had not bestowed charity upon him or been afeared... then all would have remained hidden from us. We would never have discovered the Chapel... let alone The Cup of Fioleth."

Norbert nodded his head in silent agreement; his destiny had become clear. The strange knight and the spirit of the woods, who were perhaps one and the same, had spoken words that meant much to him. As they followed the path, much overgrown with hazel and ash strewn with masses of ivy, thorns tore at their raiment. At last they came within sight of the Chapel, a squat edifice hardly bigger than a stable. This was the place where the Holy of Holies was to be found, and it seemed to ask the Questing Knights, as had Sir Percy, to forgive its lowly appearance.

Set atop two pillars, sculpted heads, their delicate features much worn, peered at the knights. A door of the darkest oak, so weathered it looked as if it might crumble into dust at a touch, was before them. Norbert examined every knot in the woodwork, even taking in the shape of the hasps that held each timber in place. A golden light seeped out from beneath the door and this, as if moved by a divine hand, swung open to reveal all within. They doffed their furred caps and Norbert passed quite easily through the opening, but Gadroon was almost bent double. As soon as they were within the inner sanctum the strains of a celestial choir could be heard, and the rich tang of frankincense was in the air. As soon as they had closed the tiny door, it was as if the world outside no longer existed.

A soft light came from the stained glass windows high in the walls above. Butterflies, the motif of the soul, fluttered in a landscape of rich vermillion and cobalt. In places the walls had crumbled, and shadows fell among the most intimate of niches. A pair of oaken settles – almost the colour of peat – stood against oak panels carved with castellated capitals and the finest tracery.

Above the altar were sculpted a score of angels, each holding a gold and crimson crown. They floated beneath an azure canopy patterned with stars and *fleurs-de-lis*. Behind the altar was a frieze of a huge sun, its rays reaching out to the sides of the chancel. Beside this was a full moon with a crescent within it. The combined power of the two luminaries seemed to be concentrated upon the very centre of the altar cloth, a space the size of a man's hand. A pale glow came from this, and a great pentacle, woven on the green and gold frontal, grew brighter by the moment. The Holy of Holies was about to appear before Norbert and Gadroon! Spellbound, they knelt before the altar, awaiting that moment. All around the light within the chapel grew brighter and more intense.

Then, as suddenly as it had come, the light was gone! All became dark and a heavily mailed fist extinguished the tapers upon the altar. A great warrior in full armour now stood before them. He held no sword, for he had no need of any weapon to demonstrate his great power. The eyes regarded Norbert and Gadroon, not with hostility, but indifference. His voice, when they heard it, echoed in the Chapel like thunder in the mountains.

"Why do ye come? Are ye true seekers... or fools who would pry here... in the most sacred of all places? Answer me! And that directly... for know ye that only the truth may be spoken here in the blessed light. Nothing less will do."

Gadroon sought to answer these questions as plainly as he could.

"We are here to know The Cup of Fioleth... that in doing so we may protect Camelot and all our Company from harm."

The warrior paused, taking this in.

"I... Heldnath... am he who protects the Sacred Chalice. No mortal man... nay not even the mightiest warrior, may best me. My task is to ensure only those who are pure of heart may remain in the presence of the Holy of Holies."

Gadroon's voice rang out so that it too resounded against the walls, the voice of a noble knight, one chosen to serve only the highest in heaven.

"I speak only of that which is true. I would know no other way when I am in the presence of the Blessed Light... one so bright that the darkness trembles before it."

Heldnath took a moment to ponder this then he looked upon the two questing knights, his stern features unaltered.

"That is well spoken! Then look now upon the Face of Paradise, O noble knights! And be ye most ready with all thy praise and adoration... for naught else will thou feel from this moment on!"

And as they looked, the eyes of the mighty Heldnath grew dim and the image of the warrior began to fade. Norbert and Gadroon were left to gaze once more at the altar and nothing could have prepared them for what followed. The vision that came to them was more profound than life itself. First appeared a king and queen, one each side of the altar, rising from among the angels. The king's features were as stone, etched and unmoving, yet about the set of the mouth was a deep compassion and understanding. This was a true monarch – one who reflected absolutely the divine power.

His consort radiated beauty and calm in the iridescent blue of her eyes; truly was she the Queen of Heaven. Then the king looked upon her consort and in both their eyes only love could be seen. This was the coming together of the masculine and the feminine – the sun and the moon as one. The divine union was being made manifest before the Questing Knights. The invisible was about to be made visible – the moment of transcendence was at hand. At that instant The Holy Grail itself appeared before them.

Norbert and Gadroon became still, and the more they held that stillness, the more dazzling and resplendent did The Holy Vessel become. The Grail entered their very being, they became the cup, and the cup was within them. All was known to Norbert and Gadroon, they beheld every secret of creation, as The Grail in its turn knew every part of them. Beyond the state of ecstasy The Grail brought lay the ineffable, and the two knights experienced this also. The Goddess, her voice sounding as the music of infinity, then uttered words that would be forever etched upon their hearts.

"Such sweet waters will bathe and heal you both... such as you have never known before. The bounteous vessel can never be empty for it is always replenished with the love of Heaven. That love is now yours... for all eternity."

The knights looked upon The Goddess before them, a countenance of such beauty and that they could only gaze in silent wonder. They saw the lips that only spoke the truth, the eyes that were bounteous with forgiveness and mercy for all in the world. Their souls were caressed in such waves of bliss they wondered if they might drown in ecstasy. Norbert and Gadroon remained before the altar, blinking in the holy light as The Goddess slowly faded from the holy scene before them.

Gadroon felt as if another presence was there. The Grail Maidens! He could hear the songs of the angels above, and the soft touch of a wing against his cheek made him start. Gadroon breathed deeply to calm his heart, which he feared was about to burst. Tears flowed heavily from him as if all the remorse he had ever felt was being taken from him. He and Norbert had encountered The Great Mother of all men, the divine female, sacred womankind.

For Norbert, his own quest was nearly over. He had found that which he had been seeking – a world beyond the one he had previously known. The Quest had shown him many different aspects of the world and now he only sought a place where he could be at one with his God, that deity he had always known. He vowed to dedicate his time upon this Earth to prayer and most earnestly did he now offer up his praises. Words tumbled over and over in his brain until they became his only reality and all else about him disappeared.

*

At the same time in a darker world, another had observed the finding of The Grail. Morgan le Fay looked impassively upon the scene, then turned away. She was aware that now all had changed for her – forever. It had happened from the moment The Goddess had appeared to Norbert and Gadroon. Destiny had now decided the path that each of the knights would follow and Gadroon would be lost to her forever. How she had yearned for his warm embrace! Yet, it was never to be; now he would know the love of another, one who the universe had decided should be his. Morgan, in a rare moment of compassion vowed she would never hinder their union, though without doubt she had the power to do so. The Purple Haze she had dismissed to the infernal regions from where it had come, and thus kept that vow to Gadroon also.

Her pain was perhaps lessened a little by knowing the Company would soon be no more. Her contempt for Arthur had never for a moment lessened and for the fortunes of The Round Table she had little concern. Only for Gadroon had Morgan any respect. He had shown that he embraced womanhood in all its moods – dark and light – and seeing this, The Goddess had protected him. In her heart she knew that this was only right. She took one final look at Norbert and Gadroon as they knelt before the altar.

The knights remained in the chapel until the day grew dark and, with that, the glow of The Cup upon the altar faded. But the vision would remain in their hearts – forever. They regained their feet, stumbling a little, and with a great feeling of loss, as if part of their very being had now been taken from them. With a great effort, Norbert mouthed a few words.

"My soul was filled with the utmost bliss... will I ever know that again?"

Gadroon laid a hand on his friend's shoulder.

"We have beheld The Cup, Norbert. At least it has tarried for a little while with us."

Norbert silently acknowledged the words of his companion and together they silently left Glainseg. They rode eastwards out of the kingdom of Dolfay into the night. Norbert and Gadroon had looked, not only into the Eye of God, but upon the face of The Goddess also. Few have known such things as this.

With the dawn of the next day they took sustenance for the first time since they were at the Chapel. The holiness of that place had sustained them for many hours. They saw birds flying in the skies and heard their song as if for the first time. They smiled upon the world and each other, for the Dream of The Grail had been fulfilled for them both. And although The Quest was over, a new beginning had come for both Norbert and Gadroon. Such was the power of The Grail to bestow insight that they could each see the soul of the other.

Gadroon knew Norbert wished to lose himself in his God, and to embrace a kingdom of belief where all questions were answered. For him, the material world was as some thicket that trapped him and gave him pain. For his part, Norbert could see that for Gadroon, only the company of his love and a reuniting with Willowpetal would satisfy him. All that remained now was their return to Camelot and such happenings as would come about upon that final part of their journey.

XVIII

Now Gawain rides in the world's wilderness,
Alive by the gracious mercy of God.
He slept under roofs, he slept under trees,
And he knew adventures, and won victories...

The return to the kingdom of Longres was not to be without further trials. Gadroon realised what might lie ahead as soon as they entered the kingdom of Tomberg. The Winter had not been marked with snow – as the previous year – but endless rains. The clouds were constantly threatening to bring more storms, and every rut brimmed. What had been a dry cleft months before, was now a muddy pool. Riding was difficult, and in many places walking would have been almost impossible. When they arrived at the ford across the River Perogel, they could see the water was perilously deep. Gadroon paused, staring at the torrent before them.

"If we are to survive the crossing, it will only be thanks to our horses. My own is a strong swimmer and will bear me up. What of your steed, Norbert?"

"He has carried me this far... and I have always trusted him..."

"Very well. Let us delay no longer. Onward!"

Gadroon slid his horse into the water and Norbert, not quite so smoothly, followed. As they set out from the bank all seemed to be well, but as they reached mid-stream the current was fiercer than they had realised. Gadroon's mount kept upright, but it was soon evident that Norbert's horse was floundering in the rushing waters. Gadroon moved his horse as close to Norbert as he dared, crying out to him as he did so.

"Climb astride my horse, Norbert! Thine is full of fear! She will drown with thee upon her back!"

Norbert did as he was bid and straightway his horse swam to the other side and succeeded in pulling itself up onto the bank. With two riders upon it, Gadroon's mount made slow progress, but after some anxious minutes they were out of the river and on solid ground. The pair made a sorry sight as they stood upon the bank, soaked to the skin and shivering. The animals busied themselves with shaking the water off themselves, most of it upon their riders.

Gadroon, as always, was one for stiffening the upper lip and putting the best foot forward, and not in any particular order. They squelched on into Dolfay and by noon were only a few leagues from the Amuthdel Bridge. A fair few of Norbert's fears returned as they drew closer, but these were quickly dispelled. Fortune also put in an unscheduled appearance, for a little distance from the way they found a shepherd's hut. Even more splendidly, they came upon the embers of a fire within, still red at the heart.

They dismounted, put the horses to graze and busied about, looking for dry wood. This they succeeded in doing and soon had a good blaze going. They both stripped off their wet garments and, each finding a blanket in their pack, wrapped this about them. Soon their sodden clothes were steaming and the inside of the hut was like a Medieval sauna. An hour later they were warm and dry, and Gadroon chose this moment to share his plans.

"By the look upon the face of the Moon I would say it is now near the middle of Gaefyd. We have but fifteen days to make our journey back to Camelot and thus we can brook no delay. We must follow the way across the kingdom of Tomberg... of this we have no choice. Neither have we the time to seek out any path to avoid Meutreville... so we must ride through the town howsoever all may be there."

Norbert agreed.

"That all seems most wise."

Gadroon allowed himself a smile.

"If we were less pressed... I would make our presence known in Valentin and surprise the good mistress Athilde in her cottage.... Nouvin also, perhaps..."

Norbert tutted a little before questioning Gadroon.

"And when we reach the Bridge of Goffrow?"

Gadroon sighed impatiently.

"It is there we must make our choice. I am certain it would not be wise to go north and enter the kingdom of Anghard. Who knows what has transpired there since the fall of Brime and his henchmen? There are likely to be many a knave roaming the land... and up to much mischief, no doubt. It may be that Queen Lardiana rules the kingdom now... but I find that hard to believe. The town of Malfaise is likely to be more of a den of thieves and wickedness than it was when we were *detained* there before."

Norbert shivered involuntarily at that memory.

"It seems most likely to be so."

"Therefore we must strike out east... and ride across the kingdom of Tomberg..."

Somewhat resignedly, Norbert nodded in agreement.

"Where does this eastern way lead?"

"It is hardly *a way*... more a cattle path. I have ridden there once, many years past and that was in the Summer months. There is an ancient gate... Hynporth, leading from Tomberg into the kingdom of Gwagmar. The way becomes a little better after that... as I recall. We must continue until we reach the Tower of Argollen. When we reach there we will know we are on the right road at least. A short way after that we shall find ourselves in the southern parts of Longres."

"I for one shall feel much safer then..."

Gadroon shrugged.

"Let us hope so. I know we will join the way somewhere near the Abbey and thence we may return to Camelot."

Mention of the Abbey at Piedervoux caused Norbert to assume an air of melancholy.

"It is there my heart lies, Gadroon. I am certain my destiny is in walking the cloisters of Piedervoux in quiet contemplation... among others who feel as I... and knowing that I am in the company of my God."

Gadroon sighed in sympathy.

"I confess, Norbert, that my thoughts are less exalted... they dwell the more upon my fellow mortals. Since we left Malfaise I have every morn asked but one question of the Heavens. What hath been the fate of Lapin... Hendrique... and Willowpetal?"

"That no one can tell... let us only hope they are no longer in Anghard if... as you say... it is a place of danger now."

Gadroon for a moment looked grim.

"Aye... and they were not caught in any of the fighting between Brime and our own king. Men... under any banner are not always to be trusted... as we discovered ourselves at Meutreville."

"You fear for the wench more?"

"Only do I fear for Willowpetal if... by some ill-fortune... she has been separated from her companions. They are loyal fellows and true... and would protect her..."

Norbert was inclined to be impatient, and spoke his mind – not gently.

"Surely it is not possible for you regard this wench with any deep or lasting affection, Gadroon? She is not of your breeding..."

Ignoring the rampant snobbery, Gadroon was as calm itself.

"Love is a mystery, Norbert. Why is it that we bestow our love upon one but not another? The ways of society mean little to me, old friend. I am more taken with knowing now that love conquers all... and indeed comes from the very wellspring of devotion. It would have been easier for me to have held back the oceans than to have refused the love Willowpetal offered me."

Norbert retired in some confusion, and not a little ashamed, but Gadroon did not think the less of him for the words he had uttered.

*

After breakfasting the next morning, the companions took stock of their provisions – a reasonable quantity of smoked fish, two quartern loaves and half a pasty. They would need to be on strict rations for the journey ahead, a prospect that was not to Norbert's liking. The likelihood of finding anything in the kingdom of Tomberg to supplement their rations was most unlikely.

As they crossed the bridge at Amuthdel and entered Tomberg, a steady rain began to fall. After some hours of this, it would have been foolish to continue any further, and they took shelter in a grove of beech and holly. Although they huddled as close as they were able to the trunks of the trees, the overhanging branches constantly dripped water upon the knights. There was nothing for it but to seek more permanent shelter as soon as they might.

The shepherd hut they had left behind now seemed but a distant memory as they scoured the landscape for sanctuary. When it grew dark, they began to despair until Gadroon espied a cattle bier in the near distance. When they drew near it, a forlorn sight met their eyes. One side was exposed to the elements and the roof was leaking badly. They had but little choice in the matter, and packed themselves and the horses as best they could into any part of the bier that might be dry. One corner was filled with hay, which did provide sustenance for the horses, and somewhere for their riders to lie also.

The next morning, stiff, and stinking of horseflesh, the knights surveyed the prospects for the day ahead.

The rain had for the moment ceased, although the look of the skies was not reassuring. Gadroon reckoned they would be near Meutreville before nightfall if they were not delayed by any more storms. They met no one upon the way and when this did occur the encounter was far from how they might have imagined. Norbert was suddenly aware of several riders ahead of them and hastened to warn Gadroon.

"A score of them... and fully armed. Can they be Brime's men... still loitering after the battle and looking for ways of making evil?"

Gadroon surveyed the approaching party, noting a certain noble bearing that he would not have associated with the men of Anghard.

"I do not believe they are Brimes' leavings. They have a different way about them altogether..."

As they drew, closer it became obvious this was indeed a royal retinue – a king and several knights. Of these, a pair had drawn swords and spurred their horses in front of the monarch in order to protect him if that was deemed to be necessary.

"Hie! Who goeth there in the Kingdom of Tomberg? His majesty's loyal followers would wish to know... and that right quickly."

Gadroon immediately reined in his horse.

"Peace, Sir Knight. I am Sir Gadroon and this is my companion, Sir Norbert. We be men of The Company of Camelot... as loyal to Arthur as doubtless thou art to thy own king."

This prompted some comment from some of the other knights following on. The one who had spoken still kept his sword in his grasp, and his tone was not encouraging.

"Thou art many leagues from Longres if thou truly be knights of Arthur's court...."

By this time Norbert and Gadroon were but a few yards from the king. Norbert regarded this imposing figure – bearded, with his white locks streaming to his ermine cape. His look was one of a stern leader but also a great guardian of his people. When he raised a hand all around him were immediately silent. His eyes rested upon Gadroon, not unkindly.

"I am King Tirhadeth of Tomberg. I see you have the way of knights about you and that you have journeyed far. As this is my kingdom that you travel upon I would request that you tell me your mission."

Gadroon returned the king's gaze without flinching.

"Our mission is almost over, sire. It was to seek out no less a thing than The Holy Grail. In bringing this to pass this we have averted much danger from our beloved Camelot."

At this, some of the knights silently exchanged glances of bemused contempt. The king however eyed Gadroon the more intently.

"Indeed. This is a most interesting and unusual tale..."

One of the knights laughed openly, thinking the king was mocking Gadroon. An icy look from his monarch told him this was not so, and he was immediately silent. The king turned in his saddle to address the knight.

"Sometimes, Sir Algernon... we must have faith in those things which at first hearing sound much as the words of fools... for therein the greatest truth lies. It is a gift bestowed upon those who rule to see men for what they are... noble or otherwise. I ask you and the rest of my loyal company to look upon these knights with the utmost respect. It is not often one meets with those who have sought out... and indeed beheld... The Holy Grail. I have no reason to believe they have not achieved this thing. Those chosen for The Quest are not of ordinary stock... they are true heroes... men of a special calling. I for one salute them."

The words of the king, spoken with such simple truth, moved the knights to draw their swords as one and salute Norbert and Gadroon. With one voice, they raised a momentous cry.

"All hail, the Knights of The Quest! May their fame resound in the world forever! Even unto the highest heaven!"

Norbert was wonderfully moved, almost to tears. Gadroon bowed his head to King Tirhadeth.

"I cannot speak words to equal thine, sire. The splendour of your office tells of itself. I can only thank the great king I see before me... and humbly request that we may be allowed to pass through thy kingdom."

The king smiled benignly.

"With my blessing thou certainly mayest, Gadroon... and thy companion Norbert also. I and these knights you see before you fought alongside Arthur at The Plain of Wythlon. Tomberg has never boasted a great army, nor even a great martial spirit... I freely admit that. Yet we mustered a force to serve alongside your king and did as we were able to gain victory. Several of our knights fell and were duly mourned. Never will the great deeds of that day be forgotten... for I have ordered the chroniclers to record these events. I am proud to have seen that day... and grateful to all heaven to have been spared also."

Gadroon spoke quietly to the king.

"I have heard of this by way of one who was at the battle... a brave page in the retinue of Sir Edmund Bascoombe. He spoke at some length of the great deeds of the men of Tomberg..."

The king appeared to make a decision and, removing his gauntlet, drew something from beneath his jerkin. This he handed to Gadroon, while the knights in his retinue stared, somewhat amazed.

"You hold there the royal seal of Tomberg and I entrust thee with this, Gadroon. Present it to your king as a token of the great trust betwixt the kingdom of Tomberg and that of Longres. Will thou do this service for me?"

211

Gadroon examined the seal – gold, and flecked with stars, a worthy symbol of any monarch.

"I will most certainly, your majesty. I know too that King Arthur will return thy loyalty twentyfold."

The king took this in, and looked evenly upon Gadroon.

"Well spake... thou knowest true the heart of thy liege. But... enough of this talk of war... we must see now to the peace. We return to Diohan this day... having spent a little time in Meutreville and seeing what may be done to ease the plight of my people there. Sorely have they been used and great are still their needs. But good will come from evil... of this I am certain. We shall journey to Malfaise in the Spring to speak with Queen Lardiana who now rules there, I am told. Together we shall ensure that justice is done for both our peoples. I for one am sure this will be fulfilled."

Norbert suddenly felt inclined to put in his groat's worth.

"It is God's will, sire... that peace reigns in the land... and I am certain the hand of God guides all noble monarchs to this great purpose."

King Tirhadeth inclined his head in Norbert's direction.

"Indeed words of great sanctity and even greater truth, Sir Norbert. We thank you for them. This has been a fine meeting. And what way do you take after you have passed over the bridge at Goffrow?"

Gadroon answered swiftly.

"We think it not wise to enter Anghard at this time, sire. We are but two and there may some abroad in that land who have no love for Arthur's knights."

The king assented.

"Thou art wise in this... you will travel to the Dwyclun Marshes and cross the Eastern part of our kingdom perhaps..."

"Indeed, sire... and then to the Tower of Argollen in the kingdom of Gwagmar. From there we travel north into Longres and join the Eastern Way that leads to Camelot."

The king nodded in assent.

"Then I wish you all fortune, Gadroon and Norbert... and mark ye that none shall harm you in Meutreville nor in any of our lands. I shall send word also that if you wish for sustenance anywhere upon the way then you shall be given it."

Gadroon bowed to King Tirhadeth.

"Your majesty is most gracious and kind."

"A king must serve his kingdom constantly... and aid the traveller therein where he may. Now... our home... the castle at Diohan lies to the south and we journey there this moment. Come, men!"

King Tirhadeth tugged at the reins of his horse and his retinue made ready to move off. Norbert and Gadroon drew to the edge of the way to allow them to pass. The king raised his gauntlet, the knights saluted most formally to them, and the men of Tomberg passed on their way to the south. The two companions watched them go, before continuing on their own journey.

The Goffrow Bridge was soon far behind them and as they rode, Gadroon told Norbert the legend of the Tower of Argollen.

"It is said that in far off days when there was a king ruling Gwagmar, he ordered the tower to be built next to his palace. He did this so that he might always know of the approach of any enemy who ventured forth from any of the surrounding kingdoms. As it came about... that time was one of peace and no army ever came to wage war against Gwagmar. Thus the tower eventually fell into disrepair... and not long after... the dynasty of those kings came to an end also."

"Is it not so that works of men fall always into dust 'ere long?"

"Much does so, it is true. None have ruled Gwagmar for many hundreds of years. Travellers told tales of those who lived here as being no better than the animals of the wild. Nothing but marsh covers the land as far as the Southern Seas. It is said that those who once were there hunted the waterfowl and fish from huts they built on stilts."

Norbert shuddered, perhaps at the thought of eating raw fish. It would take some time before Sushi became fashionable in the West.

"It is as well we shall not tarry long..."

"Not an hour longer than we need. But I would rather be here than any place in Anghard. Although we are many a league from the border, I still feel the shadow of evil lurking there. It will be of great import how all will be after King Tirhadeth hath spoken with the new queen. I pray this will bring about a new era of peace and goodwill between all."

*

Another day and night passed before they came to the Mound of Annoeth. Upon its summit was a ruined stump all that remained of the Tower of Argollen. They rested the horses and took provisions from their packs. True to his word, King Tirhadeth had by some means sent word to his people and the first cottager they encountered provided the knights with fresh bread and smoked meats for their journey. This they now ate gratefully, while Gadroon almost sniffed the air with anticipation.

"I do believe, Norbert, that we are about to know the wondrous power of all that we encountered at the Chapel of Glainseg."

No sooner had Gadroon spoken than the sun thrust aside the clouds on the horizon and revealed his golden splendour. Out of this globe of golden light came the silhouettes of two figures on horseback. As they burst into view, a halo of topaz about them, the knights knew them... Lapin and Hendrique! They sprang down from their mounts and for a long moment, all was embracing and joy. Gadroon beamed upon them, his features almost as bright as the sun above.

"My fine fellows! You are safe and well! All we had hoped for has come to pass!"

Norbert was even moved to perform an impromptu jig that delighted all the company, particularly Lapin.

"Now I remember, Sir Norbert... you danced so well at Charbon and led the lords and ladies... like a young deer a-prancing in the meadow..."

Norbert grimaced.

"Do not remind me, Lapin... I beg of you..."

Gadroon joined in with the laughter, but he could not help looking in the direction of the woods, from beyond which Lapin and Hendrique had ridden. His heart beat faster. Surely Willowpetal would not be far away? Lapin met the knight's questing eyes coolly.

"What can it be that ye seek, Sir Knight? A spirit of the woods, perchance? A pretty nymph made from roses and rainbows... a maiden of mist and morning's beauty..."

Gadroon for a second lost his good humour.

"Lapin! Do not jest!"

The other roared with laughter, a great music that filled every corner of the glade where they stood, and even further. Lapin was beside himself with mirth, he could hardly stand up.

"The jester not jest? The knight not be noble and knightly? The earth be not to stand upon? What can this be? I swear the world is forthwith wrong side up and we stand in the sky... nay, upon the Moon."

Gadroon could not help but smile at this, his good humour returning in an instant.

"I beg thy pardon... O Master of Mirth... I merely wished an answer to my question... one to which thou knoweth the answer, methinks..."

Lapin's grin was like a slice of cantaloupe.

"That I do, O Crown of Chivalry! Know ye not that Willowpetal never ceased to talk of thee... daily... hourly... and of the great love she felt for thee. Why... if her words were wimples then the Earth would be filled with none but nuns!"

Gadroon shook his head in disbelief.

"Cease... I beg thee... my own love for Willowpetal has sustained me through all. Now... riddle me no more... tell me..."

"Aha! Thy request to riddle me not, I grant thee! The better to bring thee the answer to that which thou enquire!"

He bowed low, doffing his plumed and bebobbled hat as he did so. From out of the woods a vision appeared. Gadroon beheld the sight he had prayed for, the moment The Goddess had told him would come. He almost wept, such was his happiness, and he thought his heart would rend asunder, so much did it pound beneath his doublet. Willowpetal herself was walking towards him! She carried a bunch of snowdrops of the purest white, a posy that echoed her smile. The two looked upon each other and the world about them melted as if into nothing. Did the lovers hear but a single word as Hendrique began to tell of his adventures?

"When we left Malfaise we made to travel into Tomberg and thence to seek out the court of King Tirhadeth at Diohan. We three travelled south through Anghard... following the way alongside the River Dwylon. We were on foot... the journey most difficult. We slept where we could... and sometimes Lapin and myself would earn a few silver pennies in some tavern along the way by making merry for the folks there. Willowpetal would dance also."

Norbert chimed in.

"And were you all not afeared... as we... that Brime had sent men to pursue thee?"

216

"Aye. We knew we must take care... for if word was about in Anghard that we had helped to free two knights of Camelot from King Brime's dungeons, then our fleeing from Malfaise might well bring a hue and cry after us. Then... all our lives would be worth less than a copper coin. But Lapin said it would take some time before our going was noticed... dispute as to whether we had freed the knights... and further days to make up a party to search for us. All in all, we were safe enough. "

Lapin suddenly bounded up and Hendrique knew his role as the storyteller was about to be usurped.

"What dost thou, Lapin?"

"I will carry the tale and vow to thee not to make it as tall as perhaps this very tower once was. When we knew an army had taken up arms against Tomberg we had no wish to be swallowed like bream by the likes of Brime. Not netted would we be... and now you see us safe in this place... where none would believe we would be."

"But that was many months ago... how didst the three of thee keep from being starved?"

Lapin smiled his jester's smile.

"Indeed... no peace would any one of us have if we were not all of a piece. Where wouldst go to feed the soul, Sir Norbert? Why... to the abbey... and there we were given alms by good Abbot Speckle whose body is like the abbey itself... most copious. His cope doth cope with covering all covenants with his maker... and maketh amends for every single sinner... but doth not the thinner get."

Norbert was slightly disapproving.

"I trust thou did not sharpen thy wit upon the good abbot in his presence, Lapin?"

Lapin looked mournful.

"Nay... his is a countenance too soft to sharpen a pin upon... but beneath that flush of flesh there lieth a desire for the cut and thrust..."

Norbert looked puzzled.

"How say thee? The good Abbot can be no swordsman."

"Neither a swordsmith either... a wordsmith perchance and a lover of the book. Also a cook who is a lover of game... not only 'pon the table but after the feasting...."

Norbert saw the light like lightning.

"Chess! You played the game with Abbot Speckle!"

"He and I did close in combat upon the squares... with no squire to be seen and the only knights and bishops upon the board. He loved me for that... as he hath with none to play 'pon any day... be they bishop... king... or queen! I beat him too, and he beateth me back, so we were as equals... and neither to suffer a whipping."

During all of this tumult of tomfoolery, Gadroon had taken Willowpetal's hand and, noticed by none, they had slipped away to the edge of the woods. There they sat, upon a fallen ash tree, one covered in soft ivy. All was still, only did they hear the gentle wind rustling the leaves around their feet and the sweet chirpings of tiny birds. Gadroon put his arms about Willowpetal and whispered softly to her.

"I have much that I wish to say to you."

Willowpetal looked up a little shyly.

"Then say on, Sir Knight."

A pigeon swooped low in a translucent sky.

"Even in my darkest hour I believed I would see you once more... but I did not know when..."

Willowpetal nestled against his breast.

"And every night I prayed that I would not be lost from you."

"That would never have been. I would have searched unto the ends of the Earth for thee."

The maid sat up slowly and stared at Gadroon in astonishment.

"Sir Knight... but why? You are a noble man of court. Why do you wish to keep the company of a mere maid such as I?"

Gadroon sighed.

"My Willowpetal... you are the sun... the moon and all the stars to me! It is my desire that we be together for all eternity."

Tears came into her eyes at these words.

"My lord! How can you say these things to me?"

Gadroon laughed, ripe rich peals that made the shadows scurry abroad.

"Who else would I say them to?"

Willowpetal looked at him plainly.

"Why... some fair lady at court..."

"There is none... in any court... in any kingdom... in any land... in any world... that I know... as fair as thee..."

Willowpetal searched his countenance as a woman does when she wishes to find out if a man be true. She saw straightway that he spoke only with an honest heart. At this she shed tears - those of joy. Her heart leaped within her, and in that moment she truly knew love in all its wonder. When Gadroon kissed her she surrendered all her being to him, holding back nothing of herself.

"Oh... I feel such happiness. Indeed I have dreamed again and again of this... since the night we first met..."

"Then dream no more... for all is real, Willowpetal."

They kissed once more and, as if the universe played a jape upon them, a pheasant shot out from the waving ferns. Willowpetal leapt up in alarm.

"Oh... I was so afeared!"

Gadroon laughed and the maid soon resumed her place in his arms and there the two remained until the sun was lost behind the trees. Hand in hand, they joined their companions once more. The sky was auburn and violet, the last rays of the sun gleaming upon the Tower of Argollen before the shadows began to gather. The tower, once a monument to a king's fear, was now transformed into a celebration of the love of a noble knight for his lady.

XIX

But of all her kings Arthur was always
Most glorious, as the tales tell – and knowing
A strange adventure, told of Arthur
And his knights, as surpassing strange a tale...

The party rode through the night and at dawn crossed
the border into the kingdom of Longres. Willowpetal
clung to Gadroon; she was so slight that Gadroon's
mount hardly felt any weight upon its back. By the end
of the day they were grateful to leave the rough
trackway and join the travellers' road once more. The
New Moon appeared in the Western sky. Its slender
horns encircled Venus – the Goddess of Love – clothing
her in the mantle of the Evening Star. Venus in turn
threw a radiant halo over her sister Diana.

Piedervoux lay but a few leagues ahead and
Gadroon noticed that the nearer they came to the abbey
the more Norbert's mood changed. Before he had been
content only to exchange a word or two as they rode,
but now his eyes were downcast, and a most serious air
came over him. When they halted at the day's end,
Norbert was in some anguish when he spoke to
Gadroon.

"I must go where my destiny lies... to join the order.
I cannot return to Camelot... there is nothing to hold
me there. It is God's work I must do... and not be in
the service of any king. You still have business there...
I have none."

Gadroon laid a hand on his shoulder.

"I know, old friend... I understand thee well... and I
am listening to thy words with all my heart. I would bid
thee go straightway and with all my good fortune to
attend thee... but this cannot be... not until after we
have returned to the Court."

"What sayest thou? Am I not master of my own fate?"

Gadroon was matter-of-fact.

"In order to leave the company... if that is your wish... thou must speak first with the king. Thy Oath of Allegiance and thy knightly vows demand this from thee."

Norbert was inclined to 'Faugh' and 'Pshaw' somewhat.

"Earthly concerns are no longer mine."

"They are for us all, Norbert... perchance we like it or nay. Come! Arthur will not prevent thee... of that I am certain. I will vouch for thee also... never fear on that."

Norbert was mollified, a little.

"But may I not seek audience with the Abbot... as we pass the Abbey gates?"

"Nay, Norbert... for my sake do not. Willowpetal will not be permitted to pass in there... that is the rule of the Order..."

To his credit, Norbert did not sulk, and they continued their journey, resting for the night before making good speed the next day. They came upon Chateau Charbon before noon the next day. Lapin became effervescent, donning his tell-tale titfer and capering about the more.

"Ho, Hendrique! There ahead may lie our fate... or I lieth and am ever fated to do so. But hear me... the man of jest cannot lie, for all the world expecteth all he sayeth to be *not true*. There lieth the power of wit! None may see the truth therein, unless he be born a jester too. One may safely hide one's secrets in a chest of jest. Yet for I... these things be always in my heart... not my chest. But merriment floweth in me... as it doth for the peasant who wisheth for a stream of ale... and for his lordship who desireth an ocean of wine."

All laughed most heartily at this, yet it could be seen that Hendrique looked upon Lapin with great curiosity.

"How say you, my friend Lapin? Is it that we should seek employ here... to amuse the court of Sir Edmund Bascoombe?"

"Indeed, Hendrique... my marvellous minstrel! That be the plan I have planned to make plain. I believe at Charbon we shall be met with gladness... as the dog with two tails made twice the welcome for his master. Wilt thou accompany me to the steward that we may make our plea... to be hired for the giving of glee and that most constantly?"

Hendrique was all smiles.

"Indeed I will, thou Lord of Laughter! Thy boldness knows no bounds! And once the court herein has set all their eyes upon us... we shall be found to be the merriest of entertainers that ever hath played before them. Yule tide cometh soon enough also, a time when all seek to be entertained most. And with good fortune we shall have comfortable quarters and not lack for victuals... for many months perhaps."

Lapin grasped his hand.

"Loyal minstrel! May thy lute long laud music's marvels and thy fingers never numb... to make nimble notes upon it! Come, let us seek out this fabulous fortune!"

Willowpetal was loath to see them leave and all three embraced most affectionately. Lapin smiled upon the little maid in his joy.

"Thou will have the most devoted eyes in any kingdom upon thee when thou dance now, Willowpetal! Thou hast no need to step out before the court when thou hast thine own devoted and lordly courtier!"

Willowpetal embraced Lapin and Hendrique over and over and bade them look to after one another, as they always did. She promised too that they would all meet once more at another time. At that, Lapin threw his hat high in the air.

"Are the hours not ours to do as we will? Let cockcrow and clocks be mocked! Days be as nights and noble knights be always in a daze if they wish..."

Gadroon was all good cheer as he and Norbert took their leave of the merry pair.

"I'll be brief in thanking thee fair Lapin and Hendrique... lest thy jests delay us an hour more! Thou bravely did set us free at Malfaise... thus we have saved Camelot... that debt Arthur has to thee. Were it not for thee also we should not have gained The Quest. So the Fool is as much the spirit of The Holy Vessel as all else it doth succour in this world."

Lapin could not resist a one-liner after that.

"All hail The Grail! Though at holy things some might rail and wail 'tis the tale that cannot fail!"

Gadroon held up a restraining hand.

"Peace! I have not said all! Thou hath also nurtured and kept my love Willowpetal from harm. For that alone I would give thee all my fortune and more. 'Tis I who am in thy debt as long as I do live."

Norbert thanked them too, perhaps not so eloquently but with all sincerity. His heart was heavy, knowing that soon they would all be parted, but he embraced them both as warmly as Willowpetal had done. Lapin threw his hat in the air once more, caught it deftly, and held it aloft.

"Farewell, Sir Norbert and Sir Gadroon! May the greatest good fortune go with thee! Champions of chivalry! Men of yore who for years will live... of many score!"

"I thank thee... and may Sir Edmund treat thee well!"

The companions and Willowpetal watched Lapin and Hendrique ride along the winding way that led to the gates of Chateau Charbon.

*

By the time they came to Camelot it was early eve. The Moon had grown great above them and glistened in a clear sky. They passed the gatehouse and let the horses rest in the courtyard. To the knights it felt uncanny to be back in Arthur's seat after so long an absence, and so many adventures. Willowpetal stood close to Gadroon wondering, a little anxiously, what might befall her. It was not long before the Steward bustled out of his quarters to greet them.

"Hail, Sir Norbert! All Hail Sir Gadroon! Welcome once more to Camelot! There will be great rejoicing among the Company when all know you have returned... and from your Great Quest. The Company have much to thank you for... our king also..."

Gadroon was gracious but he had the same look about him as those clever chaps who always finish the Times Crossword before breakfast.

"I thank you, Steward. Now I would send *thee* upon a mission also if I may. There are matters I would discuss with the king... brief I trust, but most urgent they are. We shall have longer audience with his majesty on the morrow of that I have no doubt... but the affair of which I speak cannot wait."

The Steward put on his thoughtful face, one he always carried in his doublet for such moments.

"Know ye the king attends the Yuletide revels in the Great Hall, as is only fitting at this time... but I am certain he will absent himself for thy sake. I am certain also he will ask this... that ye and Sir Norbert are willing to be presented to the Company this night?"

Norbert stepped up.

"Let Gadroon and his lady attend the king. I shall retire to my quarters and wait to be summoned. Then we shall both be set before the Company."

"Excellent! It shall be as you say. I will show thee to the guest chamber, Sir Norbert... and then hasten to the king. If Sir Gadroon and..."

The maid spoke up.

225

"Willowpetal."

The steward bowed to her.

"Indeed. If thou canst but tarry here for a moment..."

Norbert and the Steward hurried away, leaving Gadroon and Willowpetal alone in the shadows. The little maid almost melted into the knight's doublet, holding him as tightly as she could. Gadroon sought to comfort her with soft words.

"Fear not, my sweet one. All will be well..."

Willowpetal was all bright-eyed, but not quite so bushy-tailed.

"I have never been among grand company, Sir... kings and knights... even stewards. None has ever *bowed* to me before! I feel that I am not worthy to be amongst them..."

"There, Willowpetal. Remember that friendship and warmth are not strangers to high places also..."

A figure came out of the shadows at that moment, and Gadroon saw that it was Guinevere. He made so bold as to hail her.

"Your majesty..."

"Lancelot?"

Gadroon stepped into the light. Guinevere looked a little disappointed.

"Nay... it is I... Sir Gadroon."

"Ah... yes... of course... and returned from your great Quest. I am sure the king and all the court will be anxious to give you the highest praise..."

"Indeed, your majesty, I await that pleasure..."

"I am certain you do... and..."

Willowpetal came forward and curtseyed.

"Your majesty... this lady is my betrothed... Willowpetal..."

Guinevere smiled upon the little maid. Willowpetal responded in the way any monarch's subjects generally do, by smiling glassily.

"How charming she is. Come... let me see you in the light of the torch above... there... and so pretty in the moonlight, too. Your betrothed you say, Gadroon? Then we must straightway find a bower for the lovers in the castle... I think I may know just the place. Come... you must accompany me, my dear girl. We women must seek out each other's company and be joyful together... not always attending to the needs of our menfolk..."

Guinevere laughed, quite shrilly at her little jest. Willowpetal was quite overcome by her queenly presence and followed in Guinevere's footsteps like a docile younger sister.

"I shall join thee later, Willowpetal... my love..."

"You may certainly do so, Gadroon. We shall prepare a nest together for you and your betrothed. I shall send word to you with one of my ladies in waiting as to where this paradise doth lie..."

The two melted into the night, which was just as well as, right on cue, King Arthur and the Steward shimmied round the corner

"Sir Gadroon! Thy presence bestows such joy and gladness to Camelot! Now those days and nights of doubt we have suffered are no more. Thou hath succeeded in thy mission to seek out The Grail and discover its holiness! Longres will prosper... The Company is united and Camelot stands proud! Thou and Sir Norbert will be forever heroes in the kingdom... thy deeds recorded in the annals. Songs will be sung about thee by every minstrel in the land, of that I am sure."

Gadroon looked suitably demure.

"You are most generous in your praise, my liege. My greatest joy is to know that Camelot will be safe once again. The Purple Haze will trouble Longres no more... that I know."

"And now you must accompany us to the Great Hall, Gadroon... and with Norbert your companion... that the

Company may honour you as is fitting for heroes and great men."

"Before we do so, my liege... there is a task I must perform. I bring a token of alliance from one great king to another... this was entrusted to me by King Tirhadeth of Tomberg. I was charged by his majesty to present it to thy royal self."

Arthur paused, dramatically – just for effect.

"And who else but the Questing knight would be worthy of such a task?"

Gadroon fished around in his doublet and duly handed over the royal gift. The king held the seal gazing upon its magnificence.

"This seal will always be treasured... as a remembrance of those who fought for justice... and as a sign that harmony will be forever between our two kingdoms. I thank thee, Gadroon... thou hast brought a wondrous thing to Longres. At a time when we have been delivered from evil... this is a hope for fair times before us."

"Let us pray that this comes to pass."

"Indeed, Gadroon... well spake. And now Steward, I beg thee go to and summon Sir Norbert from his chamber. These two noble knights shall be brought to the Great Hall and there presented to the company with the greatest honour and triumph. We shall celebrate most well upon this eve..."

*

Despite the coziness of the nook she and the Queen had put together, it was a weepy Willowpetal that Gadroon came upon when he returned from The Great Hall. He wrapped the little maid in a huge hug-o-rama, for she was an ocean of emotion.

"The queen was so kind to me... not at all the grand lady I thought she would be... but so very much a friend..."

228

"I assured thee thou wouldst find a good and loving soul to take care of thee..."

"Yes, my wonderful Gadroon... you are right... but... but..."

She burrowed her head into his chest once more and sobbed the more, Gadroon was all tenderness.

"Now... tell of that which irks thee..."

"Camelot is not the place for me..."

"And neither is it for me, my darling one."

Willowpetal looked puzzled.

"What can thou mean? Camelot is your abode... as one of The Company."

"No more it shall be. Tomorrow morn I shall renounce my vows to the king. Upon the morrow we two shall go from Camelot forever... to live in the Manor the house of Montaigne doth own."

Willowpetal was wide-eyed.

"It is all thine?"

"Aye... and thine too..."

"You would give me all you own?"

"Willowpetal, I have no kin... you are all my world."

"And you are mine... but this cannot be true... it is like a dream... a tale of which only Hendrique could compose... a fabulous tale..."

"My dearest Willowpetal... my love for you is so great. I would never wish that it be a burden to you. You are free as a bird... I want you to be so. Never will I chain you to me...."

Willowpetal took both his hands in hers.

"But I would wish you to heap me with chains... and I would willingly gather them to me... and bind them tighter...."

"Is this so?"

"Yes... yes... for... they are the chains of love."

"And did I not tell Queen Guinevere that we were betrothed?"

"I heard you say these words and my heart nearly stopped in its beating."

Gadroon smiled.

"I am certain glad it did not, for I have the betrothal ring here with me."

Slowly he took the gift that had been bestowed upon him at the Chapel at Glainseg and placed it upon Willowpetal's finger. Light of an intense brilliance seemed to fill the chamber, none more so than that which came from the ring itself. The Goddess looked upon them and blessed their union, the gift of The Grail. They gazed upon each other for what may have been eternity.

"Oh... Gadroon, I love thee."

"And I thee, Willowpetal."

Soon they lay beneath the coverlet. Man and woman, god and goddess, lovers all. And they whispered together, between kisses, as lovers always do.

"I chatter so..."

"It is the sound of water cascading upon the pebbles..."

"I know nothing..."

"That is the greatest wisdom."

"I know not of the grand ways of the court, my lord..."

"They are not worth knowing, my lady..."

"I am the poor daughter of a peasant..."

"I love you whatever you be... you are all I could ever wish for."

"You are so kind to me... I would do anything for you... give you anything... all of me is yours... I beg you... I plead with you to take it... all."

Gadroon touched her skin, as smooth as ivory, looked most deeply into her eyes and saw only wonder.

*

Arthur woke the next morning with a head as heavy as Deep Purple. The carousing in the Great Hall had continued well into the small hours, so prolonged that most of the company soon forgot what it was they were celebrating. A surfeit of stoups of ale, as well as many cups of claret, had left his majesty a little jaded. Arthur looked around. Guinevere was absent from the breakfast table; she was hardly ever a permanent fixture these days. Through the fog of alcohol, Arthur reflected on his standing with the queen. On occasions like this, with a stinking hangover, and the melancholy that always accompanies it, he more than yearned for the good old days. When the Round Table had first been ordained, things were a lot simpler, particularly when Merlin was around to advise him.

Who he could turn to now? Lancelot? A man of the world certainly, forthright and decisive – but more moody than a prima donna ballerina. A bit rum in his dealings with Guinevere too. Sometimes he wondered if those two weren't a bit more than just good friends. As usual, he would have to sort things out on his own. Heavy is the head upon which the crown lieth, they say. Arthur felt like there was a JCB perched on top of his own right then. A touch of tapping on the door preceded the Steward sliding into the Royal Chamber.

"Your majesty... Pretzel the Money Lender is here."

"Why? What can he want? The royal coffers are stuffed to overflowing..."

The Steward was patience itself.

"Pretzel is not here to consult upon matters of the royal wealth, Your Majesty... but in his office as the court archivist. I believe he has discovered a pedigree for Lady Gadroon.... as the maid is shortly to be known..."

Arthur jumped out of his seat – a great mistake, as his head went and hurt a lot more.

"Lady Gadroon! I heard nothing of this..."

"Did not the Queen inform your majesty that..."

"Guinevere? I have not laid eyes upon the Queen since... since... I know not when... last St. Ringo's Day probably. She was not at my side in the Great Hall last night and..."

At that moment, the queen appeared, with Pretzel in tow. Sensing the approach of a tricky domestic, the Steward vamoosed stage left.

"Arthur! We must make arrangements for the coming marriage!"

"Marriage? Who is to be wed?"

Guinevere was in no mood for shilly-shallying.

"Lord and Lady Gadroon. There is to be a great feast... and bright bunting hung from every beam, branch and bough..."

Arthur could feel his head hurting again.

"But... I presented Gadroon to the Company last eve... he had no mistress at his side... of that I am certain..."

Guinevere was all *fait accompli*.

"Mistress Willowpetal and myself were conversing in the Bridal Chamber..."

"Bridal Chamber? Willowpetal? Come... I beg of thee, Guinevere... I am as one lost... thou speakest in riddles..."

The singular figure of Pretzel had been hovering in the wings, and he produced a pile of parchment from a leather pouch.

"If I might personally enlighten you your majesty.... Sir Gadroon of the Company is now betrothed to a serving maid formerly of Malfaise Castle..."

Arthur was scandalized.

"A lowly maid! This cannot be! One my noblest knights... of the De Montaigne lineage... about to be wed to a common... well..."

Guinevere annexed this snooty snub *tout suite*.

"Hold, Arthur... let Pretzel continue..."

"...it is fortunate that whilst investigating her ancestry... a certain lowly birthright, it is true... I came upon certain ancient charters which prove Mistress Willowpetal... is... without doubt... was once... of noble stock. To be precise... the family of... um... Le Godard de Gauloise..."

Guinevere interrupted.

"We thank you, Pretzel... but these details of Willowpetal's ancestry mean but little... only to those misguided old crocks who hold such things in high regard. She is a charming gel and will obviously make a most suitable companion for Sir Gadroon. The nuptials must follow forthwith... they have *known* each other I believe..."

Arthur was merely baffled, but knew of old there was no arguing with Guinevere once she had the bit between her teeth. He was suddenly inspired.

"A Spring Wedding... perhaps..."

"An excellent notion, Arthur! So all is settled! Come, Pretzel... I am certain his majesty has matters of state to decide upon... and I have a most pressing affair to attend to in my boudoir..."

As Pretzel and the Queen withdrew, the Steward was occupied announcing Sir Norbert and Sir Gadroon. Arthur greeted them, somewhat unsteadily.

"My noble knights! Your king welcomes you!"

On cue, both bowed low.

"My, Liege."

Arthur tried to be bluff and *sans souci* though. If quizzed, he would probably not have known much about either.

"Gadroon! Thou art to be wed...?"

Our hero did not realise arrangements had moved on so swiftly. The ladies must have been up to things without telling him, bless 'em.

"So it doth seem, Your Majesty... and the bearing of many offspring will doubtless follow... so I would humbly request that..."

"I would be their godfather? Why... that would be only an honour, Gadroon."

Gadroon kept his cool, just.

"I thank thee, My Liege... that honour would only be mine. Of greater import is that their *father* be with them... constantly. I would desire to be at Montaigne Manor... Uchelgwyn, as it is known in the old tongue. Therefore I ask to be released from my knightly vows. This boon I crave... with great regret... but the utmost..."

Arthur's expression was as various as dips at a buffet.

"I desire only thy happiness, Gadroon... though I shall sore miss thy presence in the Company. Yet... if this is the way I may best reward thee and thy service, then so be it. I release thee from thy vows forthwith."

Gadroon bowed low once more.

"I thank thee, Your Majesty... thou hast been more than munificent."

Arthur turned to Norbert, without realising he had lost this rubber too.

"At least the Company will still have thy presence, brave Norbert..."

"I fear not, my liege... I also wish to..."

"Norbert! Do not say thee as well doth desire to depart from Camelot..."

"I feel a calling, My Liege..."

"A calling?"

"One I cannot resist... it is to join those devout souls at the Abbey of Piedervoux..."

The king almost flipped his crown.

"A monk! Thou wouldst exchange thy sword and buckler for a cowl and rosary?"

"I would, my liege. This very day, if thou wilt allow it."

Arthur stood up and paced about, a move that started off his head throbbing again.

"It would be unjust to refuse... you also have been the saviour of Camelot. Thou mayest, Norbert... and with thy king's blessing."

Norbert also bowed low; it was all becoming like a variety concert.

"I thank, thee My Liege. All Heaven rejoiceth... this I know."

Arthur looked as if he wasn't sure that was the case, but let it pass. Believing that any further dilly-dallying would be an anti-climax, the two knights made to withdraw from the royal chambers. Arthur did not seem in a hurry to dismiss them, as he was busy recalling something he meant to ask.

"The Grail! The Holy Vessel!"

"Your majesty..."

"Where doth it lie?"

Gadroon realised that almost any answer he could give would be in danger of amounting to a thesis.

"My Liege?"

"I recall that The Purple Haze demanded The Grail be brought to Camelot..."

Gadroon attempted to be brief.

"Your Majesty... the nature of the Holy Vessel is not as a mundane thing... its presence belongeth only to Heaven."

When Arthur tried to think this one through, his head started hurting again.

"But... but..."

"Your majesty... The Purple Haze only demanded that a Knight of The Round Table *embarked upon The Quest...*"

That all seemed as the pikestaff to Gadroon.

"But... but..."

"My liege... Morgan le Fay – who conjured this fell thing – hath sworn that it is no more. Your majesty, no harm will come to the kingdom from The Purple Haze."

Gadroon had a slightly murky conscience when he said that. From what he knew of the vengeful Morgan le Fay, she would undoubtedly conspire to bring an end to Camelot. What good would it do to reveal these things to Arthur? Like telling a kid there was no Father Christmas, perhaps.

"Very well... I wish thee both the greatest good fortune. This is indeed a time when the Winds of Change blow this way and that..."

Gadroon regarded Arthur closely and decided they had blown his tiny mind.

XX

The world was beautiful, hung with frost,
And the huge red sun rose through clouds
And came, white and gleaming, to the sky.

At dawn, Norbert and Gadroon, accompanied by
Willowpetal, left Camelot. The maid sat upon a splendid
palfrey – a gift from Guinevere. Some leagues past
Château Charbon, the way forked. Norbert would
continue to Piedervoux Abbey and thus the two friends
would part.

"Yonder lies the Manor of Montaigne where
Willowpetal and I are bound, Norbert."

"Then it is time for farewells, old friend..."

"It seems so. We have known much and seen even
more upon our journey together. It has been an honour
to have thee as a trusted companion, Norbert. I owe
thee a great debt... one I can never repay... my life..."

Norbert had to hold back his tears when he heard
this, and found it difficult to utter even a few words.

"And to thee I owe my continuing upon our Quest
also... there were many times when thy courage was all
that saved me. More than anything you led me to the
gate of wisdom, Gadroon. I can only hope that I am
worthy enough to enter in there."

"Thou art, Norbert. Of that I am certain."

They looked upon each other most fondly knowing in
their hearts that their time together was now over, as a
dream upon waking.

"Gadroon... thou art the most noble knight I have
ever known..."

And Norbert turned away, not wishing to show to the
world the grief he felt. Willowpetal wanted to embrace
him but, before she could, Norbert had ridden away
from them. Before him lay the Abbey and the new life
that beckoned and he looked neither to right or left,

such was his resolve. Willowpetal clutched Gadroon's arm.

"Will all be well for your friend? I hope that is so."

Gadroon sighed.

"I believe it will... and that most assuredly. There is much to Norbert that I did not know when I first met him... and there is still much that will ever be hidden from me. A strong heart beats within him... and a pure one at that."

Willowpetal put her arms about her betrothed.

"And your heart is strong also and mine will always be entwined with thee."

Gadroon kissed her most tenderly and together they started upon the way that led to their new life also.

*

When the great tales are told once more – the great sagas recalled – we know once more the lives of the heroes of old. We see again the creatures they came upon and how they fought with them. We venture upon voyages into dark lands, through towering seas. Like them, we do not rest until at last we behold the great treasure that lies within the Promised Land. When day is done, our hearts are filled with joy and our spirit rests, to bathe in light.

We look again upon the stern features of the warrior who will never surrender, the fair princess whose beauty exceeds that of the dawn. Death we learn not to fear, merely acknowledge its presence and act accordingly, owning a greater compassion and understanding. Willingly do we swear an oath to our king and promise to be valiant in battle. Magnanimous are we to the defeated when we have won the peace. Life is beset with troubles: the brave endure them, the weak are harried by fate. We learn to recognise evil – in the mean and the unjust, and those who show ignorance and hatred in the world. We strive, through knowing the magnificence of creation, to be as the angels of whom the minstrels sing.

It would come to pass that Anghard would once more become a fair land, Malfaise a city of prosperity – a place of craftsmanship and artistry. A new golden age had begun, one where the old must give way to the new and Longres would disappear forever, except in the songs and poetry that magical land would inspire. In death King Arthur would once more be united with Morgan le Fay in Avalon. Thus the old legends and the great prophecies of wizard and sage had told true.

*

At Piedervoux, Norbert was reunited with Scriven. When invited by him to look upon the secret book that the monk continued to compile and illuminate, he had no fear to do so. There he saw the whole of the journey now most marvellously depicted in every detail. The interior of The Chapel enabled him to relive those wondrous moments. On the following pages he saw Gadroon with Willowpetal and one... two... three children skipping about them. The sun shone upon them and great joy was all around. To one side of the picture stood Edrith, smiling benignly upon them. At that moment Norbert clearly heard the words of the wizard speaking to him.

"Hail, Master Norbert. We meet once more... even in the pages of a great book... one that is both past and present... for does not that shape what we call the future? Thou hast found thy calling as I once did mine. Let us both use our power wisely... never to judge... but always to aid others when and where we may. Remember... Loenel will watch over you until the end of your days... that I promise."

At that moment both God and Goddess became united in Norbert's soul and he felt as if he was floating, suspended above the world. Providence, however, sprinted in at that very instant. A gong sounded from the refectory.

"I believe Supper summons us, Norbert."

"Indeed. And from Brother Plume this very morn I heard tell great tales of smoked trout and pickled beets... so let us not delay a moment longer."

*

Willowpetal had found great happiness also, more so than she could ever have imagined. Greatly loved by one and all at the Manor and round about for her simple goodness, she had inherited a magic land. Though slight, had become noticeably more rounded. The Spring wedding arrived just this side of decorum, but it was a damn close run thing.

An evening in late Summer found Willowpetal in the bedchamber gazing upon the Moon. In her cradle lay their daughter Ravenbreeze – named for her lustrous dark hair – sleeping peacefully. Her father also slept soundly near, and Willowpetal silently gave thanks to Loenel that the two she loved most in the world were there so close to her. She was not greatly surprised when she heard her prayers answered, in the comforting tones of The Goddess. Words she could hear clearly, resounded in her heart

"You deserve every part of your joy, Willowpetal... for you too have always been my handmaiden though perhaps you did not know this. You were also chosen to be a Grail Maiden and to serve in the Chapel at Glaesneg. You watched over the Questing knights when they prayed there... did you not?"

"That I did, O Queen of Heaven, and how I rejoiced to see the Holy Vessel revealed to my beloved Gadroon. You, O Loenel gave us both the hope and promise of eternal love and sealed your gift to us at that moment. For this I am grateful always and pray that you will always continue to keep my loved ones safe..."

"It was destined from the first that Gadroon could never come to harm... he was chosen... as your companion... the only one worthy to care for you. "

"...and Ravenbreeze also..."

"All Heaven will care for her also... never fear..."

And the babe moved a little in her crib and her eyes opened for but an instant. Then it seemed to Willowpetal that sparkling silver sprang from her eyes. Ravenbreeze was surrounded by a cloud of stars, which slowly ascended to join with The Goddess in Heaven above.

~oO0o~

Other Books by Gordon Strong
Available from Mutus Liber:

King Arthur: The Waste Land & the New Age

The stories about King Arthur, and the Waste Land that must be crossed in order to attain the Grail, continue to fascinate, inspiring writers from Geoffrey of Monmouth in the twelfth century to T. S. Eliot in the twentieth.

This new study of the Arthurian legends combines exciting insights into the nature of the Holy Grail, our modern yearning for spirituality and romance, and the relevance of Arthurian myth in the technological age.

Arthur and Guinevere, Merlin, Morgan le Fay, the Lady of the Lake and the Knights of the Round Table... all are brought to enchanted life on the mystical stage in the heart of sacred Albion: Glastonbury and the landscape of Somerset.

❊ ❊ ❊

This is one of the most strongly individual and imaginative reinterpretations of the Arthurian legend that I have ever encountered. It proves again how the story can be made fresh and new for any age.

~ Professor Ronald Hutton

A very different approach to the matter of King Arthur and his legends... Gordon Strong has gone for a much wider canvas, drawing on tradition but also looking at Tibetan mantras, Apocryphal texts, magical writers and mages and sages... He shows that inner themes of search and loss and captivity are universal and that the main characters are to be found echoed in many ancient sources of wisdom... a myriad of fascinating clues.

~ Marian Green, co-author of *The Grail Seeker's Companion*

ISBN: 978 09555230 14

Tarot Unveiled

The Tarot is a philosophical document, a wisdom tradition and a gateway to the unseen. It has the power to reveal the ebb and flow of existence – the divine rhythm.

An invaluable guide for the beginner and the professional reader alike, Gordon Strong perceptively explains all the cards of the Major and the Minor Arcana. A brief history of the Tarot, an intimate guide to Divination, Tarot Correspondences, numerology and Tarot meditation exercises are also included.

❈ ❈ ❈

Tarot Unveiled speaks with a friendly yet informed voice. The author's familiarity and enthusiasm provides a well-grounded introduction to the subject including practical advice for readers and guidance for the spiritually adventurous. Right from the start Gordon Strong sets the right tone by reminding his audience that Tarot is part of a magical philosophy, not just a method of divination. Unveiling the Tarot is a lifetime's journey, and this book offers a good starting place.

~ Naomi Ozaniec

ISBN: 978 09555230 21

Bride's Mound: Gateway to Avalon

With Jane Marshall
Illustrated by Jen Delyth

Bride's Mound: Gateway to Avalon celebrates one of Glastonbury's most important, but least known, mystical sites.

The destination of sea-borne travelers from the West, Bride's Mound is also the portal into the Other World, that of Avalon, the Arthurian paradise. Like Isis, Bride is the Goddess of the Moon – to the Romans she was Minerva, to the Christians, St. Bridget. She is the swordsmith, the healer and the poet, and excels in each calling.

Associated with Mary Magdalene, the Black Madonna and the Celtic festival of Imbolc, Bride is also the sister of the archangel Michael. Her colour is white like the lamb, and the snowdrop that symbolize her. Bride protects the young mother and the old sinner alike – she owns compassion and devotion. Today, she may have exchanged the mantle of Pisces for that of Aquarius, and become the independent, radical female.

Jane Marshall is the secretary of the Friends of Bride's Mound.

Jen Delyth is a Celtic artist based in San Francisco.

ISBN: 978 09555230 45

Sun God and Moon Maiden:
The Secret World of the Holy Grail

The Medieval troubadour saw the Holy Grail as a vision of heaven. In the twenty-first century, the quantum physicist locates heaven in parallel universes. The shaman, spanning prehistory and the modern world, travels in other dimensions to experience the limits of existence.

In *Sun God and Moon Maiden*, Gordon Strong argues that the metaphor of the Grail questions not only space and time but perception itself. The philosophy of Plato, the psychology of Jung and the nobility of mythic kings lie in the Grail's domain; an interior landscape where we discover gateways into Inner Space, the nature of the universe, and ourselves.

From legends of Atlantis to Arthur's Camelot, the path to Avalon awaits. In this fascinating book, drawing together mythology, magic and modern physics, Gordon Strong explains how the ancient wisdom of Qabalah, Tarot and Stone Circles open the way for new discoveries in expanded consciousness.

❉ ❉ ❉

An approach to the sanctity and mystery of the Grail which combines tradition, insight and invention in equal and exciting measure.
~ Alan Richardson, author of *Priestess: The Life and Magic of Dion Fortune*

This revealing and original study sheds important new light on the paradoxes of the Grail which we find, ultimately, are paradoxes of the Self. Joining Gordon Strong's mythic quest to unlock the secrets of its divine truth will reward the reader handsomely.
~ Geoff Ward, *Mysterious Planet*

ISBN: 978 1 908097 019

Dawn of the Goddess

The Age of Kings is over. The Goddess has decreed that a queen will rise and rule the Six Great Kingdoms. Before this age of joy and peace may come about, one great and final battle must be won. Can Paldarch the Wizard restore the Sword of Pengyron to its rightful heir?   Only with this enchanted weapon can the young monarch Huan Brynan be victorious over the forces of darkness.

But Brynan must know enlightenment, experience love and sadness and realise the eternal power of magic, before he is worthy of leading the knights of his realm to a great victory.

A veteran chronicler of myth and legend, Gordon Strong creates a vivid world of the imagination. This gripping tale transcends all limits of time and space to become a reflection of the spiritual world in our own era.

❋ ❋ ❋

This is a powerfully heroic and epic tale, rich in stirring action. The saga is enriched by love and romance – its magic the kind that makes the greatest folklore and legend so unforgettable. *Dawn of the Goddess* is eminently readable and thoroughly enjoyable.

~ Lionel Fanthorpe, Author and Broadcaster

Gordon Strong provides us with a treasure house of images, and enriches the imagination of his readers. A real gem!
~ Alan Richardson, Author of *Priestess: The Life and Magic of Dion Fortune*

ISBN: 978 1 908097 033

Also available as an EBook on Kindle and Smashwords